Passion in the Temple

The mysterious woman stepped directly in front of Michael. Gazing upon the voluptuousness of her body, he knew that he was in the presence of the goddess.

"I have never seen anyone so lovely before," Michael said, "or been so close to a goddess."

She came nearer. "Have you ever touched a goddess?"

"No."

"Or held one in your arms?"

Answering the implied invitation, he pulled her to him. She did not resist, but a sudden tensing of her right arm warned him that something was wrong. He tried to draw away, but her left arm held him. And in the light he caught the glint of metal in her right hand as she raised it to drive the dagger home!

Are there paperbound books you want but cannot find in your retail stores?

The Curse of Jezebel

A Novel of the
Biblical Queen of Evil

by

FRANK G. SLAUGHTER

A KANGAROO BOOK
PUBLISHED BY POCKET BOOKS NEW YORK

THE CURSE OF JEZEBEL

Doubleday edition published 1961

POCKET BOOK edition published March, 1977

This POCKET BOOK edition includes every word contained in
the original, higher-priced edition. It is printed from brand-
new plates made from completely reset, clear, easy-to-read type.
POCKET BOOK editions are published by
POCKET BOOKS,
a division of Simon & Schuster, Inc.,
A GULF+WESTERN COMPANY
630 Fifth Avenue,
New York, N.Y. 10020.
Trademarks registered in the United States
and other countries.

ISBN: 0-671-80921-0.
Library of Congress Catalog Card Number: 61-12582.
Cover illustration by Robert Berran.

Printed in the U.S.A.

Author's Note

THE HISTORY OF AHAB AND JEZEBEL, AS TOLD IN THE
Old Testament Book of Kings, is one of the great dramatic stories of the Bible. And yet the biblical writer
omitted much that adds breadth, color, and suspense to
the scriptural account. Modern historical and archaeological research has revealed that Ahab was one of the
truly great kings of Israel, a statesman and warrior
whose major mistake seems to have been his marriage to
Jezebel in order to form a political alliance with the
important Phoenician city-states of Tyre and Sidon.
Through this marriage an alien religion was introduced
into Israel, earning for Ahab the condemnation of the
great prophet Elijah and the wrath of God.

The biblical account does not mention the battle of
Karkar fought in 853 or 854 B.C., one of the few dates
which can be established accurately in all of biblical
history. Yet this crucial defense of the northern entrance to Israel by a confederation of twelve kings—
perhaps the first time such an alliance had ever func-
tioned effectively—was one of the more important
battles of ancient times. Though Shalmaneser III
claimed the victory in his account chiseled upon the
famous "Black Obelisk" which now rests in the British
Museum, the fact remains that he retreated to the
northeast immediately after the battle and Israel was
saved from destruction for over a hundred years, until
the Assyrians invaded and conquered it in 721 B.C.

In reconstructing the classic biblical story, I have
drawn upon hundreds of sources which it would be

v

impractical to list here. In every instance I have sought to portray people, things, and, above all, places as accurately as it is possible to describe them from the study of source references. For example, thousands of ivory splinters from the furniture brought to Samaria by Jezebel were found when the city was finally excavated by archaeologists, largely from Harvard University, during the past fifty years, along with many small plaques and panels portraying vivid scenes of the period. The actual tunnel by which, in the story, Michael was able to enter the palace, was discovered also during these excavations. Archaeological discoveries in recent years confirm the fact that Ahab turned Megiddo into a heavily fortified center for chariot warfare, enlarging upon the original fortifications built by King Solomon.

But however fascinating the actual locales, to a novelist the task of portraying the people who walk the scenes of his story is always an exciting challenge. All major characters in this novel are taken from the biblical account and the roles they fill are essentially those described in the Book of Kings. The name of Michael is recorded among the sons of King Jehoshaphat of Judah, and Miriam is a name honored among the Hebrew people since their beginning. As always, I have sought to incorporate the biblical account into the fictional structure of the novel in such a way that its original identity is retained unimpaired. In *The Curse of Jezebel* this was less difficult than is sometimes the case, for in the Book of Kings, truth is often stranger and more dramatic than fiction.

—Frank G. Slaughter

The Curse of Jezebel

Chapter 1

SPRING WAS STILL A MONTH AWAY ONE AFTERNOON when two horsemen drew their mounts to a stop on the crest of a hill in the rolling country of central Canaan. Earlier they had crossed the border between Israel and Judah just south of the ancient city of Bethel and all that day they had ridden leisurely through a region sacred to all worshipers of the Hebrew God, Yahweh. Abraham, the father of his people, had made a sacrifice to the Lord upon a high place in this area when he had first come into Canaan from Haran, far to the northeast near the ancient Hittite capital of Carchemish. Here he and his tribe had grazed their flocks and herds, moving slowly southward to establish themselves finally in the pasture lands around Hebron and Mamre. And to this region, many centuries later, the Children of Israel had returned from captivity in Egypt, to wrest a new homeland for themselves from its Canaanite inhabitants.

Since the death of Israel's great King Solomon nearly a century and a half before, the country had been divided into a southern kingdom called Judah, with its center of government and worship at Jerusalem, and the northern kingdom of Israel, ruled by Ahab from his

1

new capital at Samaria. Under King Ahab, Israel once more stretched from Dan in the north to Beersheba in the south, for, although Jehoshaphat ruled in Jerusalem, it was a vassal and friend. The border between the two kingdoms was no longer fortified as it had been in the days after Solomon's death, when brother in the north often fought his counterpart in the south. Nevertheless, a new threat faced all of Canaan, for the armies of Shalmaneser III, King of Assyria, were poised for an invasion from the north which the ruthless monarch of the land between the Tigris and the Euphrates rivers confidently expected to take him to the lush delta of the Nile in Egypt.

Affairs connected with the imminent invasion by Assyria caused Prince Michael of Judah to be on the road today. Recently returned from a journey to the Assyrian capital of Nineveh, where he had studied Shalmaneser's methods of warfare with thousands of chariots and great engines of war that could lay siege to even a walled city and batter down its defenses, Michael had been sent by his father, King Jehoshaphat, to inform Ahab of the Assyrians' strength. Privately, he had also been instructed to assay the forces being trained by the Israelite monarch and eleven other kings who had joined in the first confederation ever attempted by the people of this area for their common defense. As yet Jehoshaphat had not joined the confederation, and upon Michael's report of his findings in the northern kingdom would depend important decisions that must shortly be made before the attack by Assyria was launched.

Sitting in the saddle with the wind that swept across the hilltops ruffling his dark hair, Michael was a fine example of the stalwart fighting men of his race—descendants of those who, under the leadership of Joshua, had wrested from the Canaanites control of the land promised to them in Egypt by God. Though third

2

in line of succession among the five sons of Jehoshaphat, and therefore far removed from any possibility of succeeding to the throne of Judah, Michael had early exhibited such intelligence and aptitude for military strategy, as well as prowess in actual battle, that at thirty he was commander, after his father, of the armies of Judah. Behind him rode his servant Aaron, a powerful, somewhat dour man who was never willingly very far from his master's side. Originally from Edom, the largely desert wasteland to the south of Judah, Aaron had been Michael's personal slave since the young prince's boyhood. Long since given his freedom, the servant had refused to leave his master and a warm bond of affection and respect existed between them.

The country here on the crest of the central ridge was rough and mountainous, the track they were following sometimes little more than a path winding along the hilltops whose sides were pocked with caves to form the sort of wilderness favored by robbers for their hiding places. From the height where they had paused for the horses to rest after a steep climb, Michael could see almost the whole of Judah. Far to the southeast a glint of color with almost the sheen of molten lead marked the location of the Salt Sea, sequestered in its own cup of hills. To the east, toward the Jordan Valley, lay a highly cultivated area enclosed in a valley protected by a ridge of high land that hid the river itself from view. On the west, a long line of hills marking the coastal ridge hid the Great Sea and the port of Joppa that served Jerusalem as an outlet to the Mediterranean and the Phoenician cities of the coast to the north, as well as Egypt.

To the north loomed another range of hills, rendering this area relatively inaccessible and well suited for the purposes of the hunted men who eked out a precarious living from pasturing small herds in pockets of grassland and from what they could steal in swift forays upon small caravans. Michael and Aaron had no particular fear of robbers, for they were superbly mounted and fully armed with weapons they knew well how to use. They rode, however, with spear in hand, the butts resting in metal sockets welded to the right stirrups for that purpose.

"Look there, master," Aaron said. "To the north."

Michael shaded his eyes and looked in the direction Aaron was pointing. What appeared to be a small caravan, or rather a file of people, for most of them were walking, was making its way slowly along a road that traversed a small valley or glen lying between the hills.

"It could be what was left of a caravan, after being attacked by robbers," Michael said. "Some are being carried while others are limping with crutches and sticks."

"Certainly they are no threat to us."

"But they may need help. We will ride down and see." Michael touched his heel to the horse's flank and guided it down the slope. Halfway down, however, the picture ahead suddenly changed. From a hiding place among the rocks, or from one of the caves that dotted the hilly region, six or eight men had suddenly appeared. And as they raced down the hillside toward the caravan, the sun gleamed on naked swords and knives in their hands.

"Robbers!" Aaron exclaimed, indignantly. "As if the people in that caravan didn't have enough trouble already."

"They haven't seen us yet." Michael spurred his horse into a run. "Attack with your spear, then turn and ride back with the sword. If we take them by surprise, the odds will be less uneven."

The two had fought side by side on more than one occasion and Michael had no doubts concerning Aaron's ability to carry his share of the responsibility.

4

But long before the two riding furiously down the slope to aid the intended prey of the robbers could reach them, the conflict had begun.

Not that it could be called much of a battle, Michael thought as he spurred his horse on, shifting his spear into a position where he could jab and thrust at first opportunity. The group being attacked numbered about fifty people, most of them old men and only a few armed. Almost half, he saw as he came nearer, appeared to have been wounded. Some were being carried on litters and few were in any condition to defend themselves.

A tall man with golden hair and beard seemed to be the leader of the caravan. Although armed only with a cudgel, he was laying about him with powerful strokes that, however inexpert, still managed to hold two of the attackers at bay by the very force and energy of his defense. What startled Michael most was the sight of a strikingly beautiful girl who had seized a sword from the hand of one of the robbers felled by the golden-bearded man's cudgel. Though obviously untutored in the weapon's use, she slashed away at the invaders, rushing here and there with all the grace of a lioness at bay to jab at the robbers when they tried to harm the helpless men lying upon the litters.

Michael and Aaron had purposely made no sound beyond the clatter of their horses' hoofs upon the rocky hillside. And amid the groans, the shouts of pain, and the curses of the thieves as they tried to subdue the man and the woman who, almost alone among the intended victims, dared to resist, their presence went largely unmarked until they were upon the attackers.

Michael rode one wiry fellow down and heard him scream as the horse's hoofs crushed his chest against the rocky ground. At the same time he hurled his spear at a man he could not reach who was about to cleave the skull of the golden-bearded warrior with a heavy sword. The spear point, made of Damascus metal and honed to the sharpness of a razor, went through the robber's body and he dropped the sword with a scream of pain and staggered back, gripping the shaft with both hands.

Beside him, Michael saw Aaron beat down the attack of a robber, laying the man's skull open with one blow before riding on to hammer a small shield from the arm of another, breaking the bone like a green stick cracked over one's knee. The battle was finished almost as soon as it had started, with two of the attackers groaning on the ground and two more past making any sound. The rest promptly took to their heels and Michael wheeled his horse around to see whether any more needed to be dispatched.

The man with the golden beard was wiping blood from his face where one of the attackers had managed to lay open a small cut above his ear. The girl was nowhere to be seen, but as Michael turned in the saddle to look for her, Aaron shouted, "Over there, master! They took the girl with them!"

Michael wheeled his horse and went charging up the hillside toward the small knot of robbers scrambling uphill for the safety of the cave in which they had lain in wait for their victims. There they could easily hold off a dozen attackers, he knew, since only a few could approach at a time. A tall robber was carrying the girl, and when Michael estimated the distance yet to be covered he saw that the man would be able to take cover behind a large boulder long before he would be able to close with him. There was only one thing to do and, even though it posed a danger to the girl struggling in the robber's arms, he did not hesitate.

Michael's short bow was across his back and a quiver of arrows was attached to his saddle. Even as he swept the bow from his shoulder, his other hand was reining in his horse to form a stationary perch from which to shoot. Trained for just such an emergency as this, the animal plowed its hoofs into the rocky shale and stopped short, leaving Michael both hands with which to seize an arrow from the quiver, place it in the bow, draw back the string, and loose it.

He did not dare aim at a vital spot because the arrow might strike the girl struggling in the robber's grasp. The point struck the fleshy part of the man's lower leg, penetrating half through it. He went down, dropping the girl, who tumbled down the rocky hillside with a limpness that told Michael she had been knocked unconscious. The robber was not seriously wounded, but the arrow protruding from his leg removed all further interest he had in the girl. Struggling to his feet and groaning at every step, he scrambled up the hill to the protection of a large boulder before Michael could send another arrow after him.

Michael dismounted and knelt beside the girl just as Aaron came riding up the hill. She was breathing, he saw, and beyond a few scratches upon her face and arms did not seem to be badly hurt.

"See to the others," he told Aaron. "I will carry her down."

As Aaron rode back down the hill, Michael gathered the girl up in his arms and rose to his feet. The rich cloth of her robe told him she was well above peasant status and he fancied that he could see breeding, pride, and gentleness of upbringing written in the high cheekbones, the slender neck, the graceful carriage of her small head and the dark masses of her hair, over which she wore a cloth of *byssus,* an expensive fabric woven by the looms of the Phoenician weavers on the coast.

Michael had taken only two steps when the girl's eyes opened. As he had surmised, they were dark and very lovely, dilated now by the shock of what she had been through. For only a moment did they remain so, however. Suddenly the pupils contracted as she jerked

7

one arm loose and struck at his face, raking him across the cheek with the heavy signet ring she wore and bringing blood. Michael grimaced with pain and instinctively held her closer, which only made her struggle the more.

"Be still, you little fool!" he snapped. "I am no robber."

"Put me down then," she said sharply.

Michael was glad enough to put her down. Carrying her while she flailed at him and raked the skin of his face with her ring and bracelets was somewhat like trying to subdue a wildcat with his bare hands. She staggered a little, but when he put out an arm to support her she thrust it aside and took a few wavering steps. Then, gaining her balance, she started down the hillside toward where Aaron was helping the golden-bearded man stop the flow of blood from the cut over his eye.

Michael did not join them, but went along the line of people, most of whom were now sitting on the rocks beside the road nursing their wounds and bruises. A few were trying to straighten out the litters which had been dropped in the surprise of the robber attack and help those who had been carried upon them. Two of the travelers, he saw, had been killed by the swords and knives of the robbers and two more were bleeding profusely from cuts on their bodies. Tearing strips from their garments, he helped bind the wounds, as he had often done for fellow soldiers injured in battle. Only when the flow of blood had been stanched did he turn to the others.

The girl, he saw, was finishing the task of bandaging the wounds of the tall man with the golden beard. He did not appear to be badly hurt otherwise and when she had finished, he held out his hand to Michael.

"You saved our lives, noble sir," he said. "Be assured the Most High will bless you for it." His speech was cultured, certainly not that of the casual traveler. "I am Micaiah," he added, "formerly chief among the priests of Yahweh in Samaria. These others are my brethren, all that are left of two hundred."

Michael frowned. "Who in Israel dares to make war on priests?"

"Jezebel!" the girl said sharply. "Who else?"

"The queen? She does not even worship Yahweh."

The tall priest looked at him keenly, taking in his noble bearing, the luxury evident in the trappings of both men and horses, and the confident manner in which Michael spoke. "I am remiss in courtesy, sir," he said. "This is the lady Miriam of Jezreel, daughter of Naboth, a prince and elder in the congregation of Israel."

"I am Michael and this is my friend Aaron." Michael did not identify himself further. "We are traveling from Jerusalem to Samaria."

"All of us can thank the Most High that you chose this day for your journey then," Micaiah said. "But for you, Yahweh would have few priests today in Israel."

"Are you traveling to Judah?"

"We hope to find refuge for the others among our fellow priests there," Micaiah explained. "I shall return to Samaria with the lady Miriam as soon as they are safe."

The girl had spoken only once since he had set her down, but Michael knew she had been observing him closely. "I will wipe away the blood from your cheek, sir," she said now, "before it stains your tunic."

"It seems I suffered my only wounds today at the hands of a friend instead of the enemy," Michael said with a smile. "May I always have such good luck."

She flushed but did not answer. Going to a waterskin that had fallen to the ground during the melee, she took a piece of cloth and, soaking it in the water, gently sponged away the blood from his cheek. Michael was acutely conscious of her nearness and of the warmth of her breath upon his face when she leaned close to apply the damp cloth.

"Even in Judah we know of the noble Naboth," he said in a low voice. "Of all his possessions, I am sure he prizes his daughter most."

He saw the quick color stain her cheeks but she did not answer. When she had finished and stepped back, Michael saw that Micaiah was studying him thoughtfully. "You have helped us already, so I hesitate to ask a favor of you," the priest said. "We were hoping to cross into Judah before nightfall, and find shelter but, without help, I doubt if we will be able to reach the border."

"Is it possible that you would be pursued?" Michael asked. "You, the priests of the Lord in his own land?"

"It is no longer our land but Jezebel's," the girl burst out angrily. "Since King Ahab went northward to join King Irhuleni of Hamath, no one dares oppose her save my father and a few others."

"The noble Naboth helped us to escape when the queen sent assassins to destroy us," Micaiah explained. "He would have accompanied us, but if the elders leave Samaria the queen may seize the reins of government entirely."

"So he let his daughter come instead?"

"My father did not know I was going to minister to the wounded," the girl flared. "Else he would have tried to stop me."

"I was not censuring him," Michael said with a smile. "Actually I doubt if he could hardly have sent a more doughty warrior."

She blushed again, but largely from pleasure, and he saw that her eyes were even more lovely when not lit by the fires of anger.

"The border of Judah is not very far away," Michael told Micaiah. "Aaron and I will help bear the load of the litters and two of your weakest people may ride upon our horses."

It was already dark when they came to the village

10

of Ephraim, lying a little off the central highway to the east and just over the border of Judah. It was a tiny place but Michael had discovered during previous travels that it boasted a comfortable, if little used, caravansary. Here they made the injured as comfortable as possible for the night. Miriam, who surprised him further by being an excellent cook—although she belonged to one of the noblest and richest houses of Israel—prepared a savory stew from the meat of a young kid he purchased in the village.

Using rushes from a canebrake growing beside a stream nearby, Aaron had fashioned a screen to give Miriam some privacy from the others. But after all had been fed and the camp was quite save for an occasional groan from one of the more grievously wounded, she came to sit by the campfire with Michael, Aaron, and Micaiah.

"I have been talking to the people from the village," Micaiah said. "Forgive me for not recognizing you, Prince Michael."

"Prince!" the girl exclaimed.

"I am so far removed from the succession to my father's throne that my friends usually omit the title," Michael admitted.

"Are you the son of King Jehoshaphat?"

"Yes. My grandmother was a Phoenician, the daughter of a commoner named Hiram who superintended the stonemasons in building the temple."

"Prince Michael is overly modest, Lady Miriam," Micaiah explained. "His great-grandfather was not simply a superintendent of stonemasons; he was the architect and chief builder of the temple. In the course of it he came to be a devout worshiper of the Most High and married a noblewoman of Judah."

"Why are you going to Samaria?" Miriam asked.

"I have just returned from Assyria. My father and I thought King Ahab should know the strength of the army Shalmaneser is gathering to fight against the twelve kings."

"It would make no difference if the Assyrians were small in number," Miriam said. "If he chooses, the Lord will give them victory."

"Why do you say that?"

"Because King Ahab let Jezebel bring the worship of Baal and Ashtoreth into Israel and drive out the priests of the Lord."

"Do you think the Lord would let the nation be put into slavery just to punish Ahab?"

"It has happened before. In the days of the judges, the people were punished many times when they turned away from following the Lord."

"What do you say to this?" Michael asked the priest.

"If it is the will of the Most High that Israel shall suffer, we cannot avoid it," Micaiah said.

"But you did not let the queen carry out her plan to destroy the priests," Michael reminded him. "Except for you, not even these fifty would have escaped."

The priest shook his head. "Naboth deserves the credit—and I fear that Jezebel will make him suffer for it."

"Both of you can take refuge in Judah with the wounded priests," Michael suggested. "My father will see that all of you are cared for."

"Then Jezebel would win!" Miriam cried. "Only a few of us dare to oppose her now. If we leave Israel everything will be lost."

"Not everything," Micaiah reminded her. "Elijah is still there."

"What can one old man do alone?"

"You forget that he is a prophet of God," Micaiah said in a tone of mild reproof. "The people have been led astray because Jezebel gives them meat from the altars of Baal and distributes grain and wine free. But when Elijah speaks with the voice of the Most High,

12

they will listen. Remember what happened after he prophesied the drought."

"Are you saying a prophet was able to cause the rain to stop, merely upon his word?" Michael asked.

"Elijah spoke the will of God, and there has been no rain in most of Israel now for almost two years. The land is parched and nearly all the streams have dried up."

"If Elijah has the power, why does he not strike Jezebel dead?"

"Even a prophet can only speak the will of God as it is revealed to him," Micaiah explained. "Whatever plan God has for Jezebel, we will not know it until it happens—unless Elijah reveals it to us."

"Meanwhile we must keep on fighting her in every way we can," the girl said firmly.

"When I went to buy the goat tonight, I spoke to the chief elder in the village here at Ephraim," Michael told them. "Early in the morning he will send carts to carry the wounded and will guide all of them to Jerusalem. You can be sure that no priest of Yahweh will be turned away there."

"Then we can go back to Samaria," Micaiah said in a tone of relief. "Some others of the priests who escaped managed to hide themselves in the hills; they will need help in supplying themselves with food and clothing."

"It will not be safe for you and the lady Miriam to travel alone with robbers on the road," Michael pointed out. "Aaron and I are going to Samaria; you can ride with us."

The camp was settling down now and Micaiah and Aaron went to look to the wounded before going to sleep, leaving Miriam and Michael beside the dying embers of the fire. The flickering light shone upon her face, highlighting her cheekbones and the lovely lines of her head and neck upon proud young shoulders. Once

13

again he thought that she was one of the loveliest young women he had ever seen. "I suppose many men have told you how beautiful you are," he said impulsively.

Startled, she turned to face him and he saw a sudden glint of mischief in her eyes. "Do not think to impress me because you are the son of a king; you are not alone in possessing royal blood. My own family is descended from Saul, the first king of Israel, and my father is one of the elders in the congregation of Israel. I am a lady-in-waiting to the queen when I am in Samaria, though until recently I remained in our old home at Jezreel."

"Travelers say the Vale of Jezreel is one of the loveliest spots in the whole land."

"Not any more," she said with a note of sadness in her voice. "The drought has dried up even the brook Jalud that kept the valley fertile. King Ahab's garden has dried up because of the drought. His palace is next to ours and he tried to buy our property because of a large spring on it, but the land has been in our family for many generations and my father does not want to sell."

"Does Ahab hold that against him?"

She shook her head. "King Ahab is a just man. He obeys the law."

"Yet you say he let Jezebel drive the priests out of Israel."

"Only because he has been away so much of the time conferring with the confederation of the twelve kings. If Ahab had been in Samaria, it would not have happened."

"Where would you rather be? In Samaria or in Jezreel?"

"Jezreel, of course." Her eyes began to glow. "From our garden we can see the spring on the side of Mount Gilboa near where Gideon defeated the Midianites."

"I have only a vague recollection of the story," Michael admitted.

"A long time ago—in the time of the *Shophetim* before we had kings—the Midianites came against us with their camels and overran the land, killing, burning, and enslaving the people. The Children of Israel could not stand against them until the Lord selected Gideon and sent him into battle with three hundred picked men."

"I would hate to fight with those odds against me."

"The Lord was fighting with them," she explained. "He directed Gideon to divide his forces into three parts and place them on the hillsides around the Midianites, who were camped on the other side of the valley. When Gideon and his men blew their trumpets in the middle of the night and displayed burning torches they had hidden under jars, the Midianites thought a great host was about to fall upon them. In trying to escape, they fought with each other in the darkness and Gideon was able to drive them back across the Jordan and destroy most of them."

Listening to the girl's voice as she described the battle, Michael could picture vividly the three small companies of Israelites moving into position to surround the pocket where the much larger enemy force was camped. In her ringing tones he fancied that he could hear the blast of the trumpets as the Israelites smashed the jars and exposed the burning torches. He could well imagine the terror of the Midianites when a veritable avalanche of sound poured down upon them from the hillsides in the darkness, and their desperation as they fought to escape the trap and ran into each other in the darkness with the ungainly camels.

"Perhaps King Ahab can trap the Assyrians in the Valley of Jezreel as Gideon did the Midianites," he suggested.

"He does not intend to let them get that far south,"

15

Miriam assured him. "But just in case, he is fortifying the city of Megiddo across the Vale of Jezreel from us. It guards an important pass leading into the coastal plain."

"You seem to know a great deal about military strategy."

"Ahaziah and I often read the ancient scrolls of our people together," she told him. "He is particularly interested in the exploits of our warriors."

Michael could not repress a surge of jealousy. "Who is Ahaziah?"

The girl's eyes twinkled. "King Ahab's son by an earlier marriage."

"The heir to the throne?"

"Yes, but Jezebel will change that if she can. King Ahab made my father Ahaziah's guardian and the prince spends much time in our home. I have been teaching him."

"How old is he?"

"About fifteen. His left foot was twisted when he was born and he walks with a limp. The people love him though because they know he is kind and good, and the Council of Elders has assumed the responsibility of seeing that he is kept safe from the plotting of Jezebel. She would like to have her own son, Joram, chosen as Ahab's successor."

"I thought King Ahab was in the prime of life?"

"He is. But he is also a brave warrior who always rides in a chariot at the head of his troops. He could easily be cut down by the enemy."

"It seems to me that you and your father have a very important task in Israel," Michael observed.

She nodded soberly. "We do. You can understand now why I must return as soon as possible."

Micaiah and Aaron came back from their visit to the sick and Miriam bade them good night before retiring behind the shelter Aaron had prepared. Michael wrapped himself in his cloak and lay down beside the fire, with his sword conveniently at hand in case the robbers they had defeated that afternoon decided to follow and claim vengeance for their defeat. But nothing troubled them during the night and in the morning the carts came early to take the wounded and the other priests to Jerusalem.

Before noon, Michael and Aaron, with Micaiah and Miriam, were riding back northward toward Samaria. Since there were only two horses and none could be obtained in the small village of Ephraim, each carried double. Micaiah and Aaron rode on Aaron's horse, while Michael helped Miriam to a seat behind his saddle. Of necessity they had to move rather slowly, but they made much better progress than if two had ridden while the others walked. By noon the next day, the travelers topped the crest of a hill and saw a beautiful city shining in all its splendor before them, across a small valley traversed by a ridge.

Chapter 2

SAMARIA, THE NEW CAPITAL OF THE NORTHERN KING-
dom built by King Ahab's father, Omri, was an im-
pressive sight. Even from a distance, Michael could
see that its site was a central and dominant one, much
stronger than the old religious center of Shechem which
lay in a narrow, exposed valley between Mount Ebal
and Mount Gerizim.

The hill upon which Samaria was built rose as a
round and isolated mass towering, Michael estimated,
between two and three hundred cubits above the valley
floor. Commanding a wide view and surrounded by
a large area of fertile plain where ample food could be
grown to feed those living in the city, the entire location had been shrewdly chosen for its military advantage as well as its location in an important part of
the northerrn kingdom.

A paticularly attractive feature of the city, from
Michael's point of view, was its adaptability to defense
against siege. Only a low range of hills lay between it
and the Great Sea, but, since there were no large seaports along that section of the coast, the inhabitants
had little to fear from a seaborne invasion. In addition,
the city was built well, with strong walls and luxurious

homes constructed of hewn stone and whitewashed until they shone in the noonday sun like polished ivory.

"The site is well chosen," he observed to Miriam, who sat behind him, steadying herself by holding to the belt of his harness.

"King Omri bought it for that reason," she explained. "The hill was called 'Watch Mountain' before because a signal fire built on top of the rock could be seen for a long distance in every direction, warning the people when an enemy was sighted so they could come together and defend themselves."

As they crossed the valley and approached the gate of Samaria, Michael studied the heavily fortified area that occupied the central portion of the city. Not only was there a wall around Samaria itself, but this central stronghold had another wall of its own, higher and more powerful than the other. Actually it was hard to distinguish the inner fortifications from the magnificent palace that formed an integral part of them. One wall of the palace was topped by a tower whose sides rose from the solid rock, and where it abutted upon a less steep section of the hillside Michael could see a walled enclosure where a number of large dogs were penned up, apparently as a further guard against any attempt to scale the wall of the tower.

"The new palace belongs to King Ahab," Miriam explained as they rode along the narrow saddle or ridge connecting the central portion of the city with an adjoining hilltop occupying a somewhat lower level. "The old one there by the wall is the palace of Omri."

He could see the structure to which she referred now. Considerably less magnificent and obviously older than what she had called Ahab's palace, it stood at one side of a large courtyard separated from the newer structure by a massive gate guarded by a tall tower.

"Ahab built the new palace after he married Jezebel," Miriam continued. "She knows the people hate her

19

so she had him build the tower that forms the highest point of the palace flush with the steepest part of the mountain. Her own apartments are located there."

"Why are the dogs penned at its foot?"

"So anyone who tried to climb it and kill her would be torn to pieces."

"Why should she be so afraid, if she is the queen?"

"If you were battling against the god a people have worshiped all their lives, wouldn't you be afraid?"

If Jezebel was half as bad as she was described, Michael decided, she must be a repulsive creature indeed. From what he had heard, he was already prepared to hate her quite as much as Miriam did.

"When Ahab decided to build the new palace," Miriam said, "he asked each city to give a portion of money for it. The section built by each gift was named after the city that gave it so everyone would know who had paid and who had not. The gate leading into the palace there is called the Gate of Shechem and the section at the base of the tower where the dogs are penned is known as the Wall of Jezreel."

"Was Jezreel remiss in its payments?" he asked with a smile.

"We were the first to finish them," she said proudly. "Jezreel was the old home of Omri and Ahab and our people are very loyal to his family."

The main gate of the city was bulwarked by a square tower of solid stone blocks which could also serve as a citadel in time of attack. In front of the gate was a broad open space, or esplanade, where, Miriam told him, justice was dispensed and other public activities were carried out. To one side of this was the public market, from which came a constant babel of voices as the merchants cried their wares and would-be purchasers haggled over prices.

Micaiah had decided that it was safer for him not to enter the main portion of Samaria, considering the fact

20

that he was officially a fugitive. He therefore dismounted from Aaron's horse at the foot of the slope leading to the gate and, after thanking Michael again for saving his life, strode away, his tall figure soon disappearing among the houses that covered the slope around the city wall. Michael also dismounted and led his horse the rest of the way so Miriam could ride in a more ladylike fashion when they entered the city.

Seen at close range, the wall surrounding Samaria appeared to be of almost impregnable construction. Only prolonged attack by a siege train would be able to breach it, if at all, Michael decided. The fact that the main part of the fortification was based upon the solid rock forming the rounded eminence of the hill also made attack by sapping against the walls practically impossible. Easily wide enough for a chariot to be driven upon it, the wall was further strengthened by projecting bosses on the outer surface. The length of the main fortification Michael estimated at four hundred paces, with its breadth perhaps a third of that extent. All of this was enclosed by a thick outer wall, studded with towers rising above the main fortification level. Beyond that was the inner citadel of Ahab's palace, the two making up a truly formidable set of fortifications.

At the gate of the city they were questioned briefly by the captain of the guard, a tall swarthy man who took in with shrewd eyes the richness of Michael's gear and clothing and the grace and beauty of his mount. "I have not seen a horse like that since I fought in the service of Ben-Hadad of Syria," he observed.

"They are bred in the desert country east of the Jordan," Michael explained. He was not at all surprised to find a Hittite mercenary in Ahab's employ, for many kings in this region employed these skilled fighters. With a reputation for ferocity equaled only

21

by their willingness to serve whoever paid them the highest price, they were much valued by those rulers who could afford their hire.

"The lady Miriam is well known to me." Michael noted that the Hittite gave her all the courtesy he would have given to a princess—as indeed she was. "But I shall have to ask you to identify yourself to the clerk, noble sir."

A clerk sat near the gate with a papyrus scroll beside him and his sharpened pens arranged across a small palette made from a single width of board highly polished even to the small cup-shaped depressions that held the ink.

"I am Prince Michael of Judah and this is my servant Aaron," Michael told him.

The clerk quickly wrote down his name, using the alphabet type of script which had recently been carried to all parts of the world by the Phoenicians, who in turn had taken it from the Egyptians.

"I will see that the queen is notified of your arrival, Prince Michael," the Hittite captain said courteously. "Please tell the clerk where you will be living while in Samaria."

"Prince Michael will stay at my father's house," Miriam interposed before Michael could speak. "He is our guest."

"Very well, my lady," the captain said, and there was no more question of their passing.

As he entered the city, Michael could not help admiring the ingenuity with which this stronghold had been constructed upon a hilltop accessible from only one side by means of the low ridge connecting it with the adjoining peak. The top of the hill had been leveled and its sides cut away to form steep banks, one of which was the sheer drop to the terrace where the dogs were enclosed. The outer walls lined the summit of the hill with a precision that was characteristically

22

Phoenician, but this he did not find surprising, for the men from the thriving seaport cities of Phoenicia were the most skilled builders in the world. Even the famed temple of Solomon in Jerusalem had been built by them and showed the distinguishing characteristics of their style of architecture.

There had been several additions to the walls of Samaria since the original construction, Michael saw, extending the city to include the middle terraces and even the lower slopes of the hill, but Ahab's palace still dominated the entire scene. The powerful rectangular tower Michael had noticed from the outside was its highest feature, and he did not doubt that a company of skilled bowmen, strategically posted upon it and the towers above the inner and outer gates, could have made an attack exceedingly costly to an invader, even after the main fortifications had been breached.

"I once heard Ahab's palace called the 'House of Ivory,'" Michael told Miriam. "Is it because the walls are so white?"

"No. Jezebel brought ivory furniture and paneling as a part of her dowry when she came to Samaria. The Phoenicians dote upon it but to us here in Israel it seems vain. The people gave the palace the name as a term of derision."

"I saw whole rooms paneled with ivory in Mesopotamia and also in Damascus," he agreed. "As for me, I would rather use the cedars of our own land."

As they moved through the city, Michael could see that some sort of a festival was in progress. The streets were crowded and there was much laughing and shouting. Painted women were everywhere, many of them wearing robes of the thin fabrics from the looms of Phoenicia that revealed practically their whole bodies. Winesellers moved through the crowd crying their wares and business seemed to be thriving, for many of the roisterers were already staggering, although it was

23

not yet noon. Miriam's face was set in a disapproving cast and she deliberately turned her eyes away from the painted, laughing women, many of whom hung onto drunken men as they staggered through the street.

On the lower terrace, not far from the palace itself, they came to a rambling house built upon the slope overlooking the range of low hills and towering sand dunes to the west that hid the Great Sea from view. A servant hastened to open the gate and they entered a courtyard, where one of the springs Michael had noticed bursting from the earth in many places on the hilltop of Samaria poured its waters into a pool. It was cool here, with shade trees growing in the courtyard.

"This is our home," Miriam said in a tone of warm pride as Michael lifted her down from the horse. Although there was nothing ostentatious about the house, Naboth was evidently well-to-do. Several more servants came to greet their mistress, and the house was well kept, the courtyard pleasant with the murmur of water falling from the spring into a pool and the rustle of wind in the trees that shaded it and the walls.

A middle-aged man with an iron-gray beard came from the house and Miriam ran to embrace him. He was of medium height with deep-set eyes that grew warm at the sight of the girl.

"Father, this is Prince Michael of Judah and his servant Aaron." Miriam said in introduction. "But for them, Micaiah and all of us would have been killed near the border of Judah by robbers."

"I am doubly grateful to you, sir," Naboth said warmly. "Both for my daughter and for the priests of the Most High."

"The name of the noble Naboth is well known in our household," Michael answered courteously. "Only a few days ago my father was speaking of you."

"I was proud to count Jehoshaphat among my friends as a young man. His son will always be welcome in my house. But where is Micaiah?" he asked Miriam. "I thought he was coming back with you."

"It seemed safer for him not to enter the city, so he left us outside the wall."

Naboth nodded, his eyes grave. "He was wise. What about the other priests?"

"I arranged for them to be sent on to Jerusalem where they will be well cared for," Michael assured him.

At Naboth's call, a servant brought a basin of water and moist cloths for them to wash away the dust of travel. Miriam went inside while Naboth and Michael seated themselves on a bench under the shade of a tree beside the pool, and shortly another servant appeared with cooled wine and spiced cakes as refreshment. The courtyard was completely enclosed by a wall, but the sounds of merriment from the city still floated down from the upper levels where the busier parts of Samaria were located.

"Is this your first visit to Samaria?" Naboth asked.

"Yes. My travels have been in eastern lands or to the south."

"Have you been to the east recently?" Naboth's interest showed in his face.

"I returned from Assyria only a few days ago," Michael said. "My purpose in coming here was to see King Ahab, but your daughter tells me he is in the north."

Naboth lowered his voice. "I sent a messenger a few days ago asking him to return; we are expecting him tomorrow. Someone must hold Queen Jezebel in check and only Ahab can do it now."

"Miriam told me Elijah is in this area. Surely the people listen to a prophet of God."

"Even Elijah can no longer speak publicly without being in danger of his life. The queen has stirred up the people against even him."

"In Judah Elijah is regarded as the holiest of all

the prophets. We would no more let harm come to him than we would allow the holy Ark in the temple to be defiled."

"Israel is not Judah, Prince Michael, and Ahab is not your father," Naboth said. "The people have suffered greatly because of the drought Elijah predicted two years ago as a punishment when they followed false gods."

"Surely they don't blame Elijiah himself for the work of the Lord."

"Ever since the kingdom was divided and Jeroboam set up the golden calves to be worshiped at Bethel, many have sought easier faiths than obedience to our ancient laws," Naboth admitted. "When Elijah came into Israel, we who hold the old ways hoped he would be able to turn them back, but I am afraid it will take some great cataclysm, some startling miracle, to accomplish that."

"Your daughter thinks the Assyrians might even conquer Israel and enslave the people as a punishment for their sins."

"It could happen. She has been reading the scrolls of our history with Ahaziah. In former days God often took a direct hand in the affairs of Israel and we were much closer to him. But when the people demanded a king and Samuel anointed Saul, the Lord was displeased. Even though my family is descended from Saul, I suspect that much of what is happening now is the result of that displeasure."

Miriam came out of the house accompanied by a sturdy boy of fifteen or sixteen. She had changed from her travel-stained clothing to a lighter robe of softer material that complemented her dark-eyed beauty and brought out the rich highlights of her hair. There was a strength of character about the boy's face and a seriousness of purpose in his wide-set eyes that seemed oddly at variance with his youth. When Michael noticed

26

that he dragged one foot in a slight limp, he realized his identity.

"Prince Michael of Judah, this is Prince Ahaziah of Israel," Miriam said formally.

"Miriam has been telling me of your encounter with robbers, Prince Michael," Ahaziah said eagerly. "I wish I could have been there to help." Then a flash of pain showed in his eyes for a moment and he added, "Not that I could have been of much value."

"It wasn't much of a fight," Michael assured him. "We took them by surprise and our arms were better than theirs."

"You are overly modest, I am sure," the Israelite heir said. "Miriam told me the whole story."

"Including the fact that she fought better than any of us, and even attacked me?" Michael asked.

The rich color rose to Miriam's cheeks, heightening her fresh, wholesome beauty. "Prince Michael does not take himself or his accomplishments very seriously, Ahaziah," she said.

Michael raised his hand in protest. "In Judah I am so far from the succession to the throne that no one calls me Prince. Please—all of you—call me Michael."

The boy's eyes warmed in a smile. "I would like that. In the palace everyone calls me Prince, but I know they pity me because my foot was twisted at birth and I cannot run and fight like the other young princes. Here with Miriam and Naboth, I can forget that I am not whole."

"Solomon was not a great soldier," Michael reminded him. "Yet his wisdom made him the greatest king in the history of our people."

Ahaziah's eyes brightened. "Miriam and I were reading of him a few months ago. What you say is true."

Michael glanced at Miriam and met a warm look of appreciation in her eyes. He could see that she was very much devoted to the boy and could understand now Miriam's and Naboth's concern for Ahaziah's welfare. Should King Ahab be slain in battle with the Assyrian hordes, the young prince would make a wise and capable ruler with the guidance Naboth could give him.

"Do you live in the palace built by King David at Jerusalem?" Ahaziah asked.

"Yes. An ancestor of mine was the architect for the temple of Solomon."

"I wish I could go to Jerusalem and make a sacrifice in the temple."

"I shall be returning in a week or two," Michael told him. "Why not go with me then? Perhaps the lady Miriam would accompany you."

"Would you go, Miriam?" The boy turned to her excitedly. "I know father will give us an escort so we need not worry about thieves."

"All in this household is yours to command," Miriam reminded him. "I would be happy to visit Jerusalem, but with Michael and Aaron we would need no other escort. Perhaps we could even go on to Jericho. where Joshua sounded the trumpets and the walls came tumbling down."

"Have you seen it?" Ahaziah turned to Michael eagerly. "Jericho, I mean?"

"We have a small winter palace there," Michael told him. "In Judah, Jericho is called the 'City of the Palms.' Even in the dead of winter, the sun is warm there and it is almost like it is here in summer."

"Could I even go to Ezion-Geber?" Ahaziah asked. "And see the place where the ships of Tarshish sailed to Ophir for ivory, apes, and peacocks?"

"I am afraid that journey will have to wait a little while," Michael told him. "When the kingdom was divided, the Edomites retook much of that region. But if your father is successful in turning back the Assyrians, we hope to send an army into the Arabah—as

28

we call the land south of the Salt Sea—to retake the port of Ezion-Geber."

"Can one really float in the Salt Sea without swimming?" Ahaziah asked. "Or is that merely a tale?"

Michael smiled at the boy's enthusiasm. "I can vouch for the fact that it is no tale. When you dive into the water it is like striking a wall of stone. And it is impossible to drown there since you cannot sink."

"I must see it all." Ahaziah exclaimed happily. "When I am king, I will embark upon a long journey and visit all the great places of our history, perhaps even the cities of the Nile where our people labored as slaves."

"We are at peace with the Pharaohs so I am sure you would be welcome," Michael agreed. "You might even visit the cities up the river and see the great tombs built by the ancient kings of Egypt."

Miriam and the boy left the house on an errand, leaving Michael alone with Naboth. "Ahaziah is a fine young man," Michael observed. "Israel will have a good king after Ahab."

"Miriam is largely responsible for that," Naboth told him. "Ahaziah's mother was Ahab's first wife; she died a few years after his birth and when Jezebel became queen the boy was deliberately neglected. The palace children avoided him because of his limp and he was a moody and unhappy lad until I persuaded Ahab to let Miriam become his teacher and nurse. She recognized his intelligence and stimulated his interest in things of the mind rather than the body."

"Then King Ahab has accomplished some good after all."

Naboth gave him a keen look. "Don't let yourself be prejudiced too much against Ahab because of Jezebel. Israel was never really stable after the separation from Judah until the time of Ahab's father, Omri, and even he was a soldier with little understanding of statecraft. Ahab has done much for Israel and for Judah as well."

"I know my father admires him very much."

"Taking both the northern and southern kingdoms together, their extent is almost as great as it was in the time of Solomon. The whole land was prosperous, until the drought came."

"Why doesn't Ahab control the queen? Surely if he is as strong as you say he is, he should be master of his own household."

"Ahab's marriage to Jezebel was a political union, designed to strengthen Israel and promote trade through treaties with the kings of Tyre and Sidon," Naboth explained. "I doubt if Ahab ever loved Jezebel, at least not for very long. She is one of those women of rare beauty who seem to possess nothing but ambition and are incapable of real love. Ahab gave her a son in Joram but she has raised the boy in her own way."

"If Ahaziah does not inherit the kingdom, will it go to Joram?"

"Yes. And you can be sure Jezebel will do everything in her power to see that her son becomes the heir."

"Even to murdering Ahaziah?"

"One who would destroy more than a hundred unarmed priests of Yahweh would hardly balk at murder."

"But why would Ahab let her do it?"

"The northern tribes who make up Israel are not like the southern tribes in your father's realm. For one thing, you have the temple at Jerusalem with the Ark of the Covenant symbolizing the presence of the Most High, and many scholars to read and interpret the law. For another, Judah's allegience to Yahweh has been unbroken for centuries and you have not been exposed to the other religions of Canaan as we here in the north have. In fact, Jeroboam deliberately set out to draw the people away from allegiance to the temple at Jerusalem almost as soon as he was made king after

Solomon's death, lest they be drawn to Judah because of the temple."

"Perhaps that explains why the people of Israel have been so easily led astray."

"Ours is an austere faith, Michael, requiring strict obedience to the law, while the Canaanite religions like the worship of Baal and Ashtoreth encourage licentiousness and wanton behavior. In justice to Jezebel, it must be said that the people did not need much leading to desert our ancient faith."

"Is Ahab loath to control her because of the alliance with Tyre and Sidon?"

"In part, yes. The Phoenician cities have prospered through trade with Assyria by way of the caravan route that passes to the north. All of them except Arvad are neutral as far as the confederation of the twelve kings is concerned. But if Ahab should punish Jezebel and she complained to her nephew who now rules in Tyre, the Phoenicians might be drawn into battle against us. Ahab could hardly afford to have a rich nation that could hire Greek and Hittite warriors ready to attack Israel while he was occupied far to the north."

Michael could see now why his father had been anxious not to be drawn into the coming conflict with the powerful forces of Assyria and why his present trip of evaluation was particularly important.

"I am more eager than ever to meet your king," he told Naboth. "If my father will allow it, I might even take service under him against the Assyrians."

"You would learn much of battle craft," Naboth agreed. "Ahab is more than just a soldier. Once the Assyrian threat is removed, he could be the greatest king Israel has ever known, extending our domain even beyond that of Solomon."

Chapter 3

THROUGHOUT THE DAY EXCITEMENT OVER THE GREAT celebration in honor of Ashtoreth, the spouse of Baal, had been building to a fever-heat in the city of Samaria. The streets were jammed with drunken celebrants and, as night approached, great crowds began to move toward the temple of the goddess located in a grove on the summit of a hill across the narrow ridge from the main part of Samaria. Neither Naboth nor Miriam planned to attend the festival, but, consumed with curiosity about a pagan rite he had never before witnessed, Michael decided to join the celebrants pouring from the city gate.

Night had already fallen when he crossed the ridge to the rolling height upon which the temple devoted to the worship of Baal and Ashtoreth was located. Following the stream of people, he entered the grove of tall trees and came to the beautifully constructed shrine which Ahab had allowed Jezebel to have built in honor of the patron god and goddess of her country. Nor had the king acted without precedent, Michael realized, for even Solomon, one of Israel's greatest and wisest kings, had set up places of worship at Jerusalem for his pagan wives.

The central building of the temple had been built from the same blocks of polished limestone Michael had noticed in the palace and the city walls. And, like them, its walls had been rubbed until they shone like marble. A broad balcony or porch circled the building; elevated slightly above the level of the grove, its roof was made of timbers hewn from the famed cedars of Lebanon and supported by stone columns. At one side of the colonnaded balcony an area had been set apart by screens woven from rushes to form a sort of stage or dais facing the open part of the grove where the crowd had gathered. At the back of the stage was what appeared to be an alcove apparently leading into the temple itself, guarded by a curtain of rich fabric.

Beside the dais a group of musicians were playing. The music was not that of Israel with which Michael was familiar, characterized by blasts of the ram's horn trumpets called the *shophar* and the clang of cymbals. Instead it was played on flutes and harps in the Egyptian manner, with a battery of timbrels—skin-covered drums beaten by the fingers of the musicians—giving the music a throbbing rhythm that had a way of getting into a man's blood in spite of his resistance.

Reason warned Michael there was something evil here. It was apparent in the moistened lips, the burning eyes, and the shrill laughter of the drunken crowd pushing through the grove toward the stage where, quite obviously, some climactic event would occur at the height of the ceremony. Everything in his religious training insisted that this was a sacrilege, a violation of the injunction given by God to Moses that, "Thou shalt have no other gods before me." And yet the beat of his own pulse in his temples, throbbing with the rhythm of the timbrels played by the musicians, drowned out any voice of conscience. With the others he pushed on, eager to reach the front, until a sudden indrawn sigh from the massed ranks warned him that a new and dramatic event was about to occur.

A file of temple priestesses had appeared from a hidden doorway behind the stage. Their bodies were draped in diaphanous veils and as they began a slow, indescribably lascivious dance, the hoarse breathing of the crowd was like that of an animal held at bay, a deep-throated obligato to the pulse of the timbrels, the wail of the flutes, and the humming of the strings.

From somewhere behind the dais the voice of a man sounded, vibrant and throbbing, as he half sang and half intoned:

"I will summon the gods, gracious and beautiful,
Children of princes, eat of the bread with me,
And drink of the wine, my weary ones.
Come, O most favored of the gods,
Come, O most favored of the goddesses,
Come and reveal thyself to us,
Thy humble suppliants."

From the hidden door through which the dancers had filed, a strange and bizarre figure suddenly appeared. Only the body below the shoulders was that of a man. Tall, dark-skinned, magnificently muscled and wearing only the briefest of loincloths, his skin glistened with oil and he moved with the grace of a dancer or, Michael thought, a superbly trained fighting man.

From the shoulders up, the figure was that of a bull, the mask so wondrously lifelike that the jewels serving it as eyes seemed wholly alive. It had been fashioned with exquisite care by a master craftsman; even the horns arching out before the massive head were polished like silver and tipped with two glowing rubies.

"Baal!" the crowd greeted the appearance of the bull-man jubilantly. "Baal! Our father!"

Michael heard a strange voice in his ears shouting the name and realized that it was his own. Beneath it he could also hear a deep throbbing beat that he recognized as the pulse in his own temples.

"Baal!" the cry rose again. "Baal! Our Father!"

As the sound died away, the character of the music changed and, with it, the dancing of the priestesses, who had now formed a circle around the towering man in the bull-mask; where before their movements had been merely voluptuous, now they became indescribably suggestive and lewd, as they moved about the bull-god in a dance of invitation.

Michael felt a fire beginning to burn in his vitals, a flame that threatened to consume all reason and turn him into a slave of the raging desire that had seized him. When a man carrying a small wineskin staggered against him, he seized the leathern bottle from the roisterer's faltering grasp and drained it. But the wine pouring down his throat did not quench the fire within him; in fact, it only seemed to make it burn more brightly. Shouting hoarsely with the rest of the crowd, Michael found himself pushing forward toward the dais, ignoring the hands of women in the crowd who pulled at his clothing and at his body.

The priestesses dancing upon the dais were singing now in high, twittering voices:

"We are women, each the wife of Baal and his slaves.
He shall cleanse our lips with his, he shall lift us
up.
Our lips will be sweet, like the pomegranate."

The god-man haughtily refused to respond to the overtures of the women as they passed about him. One of them tore her veil with a wild cry of abandon and flung herself naked at his feet, but he spurned her. Brandishing his horns in mock anger, he drove the dancing women about the dais, tearing their robes from them until, all naked, they rushed from the stage in mock terror to the safety of the temple behind it.

By now Michael was only a few paces from the elevated stage, but the press of the crowd would not allow him to go nearer. Almost directly above him, standing upon the lower steps and towering over the people packed tightly before the small patform, was a giant Nubian. He wore a turban of white, with a single white plume attached to it by a silver pin engraved in the form of a horse's head, and a loincloth of gleaming white into which was thrust a long jeweled dagger with a curving blade. Michael had seen such slaves at the court of Shalmaneser and also in Egypt, but he had never seen one quite so tall and powerful as this giant of a man. The black ignored the crowd swirling about his knees and stared out over their heads with eyes that showed no emotion.

Repelled by the coldness of the Nubian's gaze, Michael felt a belated urge to turn back, but the crowd was so tightly packed before the stage that there was no room to move. The shouting had begun to change now. Instead of Baal, they were calling for his spouse, Ashtoreth. On the dais, the man in the bull-mask turned to the curtained recess back of the stage and his deep voice sounded again, ringing out over the crowd and silencing their premature invitations to the goddess:

"O giver of new life! O kindler of divine fire!
  She who causes the Dead Sea to spout,
  O Earth Mother from whose breast
  We are nourished and gain our strength.
  Keep not the light of thy glory from us,
  Reveal thyself that we may know thou art
    returned."

The crowd was still, every eye fixed upon the dark curtained recess. And as the people waited, hardly daring to breathe lest they break the spell being invoked by the bull-god, Michael felt his senses reel. What was happening before his eyes, he found it difficult to believe—unless a goddess was indeed to be revealed here this day in a land which Yahweh himself had promised his people should be theirs, if they worshiped only him forever.

As the voice of the man in the mask died away, a light had begun to glow at the base of the curtained recess. Slowly it appeared to creep upward, growing brighter all the while, until it filled the space behind the curtain with a strange unearthly glow. Had he been able to tear his eyes away from the curtains long enough, Michael would have seen that the slaves who had been standing beside torches burning on either side of the platform, as well as here and there in the grove, were snuffing them out with metal cups attached to long handles. Thus, as the light rose in the curtained alcove, all other illumination died away, leaving the grove and the crowd in darkness with only the space behind the curtains aglow.

Suddenly a deep "Ahh" of indrawn breath came from the crowd and a woman screamed, her voice dying away in a gurgling moan as she fell senseless to the ground. For an incomprehensible miracle seemed to be taking place behind the curtains, rendered almost transparent by the light glowing through them. The body of a woman was taking form there; though hazy and not completely defined as yet, even at that distance it was lovely beyond belief.

"Behold!" the man in the bull-mask shouted and now his voice reverberated through the grove like thunder—Michael guessed by means of a speaking trumpet built inside the mask itself. "Behold the Earth

Mother! The giver of life! Behold your goddess, Ashtoreth!"

An answering roar broke from the people as their throats gave utterance to the one word. "Ashtoreth! Ashtoreth!" they cried and Michael was not surprised to hear his own voice also shouting the name.

"Ashtoreth!" the stentorian voice issuing from the bull-mask shouted. "Reveal thyself, O Mother of Gods! O giver of life!"

Michael could not be sure, for the bull-man was now in half darkness, whether he had reached for a cord or whether it was manipulated from somewhere back of the dais itself. But suddenly the hangings that heretofore had partially hidden the woman behind them from view were drawn away. The brilliance of the light filling the recess now bathed in its radiance the body of the woman, naked in all her glorious beauty save for a tiny golden girdle about her hips and golden paint covering the nipples of her full breasts. A single blazing gem was attached to a golden chaplet in the center of her forehead and a mask of cloth attached to it hung before her eyes, leaving only dark slits through which she could see.

Michael felt a surge of desire so great that it made him tremble. Around him people were falling to the ground in obeisance before the incarnation—as they believed—of the goddess herself. Standing there while others about him were prostrating themselves, Michael was almost as conspicuous as the Nubian only a few paces away. But no power on earth could have drawn his gaze from the lovely voluptuous body revealed in the bright glow of the light that now filled the recess.

"Hail Ashtoreth!" the man in the bull-mask shouted again, his voice rolling out over the crowd. "The goddess has returned to give life."

The woman in the recess was like an incredibly beautiful statue, carved from living marble. Michael could see her breasts rise and fall with her breathing and knew she was human, but somehow she managed to keep her features immobile, showing no sign of emotion though she must be experiencing a moment of highest triumph as the people ecstatically raised their voices in shouts of acclaim.

Michael had no way of knowing the identity of the woman who had chosen to reveal herself to the great crowd that filled the grove. But the fact that she had been chosen as the earthly incarnation of the deity, her beauty, her regal bearing, and the very confident effrontery that could lead her to play the role of goddess come to earth could only mean that she was at least the high priestess. And though he did not know her name, he knew that he could not rest until he held her in his arms and possessed her, even at the risk of his life. He had known other women, but beside the earthly incarnation of the goddess they paled into mere phantoms. In the arms of such a creature, he realized instinctively, a man could experience bliss incarnate, rising to heights of ecstasy beyond which mere humans were not allowed to go.

The man in the bull-mask was kneeling before the goddess now, bowing until the jeweled horns touched the floor at her feet. When he arose and turned to face the crowd, his voice was once again magnified many times by the trumpet inside the mask.

"The goddess bids you be merry in her honor," he announced. "Let joy be unrestrained and without limit."

The answering roar from the crowd left no doubt that the people understood his meaning fully. On the dais, the lights which had illuminated the lovely glowing body of the woman were already beginning to fade, just as they had risen in intensity to reveal her. Now the hangings began to close as someone behind the dais manipulated them to shut away the body of the goddess' incarnation from sight.

His eyes still fixed upon the woman, Michael did not realize that something else was happening, something not planned for the occasion, until a sudden hush fell upon the crowd. He tore his gaze away from her just as a strange figure moved from the crowd to the steps of the platform to stand near the curtained recess where the light still coming from it would silhouette his body in stark relief.

Wiry, almost emaciated, the man wore the rough homespun robe, heavy sandals, bushy hair, and beard of a Nazarite, as those dedicated from birth to the service of Yahweh were called. His eyes were burning with a blaze of anger that made those nearest to the dais recoil. And there was an awe-inspiring majesty about him that left Michael in no doubt concerning his identity. It could be none other than the prophet Elijah, the holiest prophet in the two kingdoms whose people had long ago made a covenant with Yahweh to worship and serve only him.

"As the Lord God of Israel lives before whom I stand," Elijah shouted, "the curse of the Lord is upon you because you have gone whoring after false gods."

The people were silent before the intensity of the old prophet's rage as he castigated them for their sins. Michael saw Micaiah moving toward the dais, a look of anxiety upon his face, but found it hard to believe that even in Israel the people would dare turn upon one known from one end of the country to the other —between the traditional limits of Dan and Beersheba —as the spokesman of God.

Then a woman's voice broke the silence and Michael was sure it came from the recess where the priestess was barely visible now in the dying light that filled it.

"Kubli!" she screamed in a voice shrill with hate and anger. "Kill him!"

As if he were a giant puppet and his mistress' scream a string giving him movements of life, the tall Nubian

40

standing beside the dais began to move. Plowing through the crowd, knocking people ruthlessly to either side, he moved toward where Micaiah and a group of men had now surrounded Elijah and were trying to move the old prophet to safety. The blaze burning in the black's hitherto impassive eyes, and the obvious intensity of purpose that drove him, left no doubt of his intention to obey his mistress' command.

The Nubian's path lay right past where Michael was standing and he realized that only he, in all probability, stood between the prophet and death at the hands of the black. For unarmed as they were, Micaiah and Elijah would have no chance to defend themselves against such a giant of a man.

Tensing his body, Michael moved a little nearer the path the slave called Kubli was plowing through the crowd toward the little knot of priests that, with Elijah in the center, was moving away from the platform. As the black man came opposite him, Michael dropped to his hands and knees and launched his body at the other's legs, exactly as boys at play often trip each other unexpectedly.

If the slave had not had his eyes fixed on the struggling group of priests, he would no doubt have seen Michael's action in time to evade the barrier formed by the slighter man's body. As it was, Michael struck him full force, wrapping his arms around the other's knee as he lunged, and Kubli went down. With his own strength alone, Michael still could not have held the giant Nubian for more than a moment, but this time it did seem that the god he served was watching over Elijah. For as Kubli fell, his head struck the bottom step of the elevated stage and, when Michael rolled to his feet and plucked from his girdle the largely ornamental dagger that was his only weapon, he saw that the black would not trouble Elijah tonight. Stunned by the blow, the Nubian lay unconscious upon the ground.

41

A quick glance told Michael that Micaiah and Elijah would need no more help than he had already been able to give them by felling the giant slave. Taking advantage of the confusion and the darkness, the knot of priests was already out of sight and, in the press of the crowd, it was extremely unlikely that anyone would be able to catch them. The momentary struggle before the dais had not been perceived by many of the people packed into the grove and, with Elijah gone, the festive crowd quickly recovered its aplomb.

The man in the bull-mask was quick to take advantage of the prophet's disappearance. Moving to the front of the platform, he shouted again, "Who can stand against Baal and Ashtoreth?"

"The gods are invincible," a voice from the crowd answered the cue. "None can stand against them."

"Then let joy be unrestrained without limit in honor of the goddess," the bull-man shouted and, as if in reaction to the brief moment of guilt and fear brought about by Elijah's dramatic appearance, the people once again began to laugh and started jostling each other good-naturedly as they scattered through the grove in the darkness.

Michael did not remain near the fallen slave, lest some of the guards posted in the grove identify him as the one who had sent the man crashing to the ground. Nor did he join the people leaving the area around the stage, for he was moved by another purpose. The dais was empty now; the priestess with the lovely body had disappeared and the lights no longer illuminated the recess in which she had stood. The man in the bull-mask, too, had withdrawn through the doorway by which he had gained the stage, leaving it empty, and no one bothered Michael when he climbed the steps and crossed the elevated platform toward the door at the back of the alcove.

The servants who had snuffed out the torches when

the priestess playing the role of the goddess had first appeared were now carrying the giant Nubian away. As for the crowd, eager to obey the injunction of the man in the bull-mask, it was already spreading to other parts of the darkened grove. And the squeals of women interspersed with shouts of laughter gave an air of abandon to the scene where, moments before, people had been moaning in fear under the tongue-lashing by Elijah. It would take some more dramatic event than he had just witnessed to turn the people of Samaria back to Yahweh, Michael decided, remembering how he had himself shouted for the appearance of the goddess Ashtoreth in the fever pitch of excitement and desire generated by the scene and the loveliness of the woman chosen to serve as the earthly counterpart of the deity.

His heart was beating rapidly, but not from any feeling of apprehension, as he moved carefully along the wall of reeds toward the alcove at the back of the stage. Only a faint light shone behind the curtain and he could see that the recess was empty. But the knowledge that she who had just revealed herself must still be nearby was enough to account for the tension in his throat, the wild beat of his pulse, and the warmth of desire that still filled his loins. He must find her, he knew, find her and make sure that he would see her again.

Before the curtains hiding the recess Michael hesitated momentarily, knowing he was risking his life by going on. But the strange urgency that drove him yielded to no sense of caution and he pulled the hangings aside, revealing the small alcove they had partially hidden. It was barely large enough for one person to stand erect, and behind it a door opened inward toward the temple. With a quick glance around to make sure no one had noticed him, Michael stepped into the recess itself.

The device by which the lighting effect had been achieved was apparent at a glance. The floor of the alcove had been made from a single sheet of glass and, when he looked down, Michael saw what appeared to be the image of perhaps a half-dozen candles still glowing in the space below his feet. It took only a moment to decide that what he was really seeing was a number of highly polished reflecting surfaces, probably made of silver, by which the light of many candles had been concentrated and reflected up through the glass into the space enclosed by the curtained recess. The way in which the light had been made to increase and decrease was also explained, for the effect could easily be accomplished by removing or adding to the number of candles in the chamber below the glass plate. The fact that the effect he had witnessed had been accomplished by purely physical means did not dampen Michael's desire to explore further, however. Actually he had never doubted, after the first glimpse of lovely warm flesh, that the figure in the recess was really that of a living woman.

The door at the back of the alcove gave access to a small chamber, which had evidently been used as a waiting room for those who took part in the ceremony. A faint but stirring perfume lingered in the room, mute evidence that she who had stood only moments before upon the glass plate of the recess with her body bathed in the light reflected from below had passed through this room. Upon a stool at one side lay the bull-mask worn by the man who had impersonated the god Baal, and only a brief examination was needed to reveal how he had been able to make his voice resound throughout the grove by means of a cleverly-devised speaking trumpet built into the mask.

The room contained nothing else of importance, and with reason at last beginning to take precedence over impulse in his mind, Michael decided to go no further into the temple. Just as he was turning back toward the recessed alcove, however, another door at the back of

44

the room opened and a woman stepped into the half darkness of the small chamber, illuminated only by a small lamp burning in a bracket upon the wall. She was swathed from head to foot in a robe of rich cloth and her hair and face were almost hidden by the folds of a veil fashioned from transparent *byssus* fabric. But the voluptuousness of her body was unforgettable and Michael knew he was in the presence of the goddess' counterpart.

The priestess had apparently come to get the bull-mask and did not see Michael at first as she moved across the room toward where it lay, with the jeweled horns winking in the light from the single lamp. He had held his breath at her unexpected appearance and the sudden heady impact of the strange oriental fragrance that accompanied her. When finally he drew breath again, the woman heard the sound and whirled to face him. As the two stared at each other, with no more than two paces separating them in a small chamber, the light from the single lamp upon the wall showed him the glow of anger building up in her dark eyes.

"You!" she said in a tone of savage fury. "It was you who stopped Kubli."

"He ran against me," Michael heard himself saying. "We both were knocked to the ground." It was almost the exact truth; he could only hope the light had not been strong enough outside for her to see what had actually happened.

"Why are you here?"

"I was curious about the light—and about you."

"Why about me?"

"I have never seen anyone so lovely before," Michael said fervently. "Or been so close to a goddess."

He was sure the light of anger in her eyes had now begun to turn to one of pleasure and interest in its giver.

45

"You are very rash—and very brave," she said softly. "If the bull-god knew you were here, he would kill you."

"He is but a man," Michael said with a shrug and nodded toward the mask. "Without that, he is no longer a god."

She came nearer. "Have you ever touched a goddess?"

"No."

"Or held one in your arms?"

Answering the implied invitation, he stepped forward and drew her into his embrace. She did not resist, but a sudden tensing of her right arm and shoulder warned him that all was not what it appeared to be. He tried to draw away but her left arm was about his shoulder, holding him. And in the light from the flame of the lamp, he caught the glint of metal in her right hand as she raised it to drive the dagger home.

His training as a soldier had taught Michael to move quickly in a changing situation. Besides, while in Assyria he had spent some time training with a Greek mercenary in the armies of King Shalmaneser. A skilled wrestler in the Greek manner, the man was incredibly swift upon his feet and had taught Michael many tricks of his particular trade. That training, plus his superb physical condition, now saved his life.

Although the woman's arm was about his body, he managed to twist his right hand free and seize her wrist just before the point struck his skin. Still holding her in the crook of his left arm, he gave the wrist a sharp twist and heard the dagger fall to the floor as she gave an involuntary cry of pain.

The veil swathing her face had been pushed aside and now he found himself looking down into a pair of dark eyes in which there was no light of fear. Logic urged him to thrust her away, in case she possessed some other weapon beside the dagger which now lay

46

on the floor. But Michael was seized now with a heady excitement that knew nothing of logic, nor concerned itself with safety. Conscious only of the full lips almost touching his own and the feel of the almost naked body in his arms, he released her wrist and drew her into his embrace, even as he crushed her lips with his own.

Only for a moment did she resist, as if refusing to let herself yield to one who moments before she had sought to kill. Then her lips parted beneath his own and she clung to him, responding eagerly to the overwhelming surge of desire that was sweeping through his body like an engulfing flame. For an instant of time that seemed an eternity, Michael was lost in the warm fragrant cavern of the priestess' eager mouth, the passionate yielding of the body whose every lovely contour he knew by heart from the scene he had witnessed outside in the grove only a few moments before. His hands parted the folds of her robe and found the soft, yielding, but ardent flesh beneath. Then as he released her momentarily to seize the edges of the robe and tear them apart, stripping her naked here in the small room as she had posed in the alcove outside, she pulled herself away quickly. With a mocking laugh, she broke free of his grasp and, moving lithely across the room, disappeared through the door by which she had entered.

Michael was at the door before the sound of its closing had died away in the small chamber, tearing at the knob with his fingers. But even before he reached it, he knew it would be locked. His fists were raised to hammer upon the door and demand admission to the innermost part of the temple where the woman-goddess had fled, but reluctantly he let them drop. The small dagger with which she had tried to kill him lay upon the floor and he picked it up, holding it up to the light of the lamp on the wall. The handle was of ivory set with tiny jewels, and carved into an exquisite miniature likeness of a horse's head, the same symbol he had noted earlier attaching the plume to the turban of the Nubian slave. Thrusting the dagger beneath the girdle of his robe, he stepped through the door and the curtain hiding the alcove into the night, not depressed in the least that the woman had escaped him.

Somewhere—and he suspected before very long—he would meet her again. And this time, she would not be able to break away with only the teasing promise of a kiss and an embrace as a token of the indescribable ecstasy her yielding fully could bring to one who became her lover.

Chapter 4

MICHAEL DID NOT SPEAK OF WHAT HAD HAPPENED IN the grove when he returned to Naboth's house. The encounter with the human counterpart of the goddess Ashtoreth was much too intimate an experience to discuss with others. When he awoke in the morning, he decided to see some more of the city of Samaria than he had been able to visualize that afternoon when they had ridden in from the south. Naboth had gone out on affairs of his own, so, leaving word that he and Aaron would return sometime in the early afternoon, Michael and his servant started walking through the town.

As with all Canaanite cities, most of the streets were narrow, although a main thoroughface had been cleared through the central portion of Samaria leading to the palace fortress at the top of Watch Mountain. This roadway was wide enough for chariots to come and go and, as they walked along, Michael saw that extensive preparations had been made for the accommodation of mobile forces. Several buildings were devoted to stalls for bedding down horses, and other to garrisoning the men who fought from the chariots, as well as for the repair and upkeep of the vehicles themselves.

Although the city of Megiddo to the north was the main fortified center of the northern kingdom, Ahab had also made Samaria into something of a secondary bastion, probably because of the almost impregnable position of the palace fortress upon the hilltop and the possible necessity of defending the capital one day against an invader who might break through the northern fortifications into the rolling hill country that was the heart of Israel. The city was thronged with soldiers wearing the colorful uniforms of the Israelite warriors, as well as with mercenaries—brawny tough-looking men of many nationalities who would be able to give an excellent account of themselves in a battle.

Not far from the gate and to one side of the broader thoroughfare was the open market Michael had noticed yesterday when he rode into the city with Miriam. From it rose a constant babble of sound as trading went on from dawn until dark. Soldiers wandered through the markets and along the streets, pausing to accost the painted women who moved about with the provocative walk of the courtesan, braceleted and ankles jingling.

The city had evidently grown very rapidly in recent times for, as in Jerusalem, groups of houses were spread out well beyond the walls upon the surrounding slopes. Most of these were built of brick and solidly roofed, since the roofs here, as in every Canaanite city, were used for sleeping places in warm weather. Many of the larger houses had paved courtyards into which chariots could be driven directly, by which Michael judged that they were probably the living quarters for high-ranking officers of Ahab's army. Everywhere an almost feverish military preparation was going on, proof that Ahab realized fully the danger posed by the Assyrian hordes of Shalmaneser III.

It was almost noon and they were looking for the shop of a wineseller where they could rest and refresh themselves in the shade, when the sound of shouts came from lower down the hill and the rumble of chariots sounded through the streets. Michael and Aaron barely had time to reach the main thoroughfare before a squadron of chariots came through the street at full gallop, sending the people scattering in all directions. Standing beside the driver in the lead chariot was a tall man with a jet-black, spade-like beard. The crested helmet of a high-ranking officer was upon his head; his armor had been polished until it shone like gold and the harness of the horses pulling the chariot was also chased in gold.

The leader's bold profile, his flashing eyes, his obviously regal manner, and the magnificence of his trappings indicated that he was a person of considerable importance, in addition to being one of the handsomest men Michael had ever seen. When he saw the people of Samaria prostrating themselves upon the ground as the lead chariot passed, Michael realized that this must be their king.

Ahab rode the chariot with the easy manner of a skilled soldier, holding with one hand to a strap attached to the frame and balancing himself easily upon the swaying vehicle. In a rack beside him stood two spears and a polished shield, while a sword with an engraved golden hilt hung from his belt. Looking at the Israelite ruler, who seemed to embody every military quality which he, as a fellow soldier, would naturally admire, Michael found it hard to believe a woman could persuade Ahab to turn aside from the worship of his father's god. A natural leader of men, it seemed likely that this tall powerful man would not let himself be swayed by anything except his own decisions.

Around them the people who had prostrated themselves in the dust at the approach of the king's chariot were rising, but few shouts of greeting could be heard and none of the enthusiasm Michael would have expected at the return of a popular ruler to his capital.

51

Instead, the people returned to their work, grumbling to themselves, although no one lifted his voice loudly enough to be heard very far away.

"The inhabitants of Samaria seem to have little love for their ruler," Michael observed to Aaron as they continued in search of a wineshop and refreshment.

"Would you, if the greater part of what you earn was taken as taxes to equip chariots, buy horses, and build stables?"

"Surely they know he is only protecting them against the Assyrians."

"It makes little difference whether they are oppressed by Ahab in the name of building an army or by the Assyrians in the name of Shalmaneser. Either way the little people have nothing to gain."

It was the sort of shrewd commentary Michael had learned to expect from Aaron. The men in the chariots behind Ahab had been mercenaries, many of them the tall dark-skinned Hittites who served any master able to pay their wages. In battle they would fight bravely and well, but Ahab could not expect to wage war very long, even in defense of his country, unless his own people were fired by the fervor of patriotism.

Entering the open door of a wineshop, Michael and Aaron found themselves in a courtyard shaded by the spreading branches of a large tree. The proprietor came bearing wine cooled in a spring and poured it for them. He seemed to be in no hurry to leave after he had filled their goblets, so Michael took the opportunity to learn what he could at first hand about the feeling of the people in Samaria toward their ruler.

"Is King Ahab fortifying most of the cities of Israel in the same manner as Samaria?" he asked.

The man gave him a keen look. "Are you travelers, that you do not know what is happening in Israel?"

"It is the first time we have been to your city."

"The fortifications of Samaria are not equal to those

52

at Megiddo to the north," the wineseller said with some pride. "From there we can control the pass leading into the coastal plains southward to Egypt."

"But everyone seems to think the Assyrians will be met farther to the north."

"True," the wineseller admitted. "But King Ahab does not entirely trust King Hadad-Ezer of Syria, with whom we are in league. Only a little while ago they were at each other's throats and the Syrians still hold our city of Ramoth-Gilead across the Jordan to the east."

Michael was familiar with these facts, of course, but he preferred to maintain the fiction that he was not. "You mean the king fears his allies might desert if the battle starts and leave him to fight alone?"

The wineseller shrugged. "When you are dealing with Syrians, anything is possible."

"Does King Ahab plan to retreat to Megiddo in that event?"

"The talk among the soldiers who should know is that he is fortifying Megiddo for another purpose," the wineseller confided. "No doubt the Assyrians intend to move against Egypt if they defeat us in the north. But if they are to succeed, they must come through the pass at Megiddo with their chariots and take the coastal route southward. With the city heavily fortified and many chariots and soldiers to defend it, a large army could be bottled up and kept immobile for a long time."

"Surely King Ahab is not foolish enough to think he could stand alone against the whole Assyrian army," Michael protested.

"There is an old saying among our people, 'He who would enter the door must first buy the key,'" the wineseller said with a knowing smile. "Megiddo is the door, and the pass there is the key."

Michael understood something of Ahab's strategy

now and could admire the forethought which had directed it. In fortifying a city considerably to the south of where the expected stand against Assyria would be made by the confederation, the Israelite monarch was building a safeguard against the time when some of his allies might desert him. For the Assyrians to take such a fortified point would require weeks and perhaps months of siege, delaying them in any advance southward and causing a considerable expenditure of both money and men. Under such circumstances it would be to Shalmaneser's advantage to leave Ahab and Israel alone in return for opening the pass by way of Megiddo and allowing the Assyrian hordes to pour into the coastal plains and take the straightest and shortest route to Egypt.

"It sounds as if your king is very clever," Michael observed.

"Ahab did not originate the idea, but one far wiser than he," the wineseller said. "A long time ago, King Solomon fortified Megiddo for that very purpose, in case the alliances he had made with surrounding nations did not serve to protect us. Solomon built the first walls of Megiddo and the first stables; Ahab only took up where he stopped and then went on to strengthen the fortifications here at Samaria."

"It seems there would be little chance of an invader taking a strong point like your city," Michael observed.

"True," the wineseller agreed. "But King David took Jerusalem by means of a trick. Some such thing could happen here, so Ahab has taken no chances. Even if the walls of Samaria were breached, he could retire to the fortress there on the hilltop and hold out indefinitely. He always keeps a large store of food and weapons there and water comes from a pool in the courtyard."

It was mid-afternoon before Michael returned to Naboth's house. There he was told that a royal levee or reception had been announced for that evening in honor of Ahab's return and, as a member of the court, Naboth was expected to attend with his guest. Miriam had already been called to the palace in her capacity of a lady-in-waiting to the queen to help prepare for the affair.

Michael had brought only military gear with him but, knowing that—as a member of the royal house of Judah—something more would be expected of him on an occasion such as this, he went to a Phoenician bazaar and there purchased garments suitable for a court appearance and a gift which he thought would be appropriate for King Ahab.

Over the white loincloth that formed the basic masculine garment in all levels of Canaanite society, he wore a *chiton* or long shirt of soft material extending to his knees. It was pale yellow, a color which the Phoenician bazaar-keeper assured him was very much in favor in that part of the world. The hem was ornamented with a delicate embroidery depicting scenes of Phoenician ships and soldiers triumphing in a great battle over an enemy. Over the shirt he wore a long strip of rich fabric which, after being wrapped about his hips, passed up and around his chest to be spread over his shoulders almost like a cape. Red boots or buskins of soft leather completed his attire.

His hair was carefully combed but was not left long or frizzed and curled in the manner affected by the Assyrians and, he had noticed, many of the dandies of Ahab's court. On his head he wore a soft cap of dark purple color held in place by a fillet of gold embroidery. And since the spring evening was cool at this height, he wore a long cloak of Tyrian purple hanging from his shoulders and dropping almost to the floor. He had no way of knowing whether the beautiful high priestess from the temple of Ashtoreth would be at the levee, but as a finishing touch to his dress he thrust the dagger with the handle carved into the likeness of a horse's head into the ornamental scabbard at his waist.

The palace of King Ahab was quite as formidable and as luxurious as it had appeared to be upon their arrival yesterday. The pool the wineseller had mentioned was in the courtyard between the two palaces. Michael could see that it was quite adequate to supply the garrison with water, in case a final defense of the citadel ever became necessary. A large door of hewn cedar ornamented with bronze scrollwork gave access to a small court or foyer from which, in turn, he and Naboth entered the main court of the palace. The foyer was covered by a pattern of shells from the shores of the Great Sea set in a flooring of lime which was quite hard, the whole polished until it shone. From the foyer they came into the central courtyard, where a large number of guests were already gathered.

The court was open to the sky, but trees of many different varieties, some of which Michael remembered having seen in the Assyrian capital, furnished shade. A well at one side of the court was evidently the main source of water, the excess flowing into the large pool. The walls of Ahab's palace were painted in brilliant colors and from the inner court several doors led to other parts of the structure. The tantalizing smell of roasting meat, herbs, and spices, and the constant passage of servants in and out bearing food and drink marked the kitchen area. Another door led—Naboth told him—to the chambers of the royal family, occupying the main portion of the palace, and to the great tower atop the so-called Wall of Jezreel.

Opening directly off the court was a large audience chamber where two thrones of ivory heavily ornamented with golden scrollwork stood upon a dais. These, Michael surmised, must be part of the furniture Jezebel had brought from Phoenicia as a part of her dowry, which had led the inhabitants of Samaria to designate the palace as the "House of Ivory."

As Naboth and Michael came across the court, they were met by servants bearing trays of viands and small skins of wine, catering to the appetites of the guests who had already gathered there to await the appearance of the king and queen. Many of the women present had adopted the Phoenician style of dress, Michael saw—no doubt in accordance with the queen's wishes. Some even wore the newest fashion, using two large shawls, one dyed red and the other blue, which they wrapped about their bodies to create an infinite variety of patterns and colors, as well as to emphasize the outlines of their figures. Wide belts of soft dyed leather around their waists held the shawls in place.

None of the women, he saw, had dared as yet to take up the fashion favored by the Egyptians and the Dorians in which a tightly fitted bodice was cut away in front to leave the breasts bare. A few wore *chitons* made from almost transparent *byssus* through which their flesh gleamed with a warm color of pale rose.

Most of the women had adopted the Egyptian style of wearing cosmetics, with rogue tinting the cheeks and lips, a heavy stibium paste adding shadow to the eyelids, and a powder made of rice whitening their skins. Their hair was usually dressed in three divisions, with the heaviest falling down the back sometimes to the waist. The sides were cut shorter to form a framework for the face, the tresses falling usually only as far as the shoulders. A few had adopted the Egyptian style of hairdressing with many masses of curls brought together at the end of a sort of plait—ornaments of varying richness, depending upon the wealth of the individual's family, being fixed at the end.

Most of the women wore a great deal of jewelry, for, being near Phoenicia, they could easily buy exquisitely fashioned necklaces, bracelets, earrings of gold or precious stones, and ornaments of silver from the great stores of the precious metal which the huge vessels that sailed westward each spring to Tartessus —known in Israel as "Ships of Tarshish"—brought back to the homeland. Practically everywhere in the palace, as well as in the dress and ornaments of the nobility of Israel who thronged the court tonight, a strong Phoenician influence was evident, testifying to the strength of Jezebel's hold upon the people.

At one side of the court, a huge gold-fringed awning of rich Phoenician purple had been stretched to cover an area where a number of servants presided at huge bowls of wine and other beverages. Slaves also passed among the people bearing trays of highly spiced sweetmeats and other delicacies to titillate their appetites. Miriam was nowhere to be seen but, shortly after Naboth's and Michael's arrival, the blast of a trumpet announced the appearance of the royal party.

A file of palace guards preceded the rulers from the royal apartment, moving along a covered gallery leading to the throne room. They were dark-skinned Hittite mercenaries except for their captain, a tall Israelite with a handsome high-cheeked face, a jutting nose, and roving bold eyes. He was dressed in the briefest of military tunics beneath a highly ornamented leather harness, leaving his arms and legs bare to reveal their splendid muscular development. Something about him seemed oddly familiar to Michael and suddenly he realized why.

The body was unmistakably that of the man who had worn the bull-mask last evening during the ceremony in the grove of Ashtoreth.

The manner of the handsome guard captain was almost truculent as he let his gaze rove around the room. Michael saw more than one young matron color and glance quickly at her husband to see whether he had noticed the brief interlocking of eyes.

"This is Hamul, captain of the queen's guard," Naboth said. "Most of the men in Samaria hate him."

"The women appear to adore him."

"Many do. In fact even the priestesses of Ashtoreth are said to pine for love of him. But Hamul is clever; he hunts only higher game—the queen herself."

Miriam and a file of highly dressed ladies-in-waiting now appeared and took up positions behind the two thrones. Compared to the other women, Miriam's fresh healthy beauty stood out like a jewel amid stones of lesser value. Her robe of soft material was a pale mauve in color, gathered at the waist by a simple embroidered girdle containing no jewels. The fabric was held at the shoulders by ingeniously devised golden pins in the shape of scarabs. Sandals of soft finely tooled leather were upon her slender feet and laced about the ankles. Over the robe she wore a light cape, gathered in front with a slender golden chain of exquisite workmanship.

In contrast to most of the other women, Miriam wore no heavy cosmetics. Her eyelids might have been shadowed lightly with stibium—Michael could not be sure—but her cheeks needed no rouge and her dark hair certainly required none of the extract from the plant called *al-henna* which many women used to give their tresses a reddish tint. Her fingers and toenails were not painted and her only jewelry consisted of a few rings upon her fingers and several plain silver bracelets upon her wrist. A delicately chased gold fillet or chaplet held a small white cap embroidered with tiny pearls upon her dark hair.

Miriam's eyes met Michael's across the room, but when he smiled she only nodded and her eyes did not warm at his presence. The next moment, however, he saw her turn and smile graciously at someone who greeted her from the crowd. He was startled by her coolness until he remembered that she knew he had gone last evening to the grove of Ashtoreth. Hating Jezebel and the gods the Phoenician princess had introduced into Israel so bitterly, Miriam no doubt held it against him that he had even visited the ceremony.

Ahab appeared next. At close range, he was just as handsome as when Michael had seen him that afternoon riding the streets in his chariot, but somewhat older than Michael had realized. His dark hair was already sprinkled with gray, but his body was tall and muscular and he moved with the easy grace of a soldier, smiling and stopping to speak every now and then to people as he passed.

It was to the woman beside Ahab that Michael's gaze was immediately drawn, however. And at the sight of her, he caught his breath in an involuntary gasp of surprise.

The priestess who had revealed her nude loveliness last evening as the incarnation of the goddess Ashtoreth and Queen Jezebel of Israel were the same!

Chapter 5

NABOTH HEARD MICHAEL'S INVOLUNTARY INTAKE OF breath and asked, "Is anything wrong?"

"I am surprised that the queen is so young and beautiful."

"She is much younger than Ahab," Naboth said dryly, "though not quite so young as she appears."

Michael did not even hear the words; he had eyes only for Jezebel. Seeking something with which to compare her, he could only liken her beauty to that of the lush tropical flowers he had seen growing in the valley of the Tigris and Euphrates rivers far to the east. In every way Israel's queen was the epitome of voluptuous allure in a woman. Yet, though she was just as breathtakingly beautiful as she had been last night, she seemed to have none of the radiant vitality that had characterized her while playing the part of a goddess. Her attitude now was one of boredom, but her lips were as full and ripe as he remembered them last night and he already knew how easily they could warm with the fire of passion.

A surge of overpowering desire for this passionately beautiful woman swept through Michael, and his pulse began to hammer with a rhythm fully as compelling as the timbrels had beaten last night. Everything about his upbringing, training, and religious belief named his desire for another man's wife for what it was—a mortal sin. And yet he could no more have denied its presence or the urgency of its demand upon his body and his soul than he could have turned his eyes away from its cause.

Jezebel had not seen him yet and Michael found himself wondering whether she would remember him, for it had been dark in the small room back of the stage and they had been together for only a few moments. Then he remembered the jeweled dagger she had dropped and thought of a way to remind her of his identity, without revealing to others that they had met before.

The king and queen had now seated themselves upon the throne chairs of the audience chamber and a line of guests began to form before the dais. When Naboth took him by the arm, Michael willingly stepped into the line and began to move forward. The tall officer Naboth had called Hamul now stood a little behind and to the right of Jezebel, as befitted the captain of her personal guard. On the other side of the throne was the giant Nubian slave Michael had foiled last night in the attempt to assassinate Elijah. The slave showed no sign of recognition, however, so Michael was sure the Nubian did not know he was the one who had tripped him last night in the darkness.

When Michael's eyes met Hamul's, the other man's hand dropped almost caressingly to the hilt of the sword hanging from his elaborately jeweled leather harness. It was a gesture of contempt and challenge, but whether the action was deliberate or unconscious, Michael could not at the moment tell. In any event, it was obvious that Hamul closely observed any man approaching Jezebel who might conceivably incite her interest.

Naboth bowed before Ahab, who acknowledged the tribute with a smile and a friendly word of greeting. The elder then turned to Michael, who stood just behind him. "I bring my guest, Prince Michael of Judah," he said in introduction.

Ahab's eyes warmed in a smile. "The son of Jehoshaphat is always welcome at our court. When there is more time, we must talk together."

"My lord Ahab needs only to command," Michael said courteously. He had purposely not raised his eyes yet to Jezebel, nor did he do so now. Instead he took from a pouch attached to his belt a small packet he had purchased at the shop of the Phoenician merchant that afternoon. Remembering that Miriam had said Ahab's chief pastime, when not fighting or preparing for war, was growing vegetables and flowers in his garden, particularly the one he maintained at Jezreel, Michael had picked out a gift he was sure would please the Israelite ruler.

It was a beautiful thing, a piece of amber in whose depths was imprisoned a small flower, as perfectly preserved as if it had been placed there yesterday, although the Phoenician had assured him the flower had become encased in the gum from which the amber came before it had started to harden. The hardening process by which amber formed was known to take many, many, years, so it might well have been centuries since the flower had actually possessed life. Yet one could hardly have told it was not alive, except for its being located inside the block of amber.

Ahab took the gift and held it up to the light of the bank of candles beside the dais. The smile of a child pleased with a new toy broke over his face.

"What is it?" he inquired.

"Amber," Michael told him. "From Tarshish on the

shore of the Western Sea. They say the flower was impressed in it centuries ago when it was only a drop of gum from a dying tree."

"The flower is perfect." Ahab turned to Jezebel. "This is Prince Michael of Judah, my dear. See what a fine gift he has brought to us."

Michael's eyes met those of Jezebel. The boredom was gone now, he realized with a surge of excitement. Instead he saw in her eyes the same mocking glow that had been there last night when she had broken away from his embrace, and he sensed that she recognized him.

"Has the Prince of Judah nothing for the queen?" she said lightly to Ahab. "Or does he not approve of women?"

"No gift could possibly vie with the beauty of Israel's queen," Michael said. "But I do have something that might please you."

From the folds of his robe where he had hidden it, Michael brought out the ivory-handled dagger with which she had tried to kill him last night. Placing it upon his open palm, he extended the handle toward Jezebel.

From the startled look in her eyes, he knew she had not expected him to challenge her so openly into acknowledging, at least to him, that it had been she he had held in his arms the night before, but she recovered her aplomb quickly.

"It is beautiful," she said with a shrug. "But I have no need for weapons. My husband is quite strong and brave enough to protect me."

Ahab leaned forward to look at the weapon. "The dagger is just like the one I gave you last year, Jezebel," he said with a frown.

"Perhaps it is the same," Michael suggested.

"Did you lose it?" Ahab asked her.

"I may have," she said carelessly. "Or perhaps one

of the palace servants stole it and sold it to a ⸻
chant."

"In any event"—Michael placed the dagger upon
the arm of the chair where Jezebel sat—"I am happy
to have brought it once again to its rightful owner."

"By the fires of Baal!" Ahab exclaimed. "You have
given us fine gifts, Prince Michael, and you must have
something in return." He raised his left hand upon
which he wore several rings and, sliding one off, held
it out to Michael. "Accept this gift, please. It will
mark you wherever you go as a friend who has brought
pleasure to Ahab of Israel."

The ring was made of gold with a heavy seal, upon
which was engraved the figure of a chariot and horses,
the driver holding the reins and the soldier beside him
lifting a spear aloft as if ready for battle. The workmanship was exquisite and typically Phoenician in character.

"The king of Israel is as generous as he is brave,"
Michael said, placing the ring upon his finger.

"And I must add my thanks." When Jezebel extended her hand to him, Michael lifted it, placing it
first against his forehead in the traditional gesture of
fealty, and then pressing his lips against her fingers
before he released them. He saw Jezebel's bosom—
more than half exposd by the thin fabric of her robe
which was cut in the Egyptian style to display a
woman's loveliness to the greatest extent—rise and fall
quickly.

As Michael moved on, his eyes met Miriam's again.
From her puzzled expression he guessed that she
suspected there was more than met the eye in the brief
interchange between him and Jezebel. Once more he
was struck by the girl's quiet loveliness, so different
from the lush charms of Israel's queen, and a verse
from the beautiful love poem of Solomon came to his
mind:

*Who can she be like flush of dawn, fair as the
    moon,*
*Bright as the sun, breath-taking as a bannered
    host?*

But then another verse drove the thought of Miriam
from his mind in favor of a woman whose beauty
filled a man with a fierce madness that could not be
denied:

The joints of thy thighs are like jewels,
The work of the hands of a cunning workman.
*Thy navel is like a round goblet, which wantest
    not liquor.*
*Thy belly is like a heap of wheat set about with
    lilies.*
*Thy two breasts are like two young roes that are
    twins.*
*Set me as a seal upon thine heart, as a seal upon
    thine arm.*
For love is as strong as death.
Jealousy is as cruel as the grave.
The coals thereof are coals of fire,
Which hath a most vehement flame.

As Michael turned away from the dais his eyes
locked once again with those of the handsome captain
of the queen's guard. And from the dark look of
suspicion in the man's gaze, Michael was sure that he,
too, realized there had been more to the brief interchange when he had given Jezebel the dagger than
would appear at first glance.

Slaves were bringing on the main dishes of the
evening now, huge platters piled with the roast flesh
of both goat and bull, as well as delicate squabs basted
in their own juice, and pickled tunny, a highly prized
delicacy brought back from Tartessus by Phoenician

ships. There was also a large quantity of preserved fruits, dates, nuts and cheeses and wine in profusion —the latter cooled by snow brought down from the mountaintops of Lebanon to the north—as well as other rare delicacies of all lands.

The entertainment for the evening was provided by a number of young people who danced the traditional dances of Israel to the music of ram's horn trumpets, gongs of brass, and small round drums. Michael saw Miriam's eyes sparkle as she watched and noticed that she was surreptitiously keeping time with the beat of the music.

The entertainment finished, a somewhat awkward lull followed until someone shouted, "Hamul! Hamul!"

Others took up the cry and without much urging the tall captain swaggered into the half circle of guests before whom the entertainment was being presented. He stood there for a moment flexing his muscles, while the women about him cooed admiringly.

"I challenge any man in Israel to a wrestling match," the brawny soldier announced. Then he added rather pointedly, "In Israel—or Judah."

Michael had gained some experience in wrestling, since the Greek sport had swept eastward in recent years to engage the attention of young men throughout Canaan. On the recent trip to Assyria he had watched wrestlers among the Medes and Persians and had even spent a while sparring with the skilled Greek mercenary who taught them, learning some new tricks he had not known before. But this was no place to risk being downed by a mercenary captain merely to make a show, before he had an opportunity to talk to King Ahab about the situation in Assyria, the real purpose for which he had come to Samaria.

Jezebel's voice broke the silence that followed Hamul's challenge. To his surprise, Michael realized that she was speaking directly to him.

"Hamul is the greatest wrestler in all of Israel," the queen said. "He has thrown every man who came against him."

"Before that I was champion of the five great Phoenician cities," the captain boasted.

Michael realized that she was trying to taunt him into challenging the Israelite champion for purposes of her own. When he deliberately refrained from answering, he saw Jezebel's eyes grow stormy and her cheeks pale with anger.

"Perhaps the son of King Jehoshaphat follows his father in preferring peaceful pursuits to war," she said contemptuously.

Prudence—a voice to which, as an intelligent man, Michael had always listened—warned him he would be a fool to let himself be goaded into challenging the Israelite. But prudence melted before the sarcasm in Jezebel's voice and the slur upon his father's courage. Getting to his feet, he dropped his cloak upon a cushion beside Miriam.

"I challenge Hamul," he said quietly.

Beside him Michael heard Miriam gasp, and realized that she had not expected him to accept the dare. She even put out her hand as if to try to stop him, but Hamul had already turned to face him with a pleased smile upon his face.

"You have not been in Israel before, Prince Michael," he said condescendingly. "Else you would know that in all this land, Hamul is invincible."

Michael was loosening his leather girdle. "As you say, I have not been in Israel before," he retorted coolly. "So I do not know that Hamul is invincible."

There was a burst of laughter at the sally. When he saw the surge of livid color come into the Israelite's cheek, Michael knew the contemptuous thrust had gone home as he intended. An angry man rarely fought intelligently, and in a contest of strength with the brawny captain he had already decided that cleverness must be his major ally.

"We follow no rules here," Hamul warned darkly. "It is every man for himself."

Michael did not even trouble to answer. Dropping his robe upon the cushion beside Miriam he stepped into the open space before the dais, wearing only a loincloth. An "Ahhh!" of admiration went up from the feminine guests at the lithe strength of his body.

His muscles did not bulge like those of the Israelite champion, but rippled under his skin like the sinews of a lion stalking his prey.

Hamul had discarded armor and harness; now he started across the circular terrace to where Michael waited balancing himself lightly upon his feet as the Greek had taught him. That the Israelite was depending upon strength rather than skill to win over his lighter opponent, Michael realized as soon as they came together. Familiar with the classic holds portrayed on the walls of Egyptian terraces and tombs for many hundreds of years, as well as the newer Greek methods of wrestling, Michael did not really expect to use any of them tonight, for in a straightforward test of strength Hamul would be sure to win. Instead he was relying upon skill and the tricks taught him by the Greek mercenary to defeat the other man's strength.

As the two came together, Hamul reached out to seize Michael in his arms, obviously expecting to crush his lighter opponent in a single bone-breaking hold. But Michael dropped his body and twisted himself until his shoulder jammed the other sharply in the belly just beneath the ribs. The air went out of the Israelite with a great sigh and he sagged across Michael's shoulder. Straightening up, Michael lifted the momentarily breathless Hamul and in one smoothly flowing motion sent him crashing to the floor.

A cry of wonder went up from the onlookers, who

had expected no such rapid development as this. Hamul lay on the floor, stunned for a moment, and Michael bent over him, taking his hand to help him to his feet in a gesture of sportsmanship. He realized his mistake too late, for the wily soldier recovered more quickly than he had expected. Lunging suddenly, even as Michael was helping him arise, Hamul seized Michael around the middle and shoved him back until his foot slipped and he went down for the second fall.

The odds were even now, with three of the customary five falls still to go, but Michael knew he must end the contest as quickly as possible, lest Hamul win on brute strength once he managed to get him within the grip of those powerful hands. This time when the two came together the Israelite jabbed upward with a swift stroke, thumb extended with the obvious intention of jabbing him in the eye, a maneuver usually limited to contests to the death.

Michael was forced to twist his head sharply to save his sight, and the extended thumb of the other man slid across his ear, almost tearing it from the side of his head. The pain nearly made him cry out, but Hamil's act also gave Michael an advantage, as well as the true measure of his opponent. Obviously the Israelite captain would not have introduced such methods into what Michael had assumed would be only a sportsmanlike bout of wrestling unless he intended to cripple his opponent. And if Hamul wished for another and more brutal form of combat, Michael decided grimly, he would not disappoint him.

Using one of the tricks in the style of wrestling known to the Greeks as *pancration,* in which blows were used as well as holds, he seized Hamul's thumb and bent it sharply backward until he fully expected to hear the bone crack. There was a bellow or pain from the Israelite captain, who found himself, so to speak, spitted upon his own weapon. Taking advantage of the momentary lowering of Hamul's guard, Michael threw his right heel behind his opponent's left foot and, jerking the larger man's feet from beneath him, sent him crashing to the floor again for the third fall.

When Hamul came at Michael again, it was in a bull-like rush devoid of any skill or plan, and by thus letting his anger betray him he sealed his own defeat. Michael did not even let himself be squeezed in a wrestling hold this time. Pivoting his body gracefully, he chopped down upon the other man's neck as the Greek had taught him. The blow was just as effective as when he had seen his teacher use it in Nineveh. It drove Hamul to his knees half-stunned and, before the other could recover, Michael seized him and threw him to the floor in the final fall.

The contest was over and Michael was turning to pick up his robe when a sudden cry of warning from Miriam told him Hamul had not acknowledged that the bout had ended. He turned in time to receive a mighty blow against the side of his head that would have toppled a man twice his size and went down like a polled ox, falling upon Miriam and knocking her flat upon the cushioned divan.

Though dazed, Michael still had the presence of mind to flex his knees upon his body. When Hamul leaped at him, fully intending to finish him off as he lay upon the floor, he kicked up with a powerful thrust. Fortunately his heel caught the Israelite captain full in the groin and with a moan of agony, Hamul sank to the floor, clutching his belly and retching, obviously in no condition for further combat.

A stunned silence held the room at this unexpected ending to the tense battle. In the midst of it, Michael picked up Miriam, who had been knocked momentarily unconscious when he fell upon her. Carrying her in his arms and followed by Naboth, who picked up his robe and cloak, he moved across the court to the street outside. By the time they reached Naboth's palace, which was not far away, she was already beginning to regain consciousness.

Naboth had gone ahead to rouse a servant, leaving Michael with the girl in his arms at the edge of the terrace. Obeying a sudden impulse, he bent his head and pressed his lips to her soft mouth. For a moment he could have sworn there was a response from her own lips and that she returned the kiss, then her mouth was suddenly firm beneath his and he drew away. But when he looked down, her eyes were still closed and she gave no sign that she had been conscious during the brief kiss.

In the house, a quick examination assured them that Miriam had suffered no serious injury. When the old woman who had served as her nurse since childhood came in to look after her, Michael and Naboth went out into the courtyard on the way to their respective bedchambers.

"You have earned an enemy for life by besting Hamul," Naboth warned him gravely.

"I can fight with weapons as well as without."

Naboth looked at him appraisingly. "Somehow I got the impression that tonight was not just a wrestling bout between two men of skill. Had you ever known Hamul before?"

"No."

"It almost seemed that you had known Jezebel before, too, judging by the interchange between you when you gave her the knife."

"I saw her for the first time last night in the grove of Ashtoreth," Michael admitted.

"It is the queen's custom to take the part of the goddess during the festivals." Naboth hesitated, then went on. "Jezebel is an evil woman, Michael, able to bend most men to her will. Be careful that she does not do the same to you."

"What about Elijah and Micaiah?" Michael changed the subject. "Did they get safely away from the grove last night?"

"Yes. Micaiah told me how you tripped the Nubian slave and saved Elijah. If Jezebel hears of it, she will be sure to seek revenge."

"She thinks it was only an accident," Michael assured him. "I saw her—" He had not intended to reveal the fact that he had met Jezebel last night in the grove of Ashtoreth, but in fairness to Naboth he now had to go on and explain the circumstances under which it had taken place, at least in part.

"Jezebel tried to kill me with the dagger I gave her, because she thought I had interfered when the slave sought to kill Elijah," he admitted. "But I am sure I convinced her differently."

"Take nothing for granted where the queen is concerned," Naboth warned him gravely as they parted at the door of Michael's chamber. "When she is the most pleasant, you can be sure the dagger is only sheathed, waiting the proper moment to be plunged into your back."

Chapter 6

MICHAEL HAD BEEN STRONGLY ATTRACTED TO KING Ahab during the brief interchange the evening before. Had Jezebel been other than what she was, his innate decency would have kept him from pursuing any possible further relationship with Ahab's wife. But the fever that had entered his blood last night when she had revealed her naked beauty at the grove of Ashtoreth was like a devouring fire, sweeping away all normal restraints. He was sure, too, that it had stirred response upon her part, so he was not surprised when Hamul appeared at Naboth's home the next afternoon and inquired for him.

"The queen bids you join her for the evening meal," the captain informed him.

As Michael and Hamul walked the short distance to the palace, the Israelite captain was almost affable. "I must beg your forgiveness for losing my head at the end of our wrestling match last night," he said. "I am not accustomed to being bested, especially by tricks."

"You told me yourself there would be no rules."

"So I did. But the next time I will be warned. You

can be sure the conflict will be resumed at the first opportunity."

"Perhaps in a dark alley? When you have a knife and I am unarmed?"

Hamul shrugged. "We are men of the world. I see you understand my meaning."

"How do you know I will not persuade the king and queen to dismiss you for making threats against me?"

"I serve only Jezebel and she is well pleased with my services." The smile that accompanied the words left no doubt in Michael's mind as to their meaning. "Actually it will be well if you leave Samaria and move on soon, Prince Michael," Hamul added. "Particularly if you value your life."

They were in the palace courtyard now, near the steps leading up to the tower apartment. When Michael started toward the stairway, Hamul's hand gripped his arm. "Take care not to try and undermine me with the queen," he warned. "You would not succeed, but I would have to kill you nevertheless for making the attempt."

Jezebel was standing in the doorway of the balcony overlooking a sheer drop to the enclosure at the foot of the rock that formed the foundation of the tower. From far below Michael could hear the sound of the dogs that guarded access to the wall as they snapped and growled over their meat. As he crossed to where she stood, Jezebel turned to him. Her face was only a white blur in the darkness, but when she spoke, the low throaty note in her voice left no doubt as to her mood.

"Welcome, Prince Michael," she said warmly. "I thought we could have the evening meal together here and talk awhile."

She took a step toward him but caught her foot on a cushion and would have fallen—or so it seemed— if he had not caught her in his arms. She made no attempt to free herself, but turned in his embrace and her lips were only a hand's breath away from his own, about as close as they had been last night when he had kissed her in the temple of Ashtoreth. The memory of that other embrace was so strong that it broke down whatever barriers—and they were flimsy indeed—Michael had sought to erect against yielding to her allure. His mouth came down upon hers and when he crushed her to him he felt her arms encircle his neck and her body strain against him as it had done briefly last night. Her lips parted again beneath his own and he seemed to be drowning in a warm and depthless sea, but when his hands moved upon her body, the flesh easily tangible through the thin fabric of her robe, she pushed herself away.

"Not tonight," she said as if it were an established fact that she would yield to him at the first opportunity. "Hamul is in the palace and Ahab will return later. We have plenty of time yet, my dear." She gave him another quick kiss, her mouth open against his for only a moment, then stepped out of his embrace when he would have drawn her close again.

"You must have had some experience with women, Prince Michael," she said casually. "So you know that love is something to be taken lingeringly, and enjoyed at leisure, not impulsively like a boy with his first girl in the underbrush beside the road."

She moved into the luxurious chamber and sat upon a cushioned divan, motioning him to a place beside her. A small table had been placed before the divan; upon it were platters of meats and other viands, with a flagon of wine and two goblets.

"We can talk while we eat," she said. "I have only a little time free tonight, for Ahab and I have several things to discuss."

Michael sank down upon the divan. "I can think of better uses for the moment," he said glumly.

Jezebel laughed. "You and I are going to become great friends, Michael. Right now, though, there are many things to discuss about Judah, your father, and the coming battle with the Assyrians. For the first time in history twelve countries have joined together to resist the enemy, and Ahab has been appointed general of their armies."

"You should be proud of him. He is a great soldier."

Jezebel shrugged. "Husbands are like pieces in a game of Senit, to be moved about by women intelligent enough to use them well." Michael was familiar with the game; it was very popular in Egypt and had drifted north even as far as Jerusalem. Upon a flat board marked out in squares, pieces were moved about by the players according to numbers turned up by a throw of the dice.

"I would not let a wife pull me about like a puppet," he said, boasting a little.

"No," she agreed, "I don't think you would. A woman would have to get around you in other ways."

A belated stirring of conscience made him ask, "Don't you love King Ahab?"

Jezebel's laughter pealed out, light and airy in the half darkness. "Ahab is my husband, Michael. I was given to him as a token for sealing an alliance, like the piece of amber you gave him tonight."

"Surely you think more of yourself than that."

"I am speaking only of what Ahab thought of me when he married me," Jezebel corrected him. "What I thought of myself is quite another matter. I admit I was hurt when I discovered that my husband's gardens meant more to him than a frightened young girl of Tyre, but the pain lasted only a little while. I soon learned to adjust myself and to make the most of what I have here in Israel. Believe me, Michael, what I have is no small thing."

"Ahab is handsome, brave, and skilled as a soldier."

Michael was surprised to find himself in the role of defending the king of Israel to his own wife. "Surely you cannot help admiring him."

"My husband is a natural leader of men, just as it was destined that I should be a queen."

"When did you first know that?"

"As a little girl. The goddess herself told me."

"What more could you ask then?"

"I don't ask more—not now at least. My husband suits me just as he is, Michael. He leads the armies while I rule the country in his absence. When we defeat Shalmaneser of Assyria, the people of the twelve nations may well be so grateful to us that they will make us rulers over all of them."

"It is an exciting prospect."

"Why haven't the people of Judah joined us then?"

"My father is not sure it is wise."

"And you?"

"I lean toward King Ahab," Michael admitted, "perhaps because I am by nature a soldier and more interested in warlike pursuits. But I can also see and understand my father's thinking. If Judah joins Israel and moves north with the confederation to fight against the Assyrians, the whole southern portion of the kingdom will be left undefended. My father believes the Assyrians might send a force southward on the east bank of the Jordan to cross the river near Jericho at the fords. They could take Jerusalem easily with no one there to defend it and Israel would be caught between two powerful jaws and crushed."

Jezebel's eyes were deeply thoughtful. She was, he realized, as intelligent as she was beautiful. "Are you sure your father actually believes this?"

"We were talking of it only a few days ago," Michael assured her. "This is one of the main reasons why I came to Samaria. Besides, my father does not entirely trust the king of Syria. After all, Hadad-Ezer fought against King Ahab not very long ago and Samaria it-self was besieged. If the Syrians decided to attack Israel while King Ahab was occupied in the north with Shalmaneser's army, there would be no one to go against them except our troops in Judah."

"I had thought your father a weak-willed old fool," Jezebel admitted frankly. "Now I can see that I was wrong. Perhaps it really is best that he not join forces with the confederation."

"Have you considered that even the twelve kings may fail to stop Shalmaneser's army?"

She leaned back against the cushions and held out her goblet to be refilled. "I am not a fool, Michael. Of course I have thought of it."

"Or the fact that the people of the twelve kingdoms might not choose to make Ahab their monarch, even if he wins?"

She shrugged. "With Ahab at the head of a large army fanatically devoted to the general who led them to victory, they will have little choice."

It was an amazingly matter-of-fact statement, but Michael did not for the moment doubt its truth. Nor was it more than he expected of Jezebel, now that he had an opportunity to realize the intensive driving force of her ambition.

"Suppose King Ahab fails to win the victory and the Assyrians overrun Israel?" he said. "What will happen to you?"

"Beautiful women are never killed by a victorious enemy," she assured him. "And a queen naturally becomes the property of the new king."

"So whoever wins—in the end it will be you?"

Her laughter rang out again. "See how simple it all is, my dear? Statecraft is no more complicated than deciding what you will wear at tomorrow's banquet."

"You forget one thing—your own fulfillment as a woman."

"Fulfillment?" He saw that she was actually puzzled by the word.

"You must love someone—or you will one day. When you do, he will dominate you and your plans will fail, unless they are also what he wants."

She shook her head firmly. "I shall never let myself love any man in the way you mean—no more than Ahab will ever love a woman as much as he does the plants in his garden. After all, a beautiful woman never lacks for men, Michael. Why should she yield herself only to one?"

"And Ahab does not mind this arrangement?"

"My husband is happy with his chariots, his soldiers, and his gardens; he has one here and another in Jezreel. I do as I please."

"Have you forgotten the people?"

"The leaders among the Hebrews hate me," she admitted. "But I am still their queen and Ahab cannot afford the anger of Tyre and Sidon, so he will not divorce me. You saw last night how the people hailed me as the goddess Ashtoreth because I gave them wine and meat and told them to forget those silly commandments Moses brought down from Sinai."

"Have you no feeling for the people at all?" he asked incredulously.

For the first time she showed signs of anger, but it was only momentary. "Who thought of my feelings when I was made a token to bind the parties to a treaty?" she demanded. "I vowed then that I would think only of what I wanted—and get it any way I could."

She poured two fresh goblets of wine and gave him one, touching the exquisitely engraved silver vessel to his own. He was not surprised to see that both bore the emblem of a horse's head which by now he knew to be a Phoenician royal symbol. "To us, Michael," she said. "I am sure fate brought us together for a purpose. You are strong and capable and intelligent; you could easily succeed your father upon the throne of Judah."

"There is already an heir."

"Is he as strong as you?"

"No."

"Then he has no right to succeed your father. The strongest should always rule." She leaned across the cup and kissed him quickly. "You and I can accomplish much together. Join me in planning a strategy to defeat the Assyrians and, when Ahab is proclaimed ruler of the twelve nations, you can succeed your father upon the throne of Judah. Surely there is room to expand your kingdom southward."

"The Edomites have moved into the Negeb," he admitted. "And the five cities of the Philistines have always been a thorn in our sides."

"With the forces of Israel under your command you could easily destroy them and take their riches for yourself. Or even open the port of Ezion-Geber on the Red Sea and once again sail the great ships of Phoenicia to Ophir and the mines of King Solomon. I can send you shipbuilders and mariners to sail the vessels for you."

It was an exciting prospect to an ambitious man and, lulled by her voice and the wine he had drunk, Michael let himself consider it for a moment. But what she promised meant the removal of his half-brother Jehoram from the succession in Judah, something he knew he would never carry out illegally. Still, it seemed just as well not to tell Jezebel that as yet.

"Can nothing satisfy this driving ambition of yours?" he asked.

"Power can satisfy it," she said calmly. "Why should Assyria be the strongest nation in the world? We have more people in Canaan and greater resources than they do. Joined together in one nation, Canaan could rule the world—from the Nile to Babylon."

"With you as queen of it all?"

"Why not? A woman was once Pharaoh of Egypt. Her name was Hatshepsut and history says she ruled better than men."

There was only one answer, Michael decided; Jezebel was mad. But it was the sort of madness that had come upon many others before her, though never before that he knew of to a woman—unless it was this Hatshepsut to whom she referred. It was a madness that could plunge the world into sudden war, too, but Jezebel, sitting there beside him with her head held high, her eyes flashing, and her magnificent bosom rising and falling rapidly with the excitement of the prospect she had been painting, was obviously in dead earnest. More than that, she was beautiful—and ruthless—enough to achieve her aims and to make any man desire her enough to help her.

Entranced by her beauty and the freedom with which she had taken him into her confidence, Michael could not help being excited by her plans, in spite of his revulsion at the thought of what she had outlined for him. When she came into his arms again, he found it easy to maintain what under other circumstances he would have recognized as fiction, namely the illusion that he was acting for the good of Judah in finding out everything he could about her plans. All of this was quickly forgotten, however, in the intoxication of her embrace, until the rumble of chariot wheels in the courtyard brought Jezebel alert and out of his arms.

"Ahab has just arrived in the courtyard," she said. "You must leave now. There are things I must discuss with him tonight."

"But—"

"In a day or two he and Hamul will both go to

Megiddo," she assured him. "When they are gone I will send for you."

The grass was already wet with dew and Michael's sandals quickly became soaked as he made his way along the streets to Naboth's home and entered the courtyard around which it was built. The house was located upon the slope of Watch Mountain and across the wall Michael could see the hills to the east, stretching away in the distance and bathed in the moonlight. There, between the mighty rivers called Tigris and Euphrates, great kingdoms had arisen and overrun this land in other times. He had seen the strength of one of those kingdoms himself and knew that unless Ahab and his allies were very powerful and managed to crush the Assyrians when they attacked in the north, Canaan would be overrun again.

While his heart still beat rapidly from the excitement of Jezebel's beauty and the dream of an empire she had revealed to him tonight, plus her implied promise to yield herself to his love-making, Michael dared to let his imagination roam. Behind each of the great kingdoms that had grown up in this land during its history, he reminded himself, there had been a man so consumed by ambition that the force of it drove him to ride roughshod over opposition. If a man could do that, why not a woman? Especially a woman of Jezebel's intelligence and ambition served by men skilled in the arts of war and capable of leadership. As Naboth had said, through her beauty and sensual allure Jezebel could easily bend most men to her will. In fact Michael found himself admitting, in a moment of self-examination, that he would find it difficult to remain firm against it. That being true, there was little doubt that she would find others to carry out her plans, even though he refused to have any part of them.

At one side of Naboth's courtyard the water from the household spring had been collected in a small pool from which the animals drank. Michael knelt and buried his face beneath the surface before going into the house, lest Naboth or Miriam should be awake and see in his face the flush of excitement and passion that was no doubt still there. The water was cold, making him gasp, and as he wiped his face upon his sleeve he was conscious of a movement in the shadows near the house. Instantly he reached for the dagger attached to his belt, but the man who emerged from the shadows posed no threat to his bodily safety.

"Put your dagger away, Michael of Judah," the voice of the prophet Elijah said. "I raise my hand only against the enemies of the Lord."

In the presence of the holy man, Michael instinctively knelt, for since his youth he had been taught to revere the priests who served the Lord and the prophets who brought word of God's will to the people.

"Rise," Elijah told him. "I am no ruler of men, but a simple man who seeks to understand the will of the Lord."

Michael got to his feet. "Queen Jezebel has sworn to kill all the priests of the Most High," he warned. "Your life is in danger as long as you remain in Samaria."

"Ahab will not let Jezebel kill me," Elijah said calmly. "Even though he is concerned mainly with arms and battle, he has not wholly forgotten the teachings of his youth. Besides, he returned to Samaria because I summoned him."

"You summoned the king?" Michael asked incredulously.

"The time has come for the drought to end. The people have suffered much; now they must be shown the way back to God."

Michael looked up at the sky. "I see no sign of rain."

"Israel must first gather at Mount Carmel where God will triumph over Baal and Jezebel. Only then will the rain come and the drought be ended."

"If you can foresee the future, can you not tell what will happen in the battle with the Assyrians?"

Elijah was looking out across the valley to the eastward, toward where the Jordan lay in its deep cleft, far below the level of the hill upon which they stood. "Israel has sinned before and gone whoring after false gods," he said. "Each time when there seemed to be no hope, the Lord raised up a leader to free his people. He will not fail them now."

"But Ahab is already their leader."

"The Lord is served by divers people in divers ways," Elijah said cryptically. "Perhaps he is even being served by you tonight, Michael of Judah, stealing back after a secret meeting with Jezebel."

Guilt left Michael tongue-tied. Before he could speak, Elijah continued: "Naboth told me you were summoned to the palace. It was inevitable that Jezebel would seek you out and try to use you in furthering her dreams of ruling the world."

"Can you read her thoughts?" Michael asked.

"The minds of men are open to God," Elijah reminded him. "The fact that Jezebel does not acknowledge Yahweh will not put her outside the power of the Lord."

"Then you could stop her now if you wished?"

"Jezebel's fate was decided long ago," the old prophet told him. "The dogs that will one day eat her flesh have already been born."

Michael could not repress a shiver of dread at the words, for there was no shade of doubt in the old prophet's voice. "How do you know I will not warn her?"

"No warning of yours could save Jezebel from her fate," Elijah told him. "The wrath of God can seek one out even in a secret place, so be careful lest it be loosed against you."

Chapter 7

THE NEXT MORNING THE NEWS RACED THROUGH Samaria that Elijah had challenged the priests of Baal to a test of power to determine who would be the supreme god in Israel. Elijah himself had named the conditions for the test, according to the report, and both Jezebel and Ahab had accepted them. The contest between the two deities would be held in a week upon the heights of Mount Carmel, the bold headland jutting out into the sea a little to the northwest of Megiddo.

In the capital, the forthcoming contest was already being treated as a game, with active wagering in the streets on the outcome. In order to be in close proximity to the scene of the test, Ahab ordered the court removed to Jezreel, the ancient homeplace of his father Omri. Jezreel, Michael learned from Naboth, served in a way as capital for the northern portion of Israel, just as Samaria served as capital for the southern area. And since his host possessed an estate and a vineyard adjoining that of King Ahab, Michael was invited to travel with Naboth's household to Jezreel for the test.

During the day, Michael heard Miriam's voice from time to time giving orders to the servants as preparations were being made for the journey to Jezreel. But he rarely saw her, and even then she passed him quickly with only a nod of greeting. He had wanted to thank her for warning him against Hamul's final attack and for taking the brunt of it when he had been thrown upon her. But when she showed no warmth for him he became a little angry and did not go out of his way to speak of it.

"Lady Miriam is displeased with you, master," Aaron said as they were packing their belongings for the journey to Jezreel.

"Why?"

"Because you visited Queen Jezebel the other evening. Didn't you know she had gone to much trouble preparing a supper of dishes she was sure you would like?"

"She said nothing of it to me," Michael protested. "Besides, I could not refuse a command of the queen."

"The household gossip is that you and Jezebel were alone for a long time in the apartment on the tower."

"We were only talking, discussing the coming battle with Assyria."

"Then you were wasting time." Aaron was a phlegmatic individual who looked at things from a very practical viewpoint. "They say Hamul has sworn to kill you because the queen looks with favor upon you. In the drinking houses men are making wagers on how much longer he will let you live."

The idea of himself and Hamul fighting over another man's wife angered Michael. "Do you think I would dare cuckold a king?"

"In this case you'd be a fool not to do it if you could," Aaron said matter-of-factly. "Jezebel is one of the most beautiful women alive and you would certainly not be the first."

"How do you know that?"

"It is common talk among the servants at the court

that she has had a dozen or more lovers since she married Ahab. Hamul is the most recent."

The memory of Jezebel's beauty and her promise when he had left her last night sent a warmth glowing inside Michael's body once again, a warmth he could not have prevented from arising there even if he had tried. He made no attempt to do so, for what Aaron had said only confirmed Jezebel's admission concerning her relationship with Ahab. And since it was true that they no longer lived as man and wife—he told himself in order to assuage his few remaining twinges of conscience—there was no reason why he should feel a sense of loyalty to Ahab or any reluctance toward going on with an affair with Jezebel.

"What else does the palace gossip say?" he asked as Aaron was combing his beard.

"Queen Jezebel hates my lord Naboth and the lady Miriam, but that is hardly news."

"Why should she hate them so much, except that Naboth helped the priests escape?"

"Before the drought Jezebel wanted to buy Naboth's vineyard in Jezreel and give it to Ahab as a present to enlarge his garden there. My lord Naboth refused to sell his inheritance and the queen cannot abide anyone not letting her have her own way."

"Naboth had every right to refuse under our law."

"Jezebel does not obey the law. Besides it is no secret that my lord Naboth and a man named Obadiah helped hide Elijah and arranged for the priests to escape when Jezebel was persecuting them. The lady Miriam was with the priests when we found them on the road to Jerusalem and everyone knows my lord Naboth and Obadiah are the leaders among those who support Yahweh against Baal in the councils of Israel."

"You seem to have accumulated a lot of information," Michael observed a trifle caustically. "Is there anything else I should know?"

"It is said that the king tires of feeding the priests of Baal who follow Jezebel like dogs at her table. Everywhere she goes a dozen slaves carry a statue of the goddess Ashtoreth as if she were riding upon a chair. The priests make daily sacrifices in the queen's name and give the meat to the poor, but since the drought the price of bullocks has gone so high that King Ahab is tired of paying out such great sums to feed them. Some say that is why he came back to Israel when Elijah sent word that he was willing to challenge the priests of Baal to a test and end the drought."

"Just what kind of a test is this supposed to be?"

"Nobody seems to know except my lord Elijah," Aaron admitted. "They say in the streets that Jezebel agreed to it only because she intends for Baal to triumph at any cost. Then she can destroy Elijah and the rest of the priests of Yahweh—along with my lord Naboth and the lady Miriam."

More than once Michael had learned the truth from palace gossip relayed by Aaron and he knew that what the servant was saying might very well be true. If it were, he must do what he could to save Naboth and Miriam, even at the risk of earning the displeasure of Jezebel.

"One of the priests of Baal was boasting in the wineshops that the plan is already set," the servant added. "He said Jezebel agreed to let Elijah have his way so she can destroy him."

"How could she do that with King Ahab in Israel?"

"I did not learn the details of the plot," Aaron told him. "The priest was just getting drunk enough to reveal it when another one came and took him away."

"You still haven't told me why Miriam is avoiding me," Michael reminded him.

Aaron shrugged. "If you don't know the answer to

that question," he said cryptically, "then Jezebel must indeed have addled your wits."

The fact that Michael was traveling in the same group with Naboth and his daughter necessitated an occasional contact between him and Miriam but it was never more than that. She seemed to have lost all the warmth she had exhibited toward him in the early days of their acquaintanceship and, since she obviously had no particular desire for his company, Michael made no attempt to force himself upon her. With this state of what might almost be considered an armed truce between them, the journey northward began.

Two afternoons later, the small party in which Michael, Aaron, Naboth, and Miriam were traveling with the prophet Elijah paused in the hills above Megiddo. The city of Jezreel, and Naboth's home there, still lay several hours' journey away across the valley when Naboth ordered a camp made on the slope of Mount Carmel and announced that they would go on to Jezreel the following morning.

At Ahab's request, Prince Ahaziah was traveling with the king's party and, since Miriam was riding a donkey after her shake-up on the night of the palace fete, their progress was somewhat slow. Michael was not impatient, however; it was his first visit to this part of Israel and he was enjoying the ride through a region containing many shrines sacred to its history. Besides, he was happy with the opportunity to study the military situation here, where a climactic battle might well be fought if the Assyrians succeeded in breaking through the first line of defense being hammered together by Ahab and the twelve kings in the region far to the north around the city of Hamath.

They had made camp for the night in a small clearing not far from the road. While the servants took care of the animals and went about preparing an evening meal of roasted goat's flesh, Michael stood upon an outthrust rock studying the surrounding countryside. It was still not quite dark and only a few miles away he could see the walls of Megiddo, guarding the junction point of two of the world's greatest caravan routes.

One of these was the "Way of the Sea" leading from Damascus and the fabled lands to the east, past the lovely harp-shaped Sea of Chinnereth into the central portion of Canaan and thence southward to the so-called "River of Egypt" marking the border with that land. The other route led from the Phoenician centers on the coast eastward to the fortress cities of Megiddo, Taanach, and Ibleam, all of which had been fortified by Ahab in order to guard the fertile plain called the Valley of Jezreel where so much of the early history of the Israelites had taken place. From this point, the road turned southward to the ancient city of Shechem near which King Omri had built the city of Samaria.

In the Valley of Jezreel, Michael could see the bed of the stream called Jalud, almost dry now because of the terrible drought which had afflicted the land for several years. In wet weather, Naboth had told him, the stream was a veritable torrent, delivering its water eastward to the Jordan. A third, but minor, caravan route ran through the valley, crossed the Jordan, and joined another age-old thoroughfare called the King's Highway, leading southward into the area of Moab and the domain of the savage tribes living to the east of the large enclosed lake into which the Jordan poured. This was variously called the Salt Sea or the Sea of Judgment —because, many centuries before, the cities of Sodom and Gomorrah upon its shores had been destroyed by its overflow during a great cataclysm.

It was cool upon the hillside where the camp was located and Michael wrapped his cloak about him as he watched the servants prepare the evening meal. Miriam had walked along the roadway a little distance

—no doubt, Michael surmised, to avoid any contact with him. When he suddenly heard her cry out, he turned quickly in the direction she had gone.

The girl was less than fifty paces from the edge of the camp; he could see her clearly, standing like a statue, her eyes fixed on something upon the ground. Suspecting what had happened, he reached for his bow and quiver and began to move quietly along the path toward her, knowing that if he startled her she might try to run and bring real danger to herself.

Miriam did not move and Michael was soon able to see the cause of her fright. In front of her, hardly a full step away, a venomous serpent was coiled. As large around as his wrist, it was fully as long as Michael was tall. The flat, reptilian head was slightly raised as it moved rhythmically from side to side, the beady eyes centered upon the pallid face of the girl. Michael could see that Miriam's eyes were fixed upon the snake, her face frozen in a mask of horror and fear, while her body was as rigid as a marble statue.

Careful to make no sudden movement that might cause the serpent to strike, Michael fixed an arrow to the string of his bow. Slowly he drew it back and, aiming carefully, let the arrow fly. He had not dared to aim at the moving head of the snake, lest he miss and cause it to strike the girl. Instead the heavy arrow drove into the coiled body only a short distance back of the head, penetrating it and anchoring the snake to the ground so it could not strike.

The flat head of the serpent jerked spasmodically several times but the arrow held it firmly beyond the reach of Miriam's body. Moving closer, Michael sent a second arrow winging toward the reptile, penetrating the body nearer to the head this time and killing it instantly. Dropping the bow, he hurried forward to catch Miriam as she swayed and toppled into his arms.

He held her thus until her shoulders stopped quivering and she raised her head.

"I—I never saw one so close up." Some of the terror that had held her rigid and spellbound was still in her eyes. "It was so beautiful—and so evil—that I could not move."

Michael helped her back to the fireside, where her maid hurriedly brought cushions so she could prop herself against a rock. A cup of wine soon brought the color back to her cheeks, but her eyes were still half dazed by the close brush she'd had with death.

Remembering the way Miriam had buried her head against his breast and the softness of her hair against his face, Michael found himself experiencing something far different from the raging passion Jezebel had stirred within him, an emotion deeper and warmer than anything of its kind he had ever experienced before. Having seen Miriam menaced by death under the fangs of the serpent, he knew now that what he felt for her was infinitely more important than the purely carnal passion Jezebel had stirred within him.

If he were to earn Miriam's love, he decided, the first step must be to have nothing else to do with Israel's pagan queen. As soon as the affair here upon Mount Carmel was ended, he would discuss with King Ahab the strength of the Assyrian military forces and his father's decision to remain behind to protect the southern frontier. With that completed, he need no longer stay in Israel, where Jezebel's presence was a constant temptation. Instead he would journey back to Jerusalem and raise a small troop of cavalrymen to follow Ahab into battle. And once the Assyrians were turned back and both Israel and Judah made safe, he would ask his father to approach Naboth in regard to a marriage with Miriam.

When the evening meal was finished, they sat around the embers of the dying campfire while Miriam spoke

94

of the glorious events in Israel's history which had taken place in this region. Across the Valley of Jezreel Gideon had dared to battle the Midianites who, with their camels, had been ravaging the land. Not far away Barak and Deborah had fought the armies of Sisera and Jabin upon the plain and triumphed when the Lord sent a deluge of rain, turning the plowed fields into mud and miring the chariots of Sisera's hosts into immobility. Michael did not speak to Miriam of the decision he had made; there would be time enough for that later on. But he was sure her feelings toward him had changed since he had saved her life a second time and that she had not forgotten that other occasion near Ephraim, far to the south, when he had sat beside another campfire and listened while she spoke of the Vale of Jezreel and the exciting events that had happened there. When finally Miriam went to the tent erected for her, Michael wrapped himself in his cloak and lay down beside the fire to sleep.

The valley below was still shrouded in the haze of morning when he awakened. Around him the others were asleep and, getting to his feet carefully so as not to awaken them, he left the camp and moved along a faint path visible on the hillside. It soon began to wind upward toward the heights above and, curious to see what the area looked like from the higher elevation, he began to climb.

The going was fairly easy although the path trended steadily upward. After perhaps a quarter hour of walking, he came out in the midst of a clearing at the very top of the height forming this part of Mount Carmel. From his elevated position he could look down upon the valley, slowly being illuminated by the sun's rays as they crept over the eastern rim of hills hiding the lake called Chinnereth from view.

Villages and farms, flocks and herds, vineyards and fields gradually emerged from the morning haze as the sun's rays penetrated into the valley. From the vantage point where Michael stood it was easy to see why people would be willing to fight for this pleasant land which, according to Israelite belief, had been given by God to Abraham and his descendants forever as their own. Not only was it extremely fertile, with rich valleys separated by rolling hills, it was also one of the most attractive areas Michael had ever seen. He could easily see now why Ahab had built great fortifications to make Megiddo a center for chariot warfare. Food and forage were easily available from the fields in the valley below in normal times, although because of the drought they were now largely sere and dry. And from this central point a swift chariot force could move swiftly in any direction to counteract an attack by an enemy or launch a foray upon their own account.

From the camp below, Michael could hear the sound of voices as it began to awaken; the braying protest of a mule when a pack was placed upon its back broke the morning silence, and a displaced stone set up a great clatter as it went tumbling down the hillside. He should be getting back soon, he decided, and turned toward the path by which he had reached the spot. But there he stopped, his eyes widening with surprise.

When he'd first come upon the clearing in the half darkness of dawn, he had not realized it was other than simply an open space at the top of the mountain, or at most a lookout point from which watchmen might be posted in time of war. Now, in the light of the morning sun, he saw that the clearing was much larger than it had seemed at first glance, the presence of a rough stone altar at one side on the very topmost level of the hill marking it as some sort of shrine.

The altar consisted of a slab of hewn stone resting upon four uprights at about the height of a man's waist. It was blackened by the fires of countless sacrifices and stained by the blood of the animals that had

96

been put to death there. A number of flat stones surrounded the altar forming a sort of floor or terrace and, like a lonely sentinel, a tall gaunt tree stood beside it, the bark ripped in many places by lightning, which as Michael knew, seemed drawn to such single trees in the midst of open places.

Michael had seen rustic altars much like this in the hills where the country people gathered to worship at the high places against which the prophets had so often inveighed because they also served as shrines for the Canaanite gods worshiped in this land long before the Hebrews had come into it. Usually such shrines contained some sort of a statue, one of the multiplicity of local Baals that were worshiped in the form of rudely carved wooden images as tangible reminders of the deities they represented. There were no images here, however, by which he judged that this was probably one of the old altars where sacrifices had been made to Yahweh since ancient times.

Feeling a sense almost of awe before the sacred stones, the clearing, and the gaunt sentinel of a tree with the open sky above it, Michael moved closer to the altar. He had thought the place long since abandoned as a shrine but now he saw a pile of ashes upon the flat stones, indicating that someone must have made a sacrifice recently. Instinctively he looked around, half expecting to see the person who had been responsible for the offering appear. But only the blue sky of the morning met his eyes, with the long red streamers of dawn arching across it as the sun sent exploring fingers toward the Western Sea, still hidden behind the commanding ridge of Mount Carmel.

It must have been in just such a clearing that Abraham had placed his son Isaac upon a similar altar to sacrifice him, Michael thought. And with the thought came the memory of Miriam's voice and the light in her eyes as she had retold the ancient stories of Israel beside the campfire in the encampment at Ephraim the first time they had met and again here on Mount Carmel. He had been moved by them more than he could remember being moved by anything since one night in Nineveh, when he had listened while a ragged Greek minstrel, far away from his home shores, had sung a tale of high adventure and romance. It had been a fanciful tale in which stalwart warriors of his people had fought for ten years against the Trojans who had stolen away the beautiful wife of their king, winning finally through a stratagem involving a huge horse made of wood. But however unbelievable, it could not fail to stir the listeners.

Miriam was different from any woman he had ever known, Michael decided once again, as different as the night which had shrouded the sleeping Valley of Jezreel in mystery was from the day that now flooded it with beauty. Once again he felt a warm feeling of affection and a desire to cherish and protect the slender dark-haired girl, whose eyes could flash so quickly from warmth and pride to anger, and to share with her his innermost thoughts and ambitions. He would not wait for their fathers to carry out the traditional negotiations concerning the *mohair* or bride price, but when they reached Jezreel, he would speak to her of his love.

And yet, when he thought of Jezebel and the implications of their conversation in the palace tower, he could not control the sudden leap of his pulse or the feeling of constriction in his chest. Aaron would say he had fallen in love with Miriam, though still bewitched by Jezebel, Michael thought, and wondered if it could possibly be true that a man would be filled with tenderness and the desire to cherish one woman while his body burned with the fire of a purely carnal passion for another. Every decent instinct urged him to ignore the queen and pay court to Miriam. And yet he knew that if Jezebel were to send for him, he would go to her again as eagerly as a young man to his first embrace.

Lost in thought, and in conflict within himself, he did not realize he was not alone in the clearing until a familiar whirring sound told him a stone was about to be launched by a sling somewhere close by. Instinctively twisting his body to afford as narrow a target as possible, he had a momentary glimpse of a man dressed in a worn robe of tattered cloth, carrying a spear in his left hand and leaning forward in the act of releasing a stone from the sling held by his right.

Michael barely had time to escape the full force of the missile. Driven with all the strength of the thrower's arm it struck his shoulder and glanced off, but did not fell him, as the man had obviously intended. The pain was severe but Michael had no time to notice; he was already racing toward his attacker, seeking to clash with him before the man in the tattered robe could place another stone in the sling. When, realizing that he would not have time to launch the second missile, the other dropped the sling and drew back his spear to throw, Michael knew that his only chance lay in dodging the spear and engaging the attacker in individual combat.

"Jochail No!" A voice that sounded familiar shouted from the edge of the clearing. The man who had thrown the stone stopped with his spear drawn back ready to be launched as a tall man with a curling golden beard ran across the clearing toward them.

It was Micaiah, the former High Priest of Israel.

Chapter 8

MICHAEL HAD LAST SEEN MICAIAH IN SAMARIA, WHEN he and some others had hurried Elijah away from the temple of Ashtoreth in order to save the prophet's life. He was startled to see the tall priest here on the crest of Mount Carmel several days' journey from Samaria, until he remembered that somewhere here, according to what Aaron had told him, the test between Elijah and the priests of Baal was to be held.

"Are you hurt, Prince Michael?" Micaiah asked, anxiously, as he hurried up to where Michael was standing.

"No. But only because your friend there is a poor marksman."

"Jochai's father was one of the two hundred priests killed by Queen Jezebel," Micaiah explained. "When he saw a stranger in this sacred place, he naturally concluded you had been sent by her to desecrate it."

"Is this one of the ancient altars of sacrifice?"

"Yes. It was built long before I was born. Abraham himself may well have sacrificed upon this mountain."

"Then this must be the place Elijah has chosen for the test?"

"It is," Micaiah told him. "We have been making

daily sacrifices in preparation for Elijah's challenge to Baal."

Michael had wondered why Naboth had journeyed out of his way to make camp here when Jezreel would have been just as near, by a slightly different route after they left the caravan junction point of Engannim. Obviously the detour had been made in order to deliver the old prophet safely to Mount Carmel.

"Elijah will remain here on the mountain with us," Micaiah continued, confirming Michael's assumption, "while the rest of you go on to Naboth's home in Jezreel. We felt that it would be safer that way."

"Why wasn't I told of this?"

The tall priest hesitated. "You saved my life once, Prince Michael," he said finally. "I would not cause you pain by admitting we have had some doubts about you—since your visit to Jezebel in Samaria. It seemed simpler not to strain your loyalty."

"In other words you did not trust me?"

"Desire for Jezebel is a disease that grips a man so he cannot shake it off. You are not the first to yield —or be destroyed by it."

"Did it occur to you that I might not have yielded?"

"All of us hope you have not and will not," Micaiah assured him. "But until we could be sure, it seemed better not to reveal the hiding place of the priests here on Mount Carmel."

The sound of voices upon the path leading up to the place of sacrifice told him others were approaching from the camp below. Soon Naboth, with Elijah, Miriam, and Aaron following, appeared at the edge of the clearing. Michael made no effort to keep the tartness from his voice when he spoke to the Israelite elder.

"Micaiah was saying you did not feel it was safe to tell me why we camped on Mount Carmel last night," he said.

Naboth gave him a keen look. "Most of us were

certain you would not reveal the hiding place of the remaining priests who escaped from the queen's persecution," he said. "But some did not agree, so it seemed best to keep it a secret."

"I was one of those who did not trust you," Miriam said quietly.

Naboth and the others had moved on to the area around the altar on the other side of the clearing, leaving the two of them alone. "Was it because you thought Jezebel would be able to bend me to her will?" he asked.

"Yes."

"Do you think that was entirely fair to me?"

She studied him appraisingly, as if trying to decide for herself whether or not he could be trusted. "Perhaps not," she admitted. "But you *did* give us reason for suspicion."

"I came to Samaria on a mission for my father, to bring King Ahab information concerning the Assyrians and explain why it is better for my father and his troops to remain in Judah and protect the southern approaches to Israel. Since Queen Jezebel concerns herself with affairs of state, I naturally had to talk to her about those things." It was not a full explanation, he admitted to himself, and he saw by the look in Miriam's eyes that she was not entirely satisfied with it.

"Will you swear by the altar of our God there at the edge of the clearing that nothing else took place between Jezebel and you?" she asked.

"You ask much," he said angrily.

"Perhaps I ask much because I hoped to find much," Miriam admitted and now her voice was cold. "Too much to hope for in a man."

He took a step toward her and put out his hand to touch her in an attempt to make her understand what was troubling him, but she drew back.

102

"Do you remember last night when you saw the snake?" he asked.

"Yes." She shivered a little at the memory.

"Remember how you stood there, completely fascinated by it and unable to move?"

"I could not take my eyes away from it."

"When you spoke, your first words were, 'It was so beautiful—and evil,'" he reminded her. "The way Jezebel affects me is something like the fascination the snake had for you. I don't expect you to understand, but I did hope you would at least try."

She looked away and he saw that her gaze was upon the ancient altar. When she spoke again, she said a strange thing. "Joseph forgave his brothers, even though they sold him to the Ishmeelites—because it was the will of the Most High that he should be a slave in Egypt. Give me time, Michael. Perhaps I will understand one day."

When Miriam went to join her father and Micaiah, Michael turned to Elijah. The sun had risen above the eastern hills, silhouetting the old prophet in its rays as he stood at the edge of the clearing. Once again Michael was struck by his rock-like strength and, though he had the impression that the old man's gaze was able to pierce through the outer coverings of a man to reveal the soul inside him, he saw no light of censure in Elijah's eyes.

"Is it here that you will hold the test with Baal?" Michael asked.

"Yes," Elijah said. "This is one of the most sacred places in the whole land, after the temple at Jerusalem."

"Surely you know already that the test will turn out in your favor."

"The will of God is not to be seen or understood in the twinkling of an eye, my son," Elijah said. "Sometimes it is revealed only after a period of centuries and then through persecution and dire afflictions. When the time comes for Jezebel and the priests of Baal to be driven from the land, they will not be able to stand against the wrath of the Most High. I can only pray that it will be soon."

"And the Assyrians?" Michael asked a little tartly. "Are they also agents of God?"

Micaiah had moved over to where they stood.

"Have you no respect for the anointed of Yahweh?" he demanded angrily, but Elijah silenced him with an upraised hand.

"The answer to that question has not yet been given me," the prophet admitted. "The Lord requires much of men, Prince Michael, because he gives freely in return. He has already punished Ahab for building a temple of Baal in Samaria by bringing this terrible drought upon the land, but the time of suffering is almost over. Only one thing remains to be done before the rains can fall again. The people must see the power of the Most High God face to face and those who serve Baal must be destroyed."

"I still think it was unwise to make the test here," Micaiah said. "Jezebel will surely try to kill you."

Elijah turned his eyes upon the priest with the golden beard. "Have you yet so little faith, my son, even though God brought you safely here when others were slain before the very altars of the Most High? When it is God's will that I shall die, then I shall die. But lest you trouble yourself too much out of love for me, I will tell you it is not the will of the Most High that I perish at the hands of Jezebel or Ahab."

He looked out across the valley and when he spoke again his voice was solemn. "The people must choose between the God of Abraham, Isaac, and Jacob and the false priests of Baal. When the time of choosing comes, be assured that they will not turn away from the Most High God."

It was late in the afternoon before Naboth's party approached his home in Jezreel, having left Elijah behind, on Mount Carmel. The house was a rambling thick-walled structure surrounding a court, with a large terraced garden below it. The city—it was actually not much more than a large village—stood at the western end of a narrow depression bordered on the north by a hill which Miriam identified as Mount Moreh. Another range of hills stretched northeasterly toward a snow-capped mountain far away which Michael already knew to be Mount Hermon.

Below the house, the vineyards dropped in a series of terraced slopes almost to the valley. In one corner of the yard a large free-flowing spring poured a considerable stream of water down the hillside in spite of the drought. This not only supplied the household needs but also provided for irrigating the terraced vineyards, making the whole area an oasis of green in an otherwise parched and dry region. From a vantage point at the edge of the uppermost terrace, Naboth pointed out to Michael the adjoining palace of the king and the garden where Ahab grew his spices and herbs. Most of them now appeared to be dead from the drought, and the vines and shrubs were stunted and seemed to be barely half alive.

"I offered to divert part of the water from my spring to keep Ahab's garden alive," Naboth explained. "But a rocky ledge runs between my property and his, making it impossible without tunneling through the rock."

"That would be a formidable task."

"The queen persuaded Ahab to make a very generous offer for the land and the spring, but I prefer to save it as an inheritance for Miriam and her children. She loves Jezreel more than any other place in Israel."

"It is a beautiful spot," Michael agreed. "One of the loveliest I have ever seen. I can understand your wanting to keep it in your family."

"In times of normal rainfall the whole valley is a sea of green all the way across to Megiddo," Naboth told him. "We would live here all the time, if I did not have to be in Samaria with the Council of Elders."

Ahab, Jezebel, and a portion of the court arrived in Jezreel the day after Naboth and his family took up residence there with Michael as their guest. Since Prince Ahaziah much preferred to live in Naboth's household, with Miriam as his tutor, he moved into the house beside the gushing spring that afternoon. There he insisted that Michael tell him all about his travels in Assyria and the countries to the east and the two quickly cemented the friendship they had begun at Naboth's home in the Israelite capital.

Michael had expected a summons from Jezebel; to his surprise, it was Ahab who sent for him first. Since the king's garden adjoined the vineyard of Naboth and the houses were side by side only a few hundred paces apart, he had only to step across a low wall atop the rocky ledge between them to enter the royal enclosure. Ahab was walking in the garden, his forehead ruffled by a frown of displeasure.

"You find me in an ill mood, Prince Michael," he said in greeting. "This cursed drought has nearly cost me my entire garden."

"I hear Elijah promised that it will end soon."

"Even then it will take a year for my vines to regain their foliage and many of my rarest plants are already dead." Ahab swung his hand in a gesture that included the entire garden. "Once I had shrubs and plants growing here from all parts of the world; the flowers were as beautiful as the temple of King Solomon in Jerusalem."

"Did your not wanting this region to become a battleground have something to do with the decision to meet the Assyrian army in the northern area governed by King Irhuleni?"

Ahab gave him a keen look. "I see you know something of military strategy."

"I am a soldier above all," Michael assured him. "My own place in the succession to the throne is so far behind my brother Jehoram that I can never hope to be king of Judah, so I occupy myself helping to defend her."

"It is refreshing to find one who does not plot to advance himself," Ahab said dryly. "It is rumored that you have recently returned from a journey to Assyria."

"My father sent me to discover the strength of the Assyrian forces and to find out their intentions."

"No doubt you came here to do the same thing with me?"

Michael laughed. "Is my purpose so obvious then?"

"I would do exactly the same thing under the circumstances," Ahab told him. "Ask what you will; I have no secrets from my friends and allies. Did you discover much of value during your trip to Assyria?"

"I learned that King Shalmaneser is so confident of victory he doesn't even bother to keep secret his plan for the invasion of Canaan by way of the northern part of the Arantu Valley."

"We have learned the same thing from other sources," Ahab confirmed. "Are his armies really as large as they have been described?"

"I could not make a count for fear of arousing suspicion," Michael told him. "But I did learn that he has been building vast forces in the area around Nineveh and is calling in soldiers from all parts of his empire."

"What about his chariot corps?"

"I saw many chariots everywhere I went. Most of them are heavily armored and the wheels are guarded by bands and braces."

"The Hittites of that region have always been expert

workers in iron," Ahab agreed. "I could wish we had more like them to help fashion our weapons, but the best ironmongers in this area have always been the Philistines and they have been our enemies as long as we have been in Canaan."

"I saw one thing that might give you trouble," Michael added. "A group of Midianites from across the Jordan have been specially trained to guide camels carrying several soldiers at a time. They travel very rapidly and go where chariots could not go, giving them a force able to move from place to place very quickly."

Ahab stroked his beard thoughtfully. "If they fight from these camels, I can instruct our bowmen to aim for the animals instead of their riders."

"For the most part they use the animals to get from one place to another," Michael told him. "The camels usually stay behind the line, where they are protected."

"Still," Ahab said thoughtfully, "the ability to move a large number of men from one part of the battlefield to another could make the difference between victory and defeat."

Michael had been favorably impressed with everything he had learned so far about King Ahab's ability as a general and as a warrior. Now he was seeing at first hand how the Israelite ruler reasoned when it came to the movement and deployment of forces in battle. And he could not help feeling a considerable respect for Ahab as a soldier, whatever defects he may have had as a ruler.

"What of the Phoenician states?" Michael asked. "Can you be sure of their neutrality when they still trade with Assyria?"

"Jezebel's kinsman sits upon the throne of Tyre and Sidon so we should not be in any danger from him, and Arvad to the north is with us already."

"It was a wise move to join Israel and Phoenicia in a treaty of peace," Michael agreed.

"It is not Phoenicia, but Damascus I fear," Ahab admitted. "The city is much nearer to Nineveh than we are and Hadad-Ezer fears Shalmaneser greatly. It was he who persuaded the other states of Canaan to join him and besiege us here in Israel in order to make me become a member of the confederation."

"Can you trust Hadad-Ezer then?"

Ahab shook his head. "Only the Assyrian threat holds us together. Syria still controls territory in Gilead rightly belonging to Israel. When the Assyrians are turned back, I plan to regain it."

"Then it was really your distrust of Hadad-Ezer that led you to fortify Megiddo and Samaria so heavily?"

Ahab looked at him searchingly for a moment. "Obviously your father sent you here to learn my plans. Now that you know them, I hope you will give me your advice when the fighting actually begins."

"I hope to join you later with a small party of horsemen from Jerusalem," Michael assured him.

"You will be doubly welcome. I need men who can see beyond the battlefield and who know something of the world around them. Once I relied upon the Council of Elders for advice but lately Elijah has turned them away from me."

"Can you blame them for feeling it is you that has been turned away from them?" Michael dared to ask.

Ahab showed no resentment at the charge. "Jezebel wants me to cast Yahweh aside for Baal and certainly I would earn favor with the other nations of Canaan if I did so. Already there has been some trouble within the confederation because we worship different gods. She also wants me to rule over other nations and I am human enough to like the idea. But here in Israel we have always followed Yahweh and whenever we departed from him, disaster has come upon us. For the time being, I must walk between two paths."

"The way is usually rougher there and it is easier to stumble."

"It may not be rough much longer. Elijah offered to pray for the end of the drought if I would allow a test of power between him and the priests of Baal. Jezebel has agreed to abide by the results of the test, so the matter will soon be settled."

"What if it goes against Yahweh?"

"It will be a fair test, conducted according to Elijah's own rules. We will hold it on Mount Carmel two days from now and whichever god proves to be the most powerful, him we will serve."

"I can see nothing wrong with that," Michael admitted.

"It will be a relief to have this over and get back to the army again," Ahab admitted. "Then, when we have stopped the Assyrians, we can proceed toward our own destiny."

"Separately from Syria?"

"Unless Hadad-Ezer gives up the territory that is rightfully ours." Ahab turned toward the house. "Come take a glass of wine with me before I leave for Megiddo to inspect the chariot corps. Ordinarily I love Jezreel but the sight of dead plants always makes me sad."

"Naboth tells me he would gladly share the water from his spring with you to irrigate your garden," Michael said as they were threading their way through the parched and dusty rows of dying vegetation.

"He did make such an offer," Ahab confirmed. "But usually there is plenty of rain here at Jezreel and it would cost a great deal to tunnel through the rock. Jezebel wants me to take Naboth's vineyard and pay him a reasonable sum for it, but I will not have the breaking of our law upon my conscience."

"You might get the water you need in another way," Michael suggested. "'Along the Euphrates River I saw it lifted by means of wheels to irrigate fields and vineyards."

"But that means keeping slaves to turn the wheels and we need every man now to help defend us against the enemy."

"With a current such as rushes from the spring on Naboth's property, one wheel moved by the flow of the whole spring could very easily turn another taller one," Michael said. "In that way you could lift a portion of water over the rocky slope, so your garden could be irrigated."

"By the tents of Israel!" Ahab cried. "Is such a thing possible?"

"Not only possible but easily accomplished. Look here." Michael chose a smooth place in the path and, breaking off a dead branch from a tree, began to draw a diagram in the dust.

"This is the wheel turned by the flow of the spring," he explained. "It need not be very tall, since because of its width the weight and force of the water can act upon it effectively. The taller wheel attached to it moves in a deep ditch cut into the earth beside the spring. Buckets on this taller wheel scoop up water from the ditch and lift it above the level of the ridge between the two gardens. There the buckets empty themselves when the wheel turns downward and pour water through a trough into other ditches leading to your garden."

Ahab clapped him upon the back enthusiastically. "Could you build such a thing for me?"

"Easily, with the help of a few workmen skilled in handling wood."

"I will speak to Naboth as soon as I return from Megiddo and Mount Carmel," Ahab said happily. "Jezebel must know of this, too. She will be overjoyed." He turned to an aide who had been following them at a discreet distance. "Ask Queen Jezebel to come here at once. I have something to show her."

Jezebel came from the house a few moments later. She was wearing a cloak but Michael could see the hem of a filmy garment extending below the cloak being tossed about by her gold braided sandals. The memory of the voluptuous loveliness hidden by the thin fabric set his pulses to hammering again and the familiar warm feeling of desire stirring within his loins.

He had promised himself he would try to avoid Jezebel, after discovering the depth of his love for Miriam on Mount Carmel the afternoon when she had come so near to death under the fangs of the serpent. But now circumstances he could not control had thrown him into close proximity with the queen once again and all the allure she had for him began to hammer at his defenses. A bored look had been on Jezebel's face until she saw who was with Ahab in the garden; then she brightened perceptibly.

'What is it now, oh my husband?" she asked with a tolerant smile. "A new plant?"

"Prince Michael has discovered a way to lift water from Naboth's spring over the ridge and irrigate my garden," the king told her eagerly. "Come look at the picture he has drawn of it."

They gathered around the diagram while Michael explained it again. He found it hard to keep his attention upon the marks in the dust with Jezebel standing close to him. Her body touched his as he moved his arm to point out the several features of the diagram, and the familiar scent she always wore filled his nostrils.

"With plenty of water from Naboth's spring," Ahab said happily when Michael finished explaining the drawing, "my garden will be green the year round whether it rains or not."

"I still think it would be better to buy the land along with the spring," Jezebel said.

"I cannot force Naboth to sell his inheritance, Jezebel," Ahab said firmly. "It is against our law."

"We could even make pipes from large reeds and carry water into the palace," Michael added, thinking this might please Jezebel. "The overflow would still be enough to keep the garden green."

"Stay here and explain the wheels to her again, Michael," Ahab directed. "Women are not clever about such things. My chariot is ready outside, so I must go."

"When will my lord return?" Jezebel asked.

"When the affair on Mount Carmel has ended. If Elijah brings rain, my garden will be growing again while Michael is building the wheel to lift the water."

"Baal will end the drought," Jezebel said sharply. "Not Elijah."

Ahab shrugged. "It will be enough to have rain. Let the gods fight over who will get the credit."

Chapter 9

WHEN AHAB HAD GONE, MICHAEL TURNED ONCE AGAIN to the diagram. "Let me explain this to you once more," he suggested, but Jezebel cut him off abruptly.

"I understood it perfectly the first time," she said.

"Then why—"

"Come inside. It is time we had a long talk alone together, Michael. I was going to send for you as soon as Ahab left, but since you are here you have saved me the trouble."

Michael knew he was trapped. One part of him might warn that an affair with Jezebel meant the loss of whatever chance he had of earning Miriam's love. But the demon who had seized control in the grove of Ashtoreth at Samaria was now in power again.

The room to which Jezebel escorted him was her own bedchamber, Michael realized as soon as he stepped through the doorway. A cushioned divan occupied one side and a soft rug of combed camel's hair covered the floor. Rich draperies were drawn over the windows and a small incense burner smoldered in the corner, filling the room with a heady fragrance.

To one side was a dressing table made from the carved ivory that was a favorite source of furniture with the Egyptians and Phoenicians. It was covered with jewelry, cosmetic jars, combs, and other things favored by women for enhancing their beauty. The bench before it was also made of ivory, as was a low chest on the other side of the room. This had been left open, revealing a pile of transparently thin garments which appeared to be Jezebel's favorite costume in the intimacy of her own home.

Dominating the exquisitely furnished room was a sculptured statue standing in one corner with a small altar before it. It was the lovely nude body of a woman, obviously an image of the goddess Ashtoreth. A lamp had been cleverly placed to illuminate the marble, making the small statue glow fully as brightly as had Jezebel's own body that night in the grove when she had impersonated the goddess.

Michael stopped in the doorway, hesitant to enter what was obviously Jezebel's bedchamber, but she seemed not to notice. "Shut the door," she said casually over her shoulder. "You heard Ahab say he would be away for several days, so we will not be disturbed."

"Is this wise?" he demurred, listening to the faint voice of his conscience.

Jezebel dropped the cloak she had been wearing outside in the garden. As he had surmised, she wore one of the transparent tunics or *chitons* favored by the Phoenician women in the intimacy of their homes. Beneath it as far as he could tell, her only garment was the same small golden girdle she had worn about her loins in the Temple of Ashtoreth. The nipples of her full breasts and the area about them had been delicately painted in gold to match the hue of the girdle about her hips.

"Pour some wine," she said, sinking down upon the divan and not at all concerned that her whole body was revealed by the transparent fabric. "And don't worry about Ahab. Even if he does return, we will be notified before he enters the house."

The room, the incense, Jezebel's beauty, even the lovely statue of the goddess, had all combined to set Michael's body aflame. He went to a small table upon which a silver flagon of wine stood and poured two goblets, carrying one to Jezebel and giving it to her.

Her eyes looked up at him over the top of the cup as he sat down beside her. "Now that you have seen me again under somewhat similar circumstances, am I so different from what I was in the grove of Ashtoreth?" she asked.

"You are even more beautiful," he told her hoarsely. "More beautiful than I believed a woman could ever be."

She leaned over to kiss him but drew away when he would have taken her in his arms. "I am Ashtoreth, why should I not be beautiful?"

Again Michael's troubled conscience prompted him to ask, "Do you think our being here together is wise? Someone is certain to tell Ahab."

"My husband is more interested in armies and soldiers than he is in me, except as a means of insuring that Tyre and Sidon will not attack him. Shall I remain at home and hide my face like some proper, demure Israelite woman? Or that white-faced daughter of Naboth?" Her voice had become sharp when she spoke of Miriam and her face was momentarily contorted with a look of hate.

"Why do you dislike Miriam so?"

Jezebeel took a long drink from the cup. "Are you in love with her?"

"I've only known her for a little while," Michael said. "My father knew Naboth so I naturally went to his home in Samaria."

Jezebel seemed to accept the explanation without question, though Michael would have been the first to admit that it was not entirely true. A few days ago, in the so-called High Place on the crest of Mount Carmel, it had seemed to Michael that he and Miriam had come to an understanding, although neither of them had specified its exact nature. Now, in order not to anger Jezebel, he had denied it and the thought disturbed him. Raising his goblet, he drank deeply to still the proddings of his conscience. The wine had a strange exotic taste; obviously it had been spiced with some rare flavoring with which he was not familiar. But the flavor was pleasant and so was the sense of warmth that it sent coursing through his body.

"Naboth is the strongest among those who would have Ahab forbid the worship of Baal in Israel," Jezebel told him.

"Can you blame them when our law forbids us to worship any save the Most High?"

Jezebel shrugged. "The people in this area have always worshiped Baal in addition to the god they call Yahweh. I only seek to give them a god who will not be foreign to the other countries of the confederation."

"Is that why you fight against Elijah?"

"Of course; he stands between me and accomplishing that aim. I was not born to waste away as queen of an insignificant country like Israel, Michael. Ashtoreth has better plans for me."

"Did she reveal them to you?"

"Yes."

"How?"

"In visions, since I was a child. And especially the other night in the grove, when I took the place of the goddess before the people."

Michael decided to humor her in order to discover, if he could, what mischief she planned for Elijah, as well as for Naboth and Miriam. But it was hard to keep anything else in his mind with Jezebel lying against the cushions beside him, every lovely line of her body revealed by the almost invisible *chiton*. Besides, the soft light gave her skin a tint strangely like that of the rosy body of the statue in the corner, making it sometimes difficult to tell who was the goddess and who the human counterpart.

"Have you thought about what we discussed in Samaria?" Jezebel asked.

"Yes." He did not add that he had put the idea of taking control of Judah for himself out of his mind almost as soon as she had suggested it. But as he had expected, Jezebel assumed from the answer that he was ready to join in the gamble that could make her the most powerful woman in the world.

"Just now in the garden, Ahab asked me to join him in the northern campaign," Michael continued. "He says he needs the thoughts of one who has seen other parts of the world and knows other kinds of people."

"You should be magnificent in battle." Her eyes were warm with admiration. "The fight with Hamul the other night was thrilling. I've never had really strong men fight over me before."

It was part of her arrogance, he thought, to assume that the match with the Israelite champion had been solely for her favors. And yet he was honest enough to admit that she was largely speaking the truth.

"Where is Hamul now?" Michael asked.

"I sent him away—on a personal mission. He will not be back for several days and neither will Ahab. We are alone, with only the servants in the palace."

The implication of her words was like strong wine, warming every part of his body even more than what he had already drunk. But when he reached for her, she still eluded him laughingly.

"You are not a boy with your first girl, Michael," she said, "Let us drink to divine Ashtoreth and to Jezebel, her priestess."

118

Twice, while they had been talking, Michael had filled their goblets. Strangely enough, though, the wine did not quench his thirst but seemed to create a desire for more. Now, when he stood up to fill the goblets for the fourth time, he found himself staggering and put his hand upon the dressing table to steady himself.

He knew he could not be drunk from that small amount of wine; remembering the strange taste he had noticed in the wine, he decided that it must be due to some sort of drug she had added to it. As he turned to ask Jezebel about it, his eyes fell upon the glowing statue of Ashtoreth in the corner and he blinked in astonishment.

When he had first seen the image as he entered the room, it had appeared to be only an exquisitely lovely figurine carved from marble and cleverly illuminated to make it seem alive. Now the lovely contours of the statue seemed to glow with a light of their own like a metalworker's forge. And when he looked into the carved marble eyes, he could have sworn that they smiled at him as if the image had come to life.

Shaking his head to clear it, Michael turned to Jezebel, who lay at full length on the cushioned divan. Strangest of all, her body, too, had taken on the same luminous hue and her eyes were those of the statue, as if somehow the goddess herself had entered Jezebel's body as she claimed had happened that night in the grove.

"You and the goddess!" he exclaimed. "You are the same."

"Of course. I told you I was Astoreth come to life."

"But how?"

"You must have noticed the taste of the wine; it comes from a rare plant called the 'Flower of Dreams.' Ahab grows it in his garden but has not yet discovered its uses."

"How did you learn them?"

"My Nubian slave, Kubli, came from a land where the plant grows freely. He knows many strange things —knowledge passed down from father to son through generation after generation. Kubli brought the seeds of the plant here."

"Why do you call it the 'Flower of Dreams'?"

"Because it can lift you into another world where nothing matters except love. You have never known what it is to make love, Michael, until you have been transported by the visions this plant will bring you."

"Everything already seems like a dream," he admitted dazedly.

"You are only standing on the threshold," she assured him. "Pour more wine that we may enter that world together."

"Tell me more about this knowledge possessed by Kubli's people," he begged as he filled the cups again.

"I know only what he has told me," she admitted. "They use weapons made from long hollow reeds. With them a tiny thorn can be driven entirely into a man's body."

"Such a weapon could do little damage," he objected. "Unless it happened to strike a vital spot."

"Kubli's people cover the thorns with a special poison that only they know," Jezebel explained. "As soon as it enters the body it causes death, but no one can tell that the victim did not die in a fit. They also know how to cast a spell over an ordinary man so he will obey the will of him who casts it. Before going into battle they eat the 'Flower of Dreams' so they will know no fear and fight as ten men, keeping on until they are cut down or win the battle."

Michael had heard rumors in Assyria concerning a strange drug that could transform ordinary men into demons when going into battle. He had been inclined at the time to consider them only tales told around the campfires. Now, it seemed, there might be more to them than mere rumor.

Jezebel got to her feet in one fluid motion and went to the corner where the statue stood. Loosening the jeweled clasp that held the thin *chiton* at her shoulders, she divested herself at the same time of the golden girdle with one quick motion, letting it fall to the floor in the midst of the soft pile of fabric. Standing naked before the statue of the goddess, she raised her arms above her head.

"Look upon me, Michael," she commanded imperiously. "Look upon me and tell me that even divine Ashtoreth is not more beautiful than Jezebel, her priestess."

In the strange world to which the drug had transported him, Michael was oblivious to everything save the body of the lovely woman before him. To his tremendously lightened senses, she did seem to be the goddess herself. And when he stepped forward and took her in his arms, it was as if he were bearing divine Ashtoreth to the couch.

To Michael day and night were now one; he neither knew nor cared for their passing. Within the silken hung bedchamber his spirit was borne on the wings of the strange drug and the intoxication of love-making to a land where time did not exist and no ties bound him to reality, except Jezebel's almost insatiable desire.

A day passed and it was night again when at last the fires of her ardor began to wane. From the couch she looked up at him and smiled drowsily. "You are mine alone now, Michael," she said. "I will never let you go. No other man has ever been able to fulfill completely my every need. Together we will one day rule the world."

"What of Ahab? Have you forgotten him?"

"A word to Kubli and one of the poisoned darts

would be driven into his body with no one suspecting he died other than a natural death. But Ahab is useful to me, at least for a while. He is a natural leader of men and they follow him into battle eagerly. So long as I control him, I control the force necessary to win all I desire."

"Can you control him, if you persist in trying to separate him from his god?" Michael asked. "Wouldn't it be better to let the people of Israel go on worshiping Yahweh, rather than risk having them desert Ahab?"

"The Israelites have fought with the people of Canaan over the question of their god ever since they came into this country," she said. "Ahab must give up Yahweh if we are to make all of Canaan one single domain."

"In ten years you have not been able to make him reject the Lord," he reminded her. "Why do you think you can do it now?"

He had expected a flare-up of anger but Jezebel was too sated with passion—or too sure of herself—to resent his impertinence. "What is the hour?" she asked.

Michael went to the window and pulled back the hangings. It was still dark outside, but the moon was high in the sky and he remembered vaguely that it rose early in the evening. "It must be toward morning, judging by the looks of the moon. The second morning since I came here."

"Then the new day has almost begun. After today, neither Ahab nor Israel will follow Yahweh."

"How can you be sure?"

"It is all arranged. Since yesterday the people have been gathering upon Mount Carmel. When Elijah makes the test between his god and mine, he will be struck down in their midst by the hand of Baal."

"How could you possibly know that?"

Jezebel laughed exultantly. "Hamul is on Mount

122

Carmel with Kubli. At the right moment, Baal will strike and Elijah will die. Before this day is ended, I will triumph over the Israelite god. Then no one in all the land will be able to resist me."

The meaning of her words was suddenly clear, even to Michael's drug-fogged mind. Obviously the death that would strike Elijah would be of man-made origin. And remembering what she had told him about the giant Nubian, Kubli, and his skill with the tube-blown poison darts, he now knew exactly how it would happen.

A great urgency filled Michael now; the need to reach Mount Carmel in time to save the gaunt prophet from death. First, however, he must get out of the palace without arousing suspicion in Jezebel's mind, else he would never leave it alive. Over the next hour, he continued to ply her with the spiced wine while only pretending to drink himself. And so surfeited was she with passion that, toward dawn, she finally slept, sprawled out upon the cushions. When he was sure she would not awaken soon, Michael left the palace quickly by way of the courtyard.

Still staggering from the effects of what Jezebel had called the "Flower of Dreams," he knew he must somehow clear his brain if he were to carry out the half-formed plan that had begun to take shape in his mind as soon as she had revealed the plot against Elijah. When he reached the pool at the corner of Naboth's garden he stripped off his clothing and lay down in the cold water. The shock of it quickly cleared his senses and, when he stood up, the cool night breeze made him gasp and shiver. As he stood there, a familiar gruff voice spoke from the shadows at the edge of the pool.

"Another night and I would have gone in to bring you out," Aaron told him. "The palace slaves tell me no man has ever stayed with her so long before."

"Who is here now?" Michael asked while Aaron was rubbing his body with a dry cloth to combat the chill.

"Only a few of the servants. My lord Naboth and the lady Miriam went yesterday to Mount Carmel."

"When will the test be held?"

"Today. The priests of Baal will make their intercession first and Elijah afterward."

Michael explained quickly to Aaron how the murder of Elijah would come about. "I must get there before the test," he said in conclusion.

"Then you will have to grow wings."

"Are any horses in the stable?"

Aaron shook his head. "My lord Naboth and the lady Miriam waited a long time for you. When you did not come back, they took our horses so they would get to Mount Carmel on time. Prince Ahaziah rode with the lady Miriam."

"What about the king's stables?"

"He is away at Mount Carmel and all the chariots are gone."

"Then we must walk," Michael said. "Get me a pair of heavy sandals and take an extra pair for yourself." He had been dressing while they were talking. His slender long hunting bow stood in the corner with a quiver of arrows hanging from it; he slung both across his shoulder now.

As yet he was following no well-defined plan; in fact, his throbbing head made rational thought almost impossible at the moment. One thing, however, was certain; he must reach the place of sacrifice on Mount Carmel in time to reveal the treachery of Jezebel to Ahab and stop the proceedings that would culminate in the murder of Elijah.

"We cannot leave without eating," Aaron protested. "We will fall by the wayside from hunger."

"Get bread and meat from the kitchen and bring a skin of wine," Michael ordered. He still staggered occasionally from the aftereffects of the drug Jezebel had placed in the wine, but he was sure the long walk to Mount Carmel would sweat most of it from his body and clear his mind for the task ahead.

Chapter 10

THE SUN WAS JUST BEGINNING TO RISE OVER THE mountaintops to the east when Michael and Aaron took the road leading across the Vale of Jezreel westward toward the majestic heights of Mount Carmel that hid the sea from view. The top of the mountain was almost obscured by a haze which, as they came nearer, took on the appearance of smoke.

"My lord Naboth said many thousands have gathered on Mount Carmel," Aaron observed as he strode along beside Michael. "The haze we see must be from the campfires."

"We should have no trouble finding them, then—if we get there in time."

"At least we know where to look," Aaron agreed. "The test is being held at the old altar where we left Elijah and Micaiah on the mountaintop." He stumbled over a rock and cursed fluently. "Let us stop and rest a moment, master?"

"Elijah will be the sacrifice this day unless we get there in time to save him," Michael said without slackening his stride. "If you are willing to let the prophet die, stay behind."

"It was Elijah who challenged the priests of Baal,"

Aaron reminded him. "If the Lord does not choose to give him the victory, surely we cannot save him."

"Will Yahweh divert the poisoned dart from its target?" Michael demanded.

"Probably not. I saw Kubli practicing with the bamboo tube back of the palace the other day. Would you believe it, master? The black one can drive a thorn-pointed dart into a plank at almost as great a distance as you can place an arrow."

The plot to destroy the prophet had been planned with truly diabolical precision, Michael realized. A poisoned dart striking from the sky could bury itself unseen in Elijah's body. And when the poison brought about almost instant death, the watching crowd would naturally conclude that Baal had triumphed. At one stroke the confidence of the people in the deity for whom Elijah was the acknowledged spokesman would be destroyed.

As he hurried on, driving himself relentlessly though he stumbled at almost every other step, Michael cursed himself now for the hours he had spent with Jezebel, hours which might have saved Elijah's life. And yet, he remembered, had he not been with her at the moment when, satiated with passion, she had boasted of the plan to destroy Elijah, he could not have learned how to prevent what was destined to happen unless he reached Mount Carmel in time.

Sheer exhaustion finally caused Michael to call a halt near a spring at the foot of Mount Carmel. They drank deeply of the water and ate the remainder of the food Aaron had taken from Naboth's kitchen. At the moment, Michael never wanted to taste wine again, but Aaron had no such feeling. He drained the skin they had brought with them without taking it away from his mouth.

It was now well past noon and every muscle in Michael's body ached from the killing pace. But they were on the lower slopes of Mount Carmel now, within, he estimated, a half hour's climb of the place of sacrifice, so he pushed on. Soon, however, they ran into unexpected difficulty.

As they toiled up the slope of the mountain, the path had become more and more clogged with people. Most of these had long since given up hope of reaching the mountaintop, where the contest between Elijah and the priests of Baal was being held. But although only waiting for word of the events taking place above them to filter down, they nevertheless resented very strongly anyone else's trying to force himself past them.

"It is settled," Aaron said, dropping wearily to the ground beside the path. "You have done your best, master. No one can do more."

"If we cannot climb the path, we will go up through the brush," Michael said doggedly. "You need not come if you are too tired."

"And leave you to the mercy of your enemies?" Aaron scrambled to his feet. "They say Hamul has sworn to kill you on sight."

Michael was not thinking of the Israelite captain as he undertook the painful and laborious climb through the underbrush covering the slope of the mountain. After Elijah, his concern was for Miriam, Naboth and Ahaziah and what they must have thought while they waited for him to return. It would do no good to explain that he had been drugged or that he had tried to influence Jezebel to give up the fight against the worship of Yahweh in Israel. For, being honest, he would have been the first to admit that his efforts in that direction had been halfhearted at best. The brutal fact was that his own passions had led him into the affair, plus a perverse and, it seemed now, childish desire to best Hamul in still another contest. Worst of all, he had made no attempt to resist either urge.

What Michael had not admitted to himself as yet

was that in trying so desperately to reach Elijah and somehow prevent the death planned for the prophet, he was really seeking to redeem himself with Naboth and with Miriam, as well as in his own eyes. But with all further progress now blocked, except the slow ascent through the thorny brush lining the mountain-side, even that seemed out of the question. Then, as he stumbled around a projecting boulder, he came upon a large spring flowing from the hillside close to the path and saw several men beside it in the act of filling large containers with water. One of those he recognized—with a burst of hope.

"Micaiah!" Michael shouted, stumbling up the slope toward the spring. "It is Michael! I must speak to you."

The priest had been filling a larger jar with water. When he looked up and saw who had spoken, his face hardened into a forbidding cast.

"We have nothing to discuss," he said harshly. "I serve Yahweh, not Jezebel and Baal."

Michael had now reached the spring where Micaiah was stooping to fill the jar. "Think of me what you will; I probably deserve your curses," he panted. "Elijah is in danger and I came to warn him."

"The Most High will protect his holy prophet," Micaiah said stolidly. "Elijah needs no help from traitors."

"Will God protect him from an assassin?" Michael demanded.

The priest looked deep into Michael's eyes. What he saw there seemed to change his feelings—at least in part.

"What is all this?" he demanded.

"Jezebel has sent the slave Kubli to kill Elijah," Michael explained hurriedly, "I learned of it by chance and hurried here to warn you."

"I have not seen Kubli upon the mountaintop," Micaiah said, suspicion still coloring his tone.

"He must be hidden somewhere, waiting for the right moment."

"How do they plan to kill Elijah?"

"The Nubian is an expert marksman with a blowing tube that drives a poison dart," Michael explained. "Hamul brought him here from Jezreel for that reason."

"Hamul is at the High Place with the priests of Baal and Ahab," Micaiah said thoughtfully.

"Kubli must be hiding somewhere close by, waiting to strike Elijah down with the poisoned dart. Jezebel herself told me of the plan."

Micaiah hesitated no longer but turned to another priest who had just finished filling a large jar of water. "Give Prince Michael your jar, Ezri," he directed. "It will help him through the crowd."

The transfer was quickly accomplished and the crowd opened the way for the men so they could move up the hillside fairly rapidly.

"What has happened here so far?" Michael asked as they climbed.

"King Ahab and the priests of Baal came to the place of sacrifice this morning as Elijah requested," Micaiah explained. "We erected two altars, one for Baal and the other made from the stones of the old altar you saw here on the mountaintop the morning Jochai attacked you. Wood for the burnt offering was laid upon each of the altars and a bullock was placed on top of it but no fire was touched to either of them. Then Elijah challenged the priests of Baal to pray to their god that he would send fire from heaven to light the flames of the burnt offering."

"And then?"

"Elijah allowed the priests of Baal to pray all through the morning but they have received no answer. Now he is about to beg the Most High to send fire from heaven and burn his own sacrifice, proving to the people that he is above all others."

130

"Why are you carrying up water?"

"Elijah ordered it poured upon the altar and the wood until they are thoroughly soaked. Then, when the Most High lights the flames of the burnt offering, the people cannot fail to see that he is the one and true God."

"But suppose Elijah fails?"

"He will not fail," Micaiah said quietly. "Yahweh himself is directing his actions this day."

"Elijah will be dead if Kubli's dart strikes him down first," Michael reminded the priest. "Even if God does send the fire."

They were at the edge of the clearing now. It was packed with people, except for an open space surrounding the two altars, and the paths extending down the slope were also jammed as far as could be seen in every direction. The two altars were as Micaiah had described them, with the wood and the flesh of the bullocks lying upon them ready to be ignited. The priests of Baal—hundreds of them, it appeared to Michael—were packed around their altar.

On the other side of the clearing, where the altar of Yahweh stood beneath a tall tree, an open ditch had been dug. This was now almost filled with water and, Michael saw, the water had also soaked the meat from the bullock placed there for the sacrifice, as well as the wood to provide the fire.

Standing beside the altar, Elijah was a solitary and somehow majestic figure, even though he wore his usual robe of rough homespun and his long hair and beard were uncombed. Across the clearing, approximately halfway between the two altars, Ahab stood with his aides and the members of the court. On the other side, Naboth and Miriam were with a group of priests and elders who were watching Elijah.

The contrast between the almost disheveled appearance of the old prophet in his rough garments and the

131

rich robes of the priests of Baal and the king was startlingly vivid. It was a dramatic moment, and all eyes were fixed upon Elijah, waiting to see whether he would be able to achieve the miracle of lighting the water-soaked sacrifice without a torch.

"I would rather not be seen yet," Michael told Micaiah when they reached the edge of the crowd. "It might warn Hamul and the Nubian. Take my jar with yours and give me as much time as you can."

Micaiah nodded and the jar of water was quickly shifted to his shoulder. While the priests approached the altar and slowly poured water from the jars upon the stones and the wood, Michael moved around the edge of the open space searching for some sign of the giant Nubian. He could see nothing, however, save the crowd, the altars, and the solitary figure of Elijah standing before the altar at the foot of the single tall tree.

Micaiah was now speaking urgently to Elijah, trying to warn the old prophet of the danger to his welfare. Elijah, however, shook his head sternly and waved the priest away. The crowd was solemn as Elijah raised his arms and looked up at the sky.

Michael looked up, too, but could see nothing except a haze from the smoke of the fires on the slope below and a small cloud floating across the crest as clouds often floated across the headland from the sea during the latter hours of the day.

"Lord God of Abraham, Isaac, and Israel!" Elijah's deep voice filled the clearing and rolled down the mountainside. "I pray thee let it be known this day that thou art God in this Israel and that I am thy servant and have done all these things at thy word."

Standing with his arms upraised, holding the crowd hushed and silent by the sheer power of his voice and his will, Elijah was an awe-inspiring figure. For a moment, in the tension of waiting for the expected miracle, Michael almost forgot why he was there. Then the realization that Elijah would never make a better target than he did just now set him searching the crowd desperately once again for some sign of Kubli.

"Hear me, Oh Lord! Hear me!" Elijah implored. "Hear me that this people may know thou art the Lord God and that thou hast turned their hearts back again to thee."

As Elijah's voice died away, the crowd seemed to have stopped breathing for the moment, so tense was the scene as they waited for the answer to the prophet's invocation. And just then Michael saw what he was seeking, a sudden movement in a tall tree on the far side of the clearing near a craggy outcropping of rock. Against the dark green foliage of the tree, the velvet black skin of the Nubian slave had been almost invisible until now. In fact, Michael would not have seen him had Kubli not lifted the bamboo blowing tube, readying it to send the poison dart winging toward its target below.

Michael's action was purely from instinct; there was no time for rational thought. In one sweeping motion, the bow was shifted from his back to his hand and the arrow was strung. Even as the twang of the bowstring sounded, the arrow was on its way. A sharp cry of agony rent the silence as the razor-sharp bronze arrowhead found its target and the black body of the Nubian tumbled from the branches.

The unexpected event had no chance to stir the interest of the crowd, however, for something far more startling was already happening. From the small cloud which had been floating over the clearing, a single jagged streak of lightning darted downward to strike the tall tree beside the altar. Racing along its trunk, the crackling spark leaped to the altar itself and spread a curtain of fire over both flesh and wood, while tendrils of flame darted downward toward the wet dirt and the trough around the altar.

The crash of thunder accompanying the flash of lightning jarred the whole mountaintop and threw many people to the ground by the sheer force of its impact. The whole altar had burst into flame at the first flash of the bolt from the sky and the acrid smell of burning flesh mingled with the sharp odor characteristic of the passage of lightning. Miraculously, Elijah was not touched by the bolt, and above the moan of pure terror that swept over the crowd his voice now rose in an exultant shout:

"The Lord, he is God! The Lord, he is God!"

People were falling to the ground everywhere, prostrating themselves before the altar where the flames were now greedily licking up not only the flesh and the wood but also the water in the trenches. The crackle of fire, the hiss of water turning to steam, and the crackling of the meat as it was consumed by the flame, filled the whole clearing with a veritable avalanche of sound. Even that, however, could not drown out the voice of the people as they joined Elijah in a paean of praise and worship.

"The Lord, he is God! The Lord, he is God!"

At one side of the clearing, the priests of Baal cowered and quivered with fear. Nor did Elijah spare them in his moment of triumph.

"Take the prophets of Baal!" he ordered the people sternly. "Let not one of them escape."

A tide of Israelites swept over the cowering priests in answer to Elijah's order. Struggling, kicking, screaming, sobbing, and begging for their lives, they were swept helplessly down the hillside by the mob of angry people. Those priests not killed in the first rush of the crowd were stoned to death in the half-dry beds of streams farther down the mountain. Only when the last of his enemies had disappeared from the clearing did Elijah return to the altar where Ahab waited.

The two faced each other across the flame, the gaunt, weary prophet who had been so dramatically supported here by a sign from God and the king who had allowed his people to be led away from the worship of that same God. It was Elijah who controlled the situation now, his threadbare homespun robe far more regal than the splendor of Ahab's armor and the trappings of the royal aides.

For a moment the air between the two was tense; then Ahab stepped forward and knelt before the altar, making an obeisance before the prophet in an act of submission to the will of God. There was no sound in the clearing save the sputtering of flames upon the altar when finally Elijah spoke. His voice was tolerant and understanding, however, as if he were speaking to a child who had erred and was begging forgiveness.

"Get up and eat," he said gently to Ahab. "For there will be the sound of an avalanche of rain."

Michael looked up at the sky but saw no hint of the downpour Elijah was promising. The small cloud which had hung briefly over the mountaintop was gone now, as if its purpose had been fulfilled, and the late afternoon sky was clear and bright with sunshine. Even the haze of smoke that had lain over Mount Carmel most of the day seemed to have been largely dissipated.

Ahab's doubt was apparent in his face as he looked up at the sky, but he did not disobey the old prophet's injunction. "We will await the beginning of the rain at our camp near the foot of the mountain," he said and strode from the clearing followed by his officers. Hamul was last; when he came to where Michael stood at the edge of the clearing, the Israelite captain paused momentarily. In his hand he held an arrow, the point and part of the shaft stained with blood.

135

"Do you recognize this?" he demanded of Michael.

Michael met the other man's eyes without flinching. "Should I?"

"Just now I found it in the body of Queen Jezebel's favorite slave. She will not be pleased when I tell her how he was slain."

"If you can tell me what the queen's favorite slave was doing here, I might be able to help you discover from whence the arrow came," Michael said mildly.

Hamul did not answer, but broke the fragment of arrow over his knee and tossed it aside with an angry gesture. "You were at the palace later than I. Perhaps it is you who should tell me. But be sure that when Jezebel learns what happened here, she will break him who caused it, as I have broken the arrow."

As Hamul stalked from the clearing, Michael looked up to see Naboth watching him from beyond the altar. Hamul had spoken fairly loudly, and he suspected Naboth had overheard for there was a puzzled frown upon the face of the Israelite prince.

"Come, Micaiah," Elijah said. "We will go and pray for rain. When the drought is ended, the people will know ours is a forgiving and merciful God to those who repent and acknowledge him."

As the two moved across the clearing to its western edge where a slight elevation looked toward the Great Sea, Naboth came over to where Michael was standing. "Come to the edge of the clearing and help me look for something," he said.

Miriam remained behind with Prince Ahaziah, who had been watching everything with wide-eyed excitement. Her face was eloquent with contempt and disdain, so Michael was sure that she, at least, had no idea of the part he had played in the dramatic event which had just taken place.

At the edge of the clearing where a low cliff overhung a heavily wooded ravine, Naboth paused. "I saw

Hamul throw something over the cliff here just now," he said. "Perhaps we should climb down and see what it was."

Michael knew very well what Hamul had thrown over the cliff, but he had no choice except to follow the older man around the edge of the rock and down into a small ravine. They soon came upon the body of Kubli; the wound in his chest over the heart had obviously been made by an arrow, but the weapon itself had been removed by Hamul.

"I saw this man fall from a tree beside the clearing just before the lightning struck and ignited the sacrifice," Naboth said. "Do you have any idea why he was here?"

Michael stooped and picked up the length of bamboo Kubli had used as a blowing tube. Two of the poisoned darts were still in a pouch attached to the slave's leather harness.

"This tube can drive a dart into a cedar plank," he explained. "But the force is needed only to carry the missile, not to kill. A single prick by one of these thorns and a man will die instantly from the poison with no one knowing the cause."

Naboth studied the tube and the darts for a long moment, then took them and threw them farther down the ravine. "So that is why Jezebel encouraged Ahab to allow the test between Baal and Yahweh. I wondered why she would take a chance; obviously she had already decided to be sure of the outcome."

"Elijah was to die, apparently stricken down by the power of Baal," Michael agreed. "I happened to learn of it from Jezebel and came here on foot to try and save him."

"Then it was your skill with the bow that brought Kubli down?"

Michael pointed to the wound in the Nubian's chest. "At that distance no archer on earth could have been sure of striking a man in the heart when he could not even see him very well among the branches of the tree. Something—or someone—guided the arrow after it left my bow."

"The Lord does indeed move in mysterious ways that we cannot always understand," Naboth agreed. "I will confess that I, too, thought ill of you because you seemed to have succumbed to the wiles of Jezebel. Now I see that it was all only a part of the work of the Lord."

"Being only a man I did succumb, for reasons that seemed logical enough at the time," Michael said. "I will not deny it, even though I was still able to reach Mount Carmel in time."

"Today you were the instrument by which Israel was saved," Naboth assured him as they climbed back to the clearing. "As surely as the Lord guided the arrow that found its mark in Kubli's heart, he guided you to this clearing so you could launch it. Israel will ever be in your debt."

"Answer me one question and the debt will be discharged," Michael told him. "Whence came the lightning that struck the altar? From the hand of God or from the cloud that hung over the clearing at the time?"

"What would you say?"

"From the cloud, of course. The tree beside the altar shows the marks of having been struck many times before. Besides, everyone knows that lightning strikes often in high places where there are tall trees."

"Perhaps God selected Mount Carmel so he could show the people that he can send fire from heaven or withhold it," Naboth suggested. "Don't forget that there was no lightning when the priests of Baal prayed for fire to ignite the wood upon their altar."

"But it had obviously struck here many times before."

"Seldom does man obtain a completely satisfactory answer when he questions the way God reveals himself," Naboth assured him. "The truth must always lie in the knowledge that the Most High dwells within the hearts of all who truly love him."

They were at the edge of the clearing now. "I will go and tell Miriam what happened," Naboth added. "She, too, has sinned in judging you so harshly."

Michael put his hand upon the older man's arm. "Do not tell her—at least not yet. It is for her to decide in her heart how she feels about me, even though she knows I have sinned grievously with Jezebel."

Naboth smiled and put his arm about Michael's shoulders in a gesture of friendship and affection. "You are wise beyond your years, Michael. I would be proud to have you as my son."

Darkness was descending upon Mount Carmel, but Elijah still prayed for rain and Micaiah with him. Seven times the old prophet had sent the priest to look toward the sea, and six times Micaiah returned to report no sign of rain. But on the seventh visit, he came back and said, "A little cloud arises from the sea, like a man's hand."

Elijah rose to his feet at once. "Go to Ahab and say, 'Prepare your chariot and get down, so the rain does not stop you.' "

Micaiah did not question Elijah's order; after what had happened here on Mount Carmel today, no one in Israel would doubt Elijah for some time—unless it was Jezebel. As the priest hurried down the mountainside, Elijah crossed the clearing to where Naboth, Miriam, and Ahaziah waited. Michael stood at one side with Aaron; he had made no move to join the others, since Miriam's feelings for him showed in the way she drew away even when he passed her.

"We must go to Jezreel at once," Elijah announced.

139

"The rain is coming."

Long before they had crossed the valley, the drumming of rain upon the slopes of Mount Carmel could be heard behind them. By the time they reached Naboth's home, it had begun to fall in torrents, drenching them all.

Chapter 11

AHAB RETURNED TO JEZREEL AT NOON, HAVING GONE to Megiddo to escape the torrential downpour of the night before. A great crowd went out to greet him, for word had gone ahead of Elijah's victory over Baal and the king's submission to Yahweh. More than anything else, the people were happy at being freed from the onerous burden of supporting the hundreds of foreign priests who had been destroyed on Mount Carmel.

Michael was not surprised when a summons came early that afternoon, ordering him to wait upon Queen Jezebel at the palace. He found her in a small audience chamber but she was very different now from the seductive temptress he had left asleep in her bedchamber. Eyes flashing, she stalked back and forth like a lioness preparing to attack.

"Ahab told me how Elijah took advantage of a convenient stroke of lightning to convince the people Yahweh sent fire to light the sacrifice," she stormed.

"The priests of Baal prayed all morning and nothing happened," Michael reminded her. "Yet as soon as Elijah began to call upon Yahweh, the fire was lit. I was there and I saw it."

She wheeled upon him, hands uplifted, fingers curled like claws. For a moment he thought she was going to attack him in her fury.

"Did you dare to betray me after I took you into my confidence?" she demanded. "Hamul claims you killed Kubli."

"Hamul has reason enough to hate me," Michael reminded her. "Surely you did not listen to such a story."

She stared at him appraisingly for a moment, then shook her head. "Of course you could not have done it. How could you have known?"

"Known what?"

"Hamul is a fool—but you *were* at Mount Carmel?"

"I was curious to see how the test would end," he explained. "When you fell asleep, I decided to cross the valley to Mount Carmel and see for myself."

"What really did happen up there?"

"Just what you were told. Lightning struck the altar prepared by Elijah, setting the wood and the flesh of the sacrifice afire. It even dried up the water they had poured upon the altar. Afterward, when Elijah prayed for rain, there was a downpour."

"Was there a cloud anywhere near when the lightning struck?"

"Yes." Thinking that if Jezebel could be led to attribute the miracle upon Mount Carmel to a natural cause, she might be less angry at Elijah and the followers of Yahweh, he added, "In fact I could see that lightning had often struck there before."

His words, however, seemed only to make her more determined, as if they had led her to a decision on something she had been considering. "Hamul says you would know where Elijah can be found," she said. "Is that true?"

"Yes. In Judah, Elijah is considered to be a prophet

of God and therefore very holy, I hope to persuade him to go to Jerusalem."

Incredible as it might seem, Jezebel did not seem to know yet that Elijah was at Naboth's house, only a short distance from where she stood. Nor had it occurred to her, apparently, that Michael could possibly put concern for Elijah's safety before loyalty to her, so certain was she of her power over any man she had once held in her arms.

"Find him and give him this message for me," she ordered: "Let the gods do to me as he did to the priests of Baal and more also, if I don't make his life as one of them tomorrow."

"But King Ahab——"

"Ahab will do as I wish," she said cryptically. "On Mount Carmel he may have been foolish enough to believe the lightning was sent from Yahweh, but I can soon convince him that an affront to the gods of Tyre and Sidon is also an insult to my nephew who rules there. Ahab cannot afford to have my people against him when he marches north in a few weeks against the Assyrians."

Michael's thoughts had been racing while she was speaking, seeking some way to protect Elijah. The immediate problem was to get him safely out of Jezreel, for with Jezebel in her present mood, she would undoubtedly try to kill the old prophet if she knew he was in the city. Suddenly he thought he saw a way to take care of all these difficulties at one time. The whole thing would have to be handled delicately, however, without making Jezebel suspect his real purpose.

"Prince Ahaziah is anxious to visit my father's kingdom and worship at the temple," he said. "Do you think King Ahab would object if I invite him to go back with me?"

Michael had learned much about Jezebel since she

had tried to kill him that night in the temple of Ashtoreth at Samaria. Now he was almost able to read her thoughts as she considered the idea he had deliberately planted in her mind. With Ahaziah out of Israel, she would have more of a chance to further her own ambition for her son Joram, to be named the heir of Ahab. And with Ahab about to depart for the battlefront upon a hazardous mission, she might be able to persuade him to name his heir before he left.

"It might be arranged," she said. "How soon do you plan to go?"

"Tomorrow. My father will want to know what has happened here in Israel and I need to raise a troop of cavalry to accompany King Ahab when he moves north to join King Irhuleni before Hamath. If I ask him, Elijah might join me."

She stamped her foot in annoyance. "Would you have me let Elijah go—when he caused hundreds of my priests to be killed?"

"I am only telling you what is best for the kingdom," he said. "Surely you can see the advantage of keeping my father in a favorable mood toward King Ahab and his plan. After all, when Ahab finishes with the Assyrians, he plans to take Ramoth-Gilead from Hadad-Ezer. For that he will need the help of Judah."

More than any woman Michael had ever known, Jezebel possessed the ability to make up her mind quickly and follow her decisions with action—to her own advantage. "Elijah can leave Israel and Ahaziah also. But see that you do not try to deceive me."

"Would I deceive you when my own future is bound up so closely with yours?"

It was the one argument that he could expect to lull any reservations she might have about his sincerity.

When she smiled and went to pour two cups of wine, he knew it had succeeded.

"To our common purpose," she toasted, giving him a cup. "May it go well."

Michael drank the wine, and was glad to see that it was not spiced with the "Flower of Dreams." Apparently Jezebel did not use the drug unless things were going her way and she planned to yield herself to its influence. Now, when she needed to think calmly, she would want nothing to influence her reasoning powers.

"In a few months the people will forget Yahweh again," she said as she put down her goblet. "He is much too austere a god to claim their allegiance for long, once Elijah is out of the country."

"And then?"

It still did not seem to occur to her that he might betray anything she told him to Elijah, or use it against her. Or perhaps, so great was her contempt for the Israelite people that such a possibility made no difference to her.

"As High Priestess of Ashtoreth, I will soon order a great celebration in honor of the goddess," she said. "Food and drink will be free to all who come, and honor for women who sacrifice to the goddess in the grove of Samaria. We will see how long the men remain loyal to the Israelite god when they can enjoy the temple priestesses I will bring here from Tyre." She smiled warmly. "May Ashtoreth and Baal speed you on your way, Michael. And on your return—who knows. Perhaps we shall take another journey into the realm of dreams—together."

Chapter 12

RAIN HAD ALREADY WROUGHT A REMARKABLE TRANS-
formation in the Vale of Jezreel, the travelers saw as
their small caravan crossed the valley shortly after
dawn the following morning. Plants which heretofore
had drooped and seemed on the point of dying were
beginning to come alive, and the green of new growth,
previously hidden by the parched state of the vegetation, was beginning to peep forth. Even the air itself
had a fresh smell, as if it too had been invigorated
with new life by the rain, and the small streams they
crossed were filled to the banks, tumbling joyously
downhill toward the brook Jalud, now a raging torrent,
and thence to the Jordan in its deep rift to the eastward.

In Megiddo, Michael was able to arrange for their
passage southward with a Phoenician caravan that was
departing the following day. During the next several
days they moved slowly along the ancient highway that
traversed the hilltops of central Canaan, stopping to
trade in the cities and villages through which they
passed, as Phoenician merchant caravans had been
doing for thousands of years.

At each stop the people gathered eagerly to examine

the wares brought by the dark-skinned tradesmen: copper pots and cooking utensils from Cyprus, richly dyed fabrics from the looms of Tyre and the upper coastal cities of Phoenicia, spearpoints and arrowheads of bronze and iron fashioned by Hittite and Philistine smiths, jewelry of delicately wrought silver, and fine pottery and vases, as well as the richly dyed fabrics that were the favorite goods sold by these merchants.

Wherever they stopped, Elijah spoke to the people who gathered in great numbers to hear him. Michael had been afraid at first that the rather slow progress of the caravan southward might give Jezebel time to send soldiers after them. But as they approached the city of Samaria, where the Council of Elders had its seat and where Naboth had considerable influence, the danger to the prophet became less and less.

At Shechem, not far from Samaria, they bade good-by to Naboth, who was going on to the capital, and camped for the night outside the old city which had been sacred to the Hebrews since the time of Abraham. Miriam had naturally accompanied Ahaziah, but she and Michael had hardly spoken a dozen words together since leaving Jezreel. When she came out of the tent erected for her at the Shechem campground by the men of the caravan, he walked over to where she stood looking out across the valley toward the steep side of Mount Ebal. The rains had extended even here and small torrents like the one beside which they had camped tumbled merrily down the mountainside, watering the groves of walnut trees, pomegranates, almonds, pears, plums, and olives interspersed with vineyards that lined the lower levels of the mountainside. Michael was surprised when Miriam spoke, for her voice was almost friendly.

"How long do you think we will be in Judah?" she asked.

"Until the battle with the Assyrians is over and it is safe for Ahaziah to return to Israel."

"None of us will be safe until Jezebel is dead and Ahab orders the worship of Yahweh alone in Israel."

"Are you sure he will ever do that?"

She turned to face him. "Did Jezebel tell you differently?"

"She will not admit that Yahweh lit the fires on the altar at Mount Carmel. After all, a bolt of lightning did actually set the wood aflame."

"But the bolt was sent by the Most High, after the priests of Baal had failed."

"A cloud hung over the mountain at the time. And the bark of the tree beside the altar was scarred, showing that lightning had struck there many times before."

"Do you deny that God set fire to the wood?" she demanded, her voice frosty once more.

"I am not saying what I think, but how it appears to Jezebel," he explained. "She is already convinced that the fire was not an act of Yahweh, so she will not easily give up the battle to turn the people from God."

Miriam did not speak for a moment. "I suppose you are right," she conceded. "After all, Jezebel cannot conceive of any power greater than her own. Nor of anyone daring to resist her."

It was an accurate portrait of Jezebel's way of thinking—proving, he thought, that women understood other women and their hidden natures far better than a man ever could.

Miriam's next words startled him. "Ahaziah says Aaron told him Queen Jezebel sent a skilled marksman to Mount Carmel to kill Elijah. And that he was cut down by an arrow shot from the crowd."

"A black slave called Kubli belonging to Jezebel fell from a tree at the edge of the clearing," Michael admitted. "Your father and I examined his body and found the blowing tube he intended to use in driving a poison dart into Elijah's body."

"Did you kill the slave"

Michael hesitated only momentarily; there was no point in denying his part in what had happened. "Yes, I did."

"Why?"

"To save Elijah. Why else?"

"Perhaps to salve your own conscience—because you had committed adultery with Jezebel."

The accusation took him aback. And since it was true, he had no words to defend himself against it. Miriam seemed to accept his silence as an admission of guilt, but to his surprise she showed no anger. "Did you learn of the plot to kill Elijah from the queen?" she asked.

"Yes."

"Then she will want your life, too, when she finds out what really happened."

"Jezebel doesn't realize she revealed her plan to me," he explained. "As you say, she cannot conceive of any man failing to obey her every wish, so she does not believe I was the one who killed her slave."

"She is very beautiful," Miriam said thoughtfully. "I suppose any man would find it hard to resist her."

There seemed to be no point in trying to explain the hold Jezebel had over him. Nor could he say just what he would do if she set herself to charm him again, as she had upon his first arrival in Jezreel. Around them the campfires of the caravan flickered in the falling dusk. From the shadows they could hear the music of a harp in the hands of a traveling minstrel who had joined them, and his voice as he sang softly of Israel's glorious past. It was a moment of peace and singular beauty.

"I want you to know I don't blame you for not

149

trusting me," Michael said. "Your accusations about my relationship with Jezebel were true, but if I were in league with her I would not have tried to save Elijah or help him escape."

"You must have been tempted when she offered you the throne of Judah, in return for helping her carry out her aim to make Ahab ruler of the twelve kingdoms."

"How did you know that?"

"Jezebel's ambition is no secret to the Council of Israel. It would be logical for her to bring you into her camp and keep you there."

"Do you think I am in that camp, Miriam?"

She turned to face him once again and looked deeply into his eyes, as if seeking the answer to his question there. *"She* believes you serve her," she said finally. "The fact that you were able to arrange the escape of Elijah and Prince Ahaziah so easily proves that."

"But if I had been concerned only with keeping Jezebel's favor, I could easily have turned Elijah over to the guards at the gate of Jezreel."

"I thought of that," she admitted. "But I know something of the reverence the people of Judah have for Elijah. Your father would be very much displeased with you if anything should happen to him. What I can't understand," she went on before he could speak again, "is how you could love someone like Jezebel."

"Love?" he asked incredulously. "Do you think I love her?"

"Why else would you betray King Ahab's confidence in you?"

"I told you once before that Jezebel affects me in much the same way the serpent did when you came upon it on Mount Carmel. She is beautiful and evil—as you described the serpent." He shrugged in a gesture of bafflement. "How can I explain it to someone who has never experienced real desire and passion?"

"King David desired Bathsheba so much that he ordered her husband put in the front lines to be killed," she said, as if speaking to herself. "And yet the Most High forgave him."

"Don't forget that the son of that union became one of Israel's greatest kings."

"But Jezebel is evil!"

"The serpent was evil, too. Yet you were so fascinated by it that you could not move to save yourself."

She had been looking across the verdant glen in which the ciity of Shechem lay, the lights of oil lamps in the houses winking at them through the darkness and the trees like so many fireflies. "Are you going back to her when you leave Jerusalem?"

"No."

"Why?"

"King Ahab asked me to join him in Megiddo with my own troop of mounted soldiers for the move northward. But there is another reason—one that concerns you."

"You need not trouble yourself about me or Ahaziah, once we reach your father's capital."

Michael took a deep breath. He had been wondering how to put into words what he wanted to say to her; now he knew there was but one way—to speak out. "I want to concern myself about you for the rest of my life and yours, Miriam," he told her. "Don't you realize that I love you?"

He saw the light of anger begin to burn in her eyes once more. "A week ago you lay in Jezebel's arms, yet now you dare speak to me of love," she said bitterly. "What proof do I have that a week from now you will not be with her again?"

"None—unless you love me enough to trust me."

She did not answer at once and he saw that she was considering the thought. "Can I be sure you will

151

not go to her again?" she asked finally and his heart took a great leap, for she had put into words for the first time the fact that what was between them went beyond mere friendship.

He wanted to answer, "Yes," but he knew he could not. For in the delicately balanced game he was playing to preserve the lives of Miriam, Elijah, Naboth, and Prince Ahaziah, it might become necessary for him seemingly to adhere to the plan Jezebel had outlined to him in the palace at Jezreel, perhaps even to make love to her again. Nor did he deny to himself any longer that some perverse part of his nature deep inside him still rejoiced at the prospect.

"Would you hold me to such a promise if it meant losing my own life?" he temporized. "Or perhaps Prince Ahaziah's and you own?"

"How could I ever be sure that was the only reason?"

"Because you trust me to do what is best for all of us."

"But she would always be between us," Miriam cried, and he saw that she was very near to tears. When he moved to take her into his arms, she did not resist but buried her head against his breast as she had done that night on Mount Carmel when he had saved her from the snake. He held her there for a long moment, then took her chin in his hand and lifted it to look into her eyes. They were wet with tears and tormented by the conflicts that troubled her, but there was also a light in them he had never seen before. And when he kissed her lips, they were warm, soft, and trusting beneath his own.

"Love like ours can wait until I have cast the demon of Jezebel out of my life, dearest one," he told her confidently. "After that nothing can come between us."

Chapter 13

MICHAEL WAS DETAINED IN JERUSALEM FOR ALMOST a month training a troop of about a hundred horsemen in methods of combating the particular skills of war he had seen displayed by the Assyrians. Elijah had gone on from Jerusalem to his old home at Tishbeh, a town in the district of Gilead across the Jordan. Miriam and Prince Ahaziah were quartered in King Jehoshaphat's palace, where the young Israelite quickly impressed the nobles of Judah with a knowledge and wisdom that went far beyond his years.

Michael could have wished for more time to spend with Miriam but the duty of organizing and training the troops he was to lead took up most of his time. In the meantime, travelers reported that Shalmaneser's hordes had already started moving westward from Nineveh to the River Arantu whose valley, lying between the extension of the Lebanon and Anti-Lebanon mountain ranges in northern Syria, had more than once afforded a route of invasion into central Canaan.

When the disturbing news came that Shalmaneser had already conquered Barga, Adennu, and Argana, smaller cities belonging to King Irhuleni of Hamath, it was obvious to Michael that the Assyrian monarch was moving toward Karkar, a heavily fortified point near Hamath, in the upper portion of the Arantu Valley, serving somewhat the same function in that region that Megiddo did in the neighborhood of Mount Carmel. Guarding a point of entry into the central part of Canaan from the north near a crossing of the River Arantu, Karkar also protected King Irhuleni's capital city of Hamath. Its fall would open a path for the Assyrian forces into the very heart of Ahab's domain, hence the enemy's tactic of concentrating the attack at that point.

Michael had delayed his departure from Jerusalem a few days in order to remain there for the Passover Feast and make a sacrifice begging the favor of the Most High for the venture upon which he was embarked. As was customary, the household of King Jehoshaphat and their guests had eaten the roasted flesh of the paschal lamb and the traditional bitter herbs together. Now, as midnight approached, Michael and Miriam left the others and went out upon a small balcony high up on the palace wall, overlooking the city. From this very balcony, it was said, David had watched the lovely Bathsheba bathing upon an adjoining rooftop at a lower level and had been so smitten by her that he had taken her as his wife, even at the price of her husband's life.

Below them, few lights were visible in the city of Jerusalem, for Judah was at peace and only a small number of guards kept watch through the night. The people were in their homes, eating the remains of the paschal lamb and the bitter herbs—symbols of the years of their enslavement in Egypt—which must be finished before midnight. According to an ancient custom, the oldest member of the household retold for the children during the feast the story of how the Hebrews, as God had instructed Moses, smeared the blood of a lamb upon the lintels of their doorposts so the Angel of Death would pass over their houses when he smote the first-born of Egypt and punished Pharaoh for holding them captive.

The last act of the Passover celebration was the singing of a beautiful hymn of praise. And as the two stood upon the balcony, the soft strains of the melody began to float up from the city below. "I had forgotten how beautiful the Passover can be," Miriam said softly. "In Samaria we do not celebrate it as you do here in Jerusalem, I suppose because the Temple of God is not there to remind us."

Their eyes were instinctively drawn to the golden dome of the temple, shining in the moonlight. For a moment neither of them spoke, lost in wonder at the beauty of the structure raised by Solomon as a tribute to the God who had made a great nation from a band of former slaves fleeing the wrath of Pharaoh.

"I wish father would move to Judah," Miriam said. "But he feels he must stay in Israel and help the Council of Elders oppose the plottings of Jezebel."

She did not resist when Michael put his arm about her, and the feel of her cheek against his own was like the touch of a soft cloth from the looms of the skilled Phoenician weavers.

"Have you heard from Naboth lately?" he asked.

"No. With King Ahab away, he and the council are always busy. In his last letter he said he hoped to go up to Jezreel and see to the vineyard there."

"I think Ahaziah likes it here in Jerusalem."

"Much better than Samaria," she agreed. "When he becomes king, I am sure he will move the capital back to Jerusalem for at least part of each year. Then we will have the temple to help draw our people closer together."

"Is there any news of Micaiah?"

"I saw a priest from Samaria in the market place the other day. He says Micaiah now leads the prophets

155

of Yahweh in Israel and prophesies in the name of God."

"Micaiah a prophet?"

"Why not? He loves the Lord and has served him since his youth. Surely he has God's favor."

The volume of the music rising from the city below was increasing now, as more and more people joined in singing the hymn marking the end of the feast.

"I spoke to my father about taking you as my wife when I return," Michael said. "He has approved."

"Have you forgotten Jezebel's plans for you?"

"They were her plans, not mine. I only pretended to be interested in the hope of diverting her attention from persecuting the priests."

Miriam had drawn away at the mention of Jezebel's name and the deep unspoken communion which had existed between them there on the balcony was broken. "I wish I could believe that is true, Michael. But both of us know it is not."

"Why should she come between us here?"

Miriam shivered, although the night was warm. "Jezebel will not give you or her plans up so easily. She is relentless when it comes to getting her way."

"Don't you credit me with enough strength to resist her?" he demanded a little angrily.

"Perhaps that would be asking too much of any man." She put her hand up to his cheek and her fingers were like the touch of a feather against his skin—or a kiss of farewell. "Your love means much to me, Michael. So much that I want nothing to mar our happiness."

"But—"

"Hush and hear me out. Ever since you saved me from the robbers on the hill beyond Ephraim, I have known I belong to you. But something tells me that events have already begun to happen involving us both—things we cannot change or alter because they are the will of God."

"It seemed to be the will of God that Elijah would be slain on Mount Carmel," he reminded her, still a little offended at her suggestion that he might not be able to resist Jezebel. "Until I launched the arrow that killed Kubli."

"Your being there was a part of God's will," she said. "Father and Micaiah believe it and I tell myself it is true to soften the pain in my heart at knowing that, while we were all supporting Elijah on Mount Carmel, you were with Jezebel."

"It was as if I were seized by a demon then, but she has no hold over me now," Michael protested. "When I see Naboth again upon my return from the war with Assyria, I will pay him the bride price. Then we shall see whether you can resist both me and your father."

"Don't forget Ahaziah," she said with a little chuckle as she came into his arms again. "He made me promise not to marry anyone else but you."

Her kiss was all he had imagined it could be and she did not resist when he held her closer than he had ever held her before. When finally he released her, Michael himself was a little shaken by the depth of the emotion that had seized them both.

"Once you said that, having never known passion or desire, I could not understand how you were drawn to Jezebel," Miriam reminded him, a little unsteadily. "But I don't think you will ever accuse me of being cold again."

It was barely dawn when Michael and his troop of horsemen rode out of the city but still light enough for him to see the flash of color from Miriam's scarf as she waved farewell to him from the balcony where they had pledged their love the night before. Two days later, he rode into Megiddo and learned that Ahab,

157

answering an urgent summons from his allies. had left for the Arantu Valley in the domain of King Irhuleni of Hamath two weeks before with every chariot and fighting man he could muster. The reports said that Shalmaneser III of Assyria was concentrating every man, chariot, and camel, plus all his massive engines of war, north of the fortified center of Karkar.

Pausing only to acquire fresh supplies, Michael led his troops out of Megiddo and headed northeastward along the ancient "Way of the Sea." Through the rough hill country lying west of the Jordan, they made good time, and toward the afternoon of the first day rode through a pass in the hills and saw the lovely harp-shaped Sea of Chinnereth far below them in its deep cup surrounded by rocky cliffs showing the typical black basalt boulders of volcanic origin.

Stopping for the night at the brawling fishing village of Chinnereth on the shores of the lake, where rows of boats with their multicolored sails furled for the night were drawn up on the sand, they departed early the next morning and skirted the lake for a short distance. Ahead the Jordan tumbled into the lake from the north, its cold waters causing a sharp zone of contrast with the warm water of the lake. This made fish school there in tremendous numbers and, as they rode along the shore, they could see them leaping in the morning sunlight like shimmering floods of molten silver.

Following the east bank of the Jordan northward, they skirted groves of oleander and the balsam-like tree from which came the nut whose oil furnished the healing "Balm of Gilead," alternating with thickets of tall fan-like papyrus reeds. Approaching Hazor—whose king had once sent iron-wheeled chariots under his captain Sisera against Deborah and Barak in the time of *Shophetim,* only to see them mired helplessly in the Vale of Jezreel when Yahweh sent a great downpour of hail and rain—they left the Way of the Sea where it turned eastward toward Damascus.

As they continued northward, the Jordan widened out into an area resembling a lake, whose surface was almost hidden by a vast swamp filled with reeds. Across just such a shallow "Sea of Reeds" far to the south on the borderland of Egypt, Moses and the children of Israel had made their escape from the chariots of Pharaoh when a great wind had swept the waters back, and had seen the armies of Egypt swallowed by the flood when the wind suddenly abated.

The king of Hazor was one of those who had joined with Ahab against Assyria, so they had no hesitation in stopping there for the night. Here Michael learned that Ahab had passed through only a little over a week before, bound for Quatna, a caravan junction point near the banks of the Arantu River. This stream, he knew, flowed north in the valley between the Lebanon range, separating its fertile lowlands from the sea to the west and from the Anti-Lebanon range, crowned in this region by the snow-capped crest of Mount Hermon, to the east.

Michael was elated at having gained several days on Ahab and, with his smaller troop and greater maneuverability compared to the more cumbersome chariots. hoped to arrive at the rallying point only a little after the Israelite monarch. They were traveling through a beautiful section of country now, with snow-capped Mount Hermon on the right hand and the cedar-clad slopes of the Lebanon range on the left in what was known as Coele-Syria.

Beyond the Lebanon range to the west lay the coast of the Great Sea with the fabulously rich Phoenician seaport cities. Michael was sure that Ahab was right in feeling that Shalmaneser would choose the wider valley of the Arantu and Litani rivers for his march southward instead of the far more difficult coastal route. In fact, at several points along the Phoenician seacoast, notably the area known as the "Ladder of Tyre" opposite that city, ranges of steep hills extended almost into the sea, making travel by the coastal route almost impossible for a force of much size.

Moving steadily northward along the course of the south-flowing River Litani, Michael and his troops entered the great hollow of Syria by way of a natural bridge that crossed the river at a point near where it turned sharply eastward to reach the sea. Here they negotiated a narrow roadway that had literally been carved from the mountainside beneath a huge precipice, an area fortified in ancient times and still showing evidence of its original function as a guardian point for this whole region.

Ordinarily at this point they would have been forced to fight their way through the strategic entrance into the widening valley of central Syria. But with the kings governing the area among those joined together against Shalmaneser and his hordes, groups of fighting men were passing through without opposition every day on the way northward for the great battle.

Just north of the origin of the River Litani, the valley began to widen out with the beginning of the Arantu, which, after bursting from the earth in the form of a great spring, flowed in a northerly direction before turning sharply westward to empty into the Great Sea. Known since ancient times as the "Entering in of Hamath," this region had once been the northern boundary of Solomon's kingdom.

In the narrow part of the valley near the headwaters of the Arantu, the banks had been lined with willows, hawthorns, poplars, and walnuts, their limbs shading the turbulent flow from the great spring that gave birth to the river. Though the rugged mountain heights were generally bare, the smaller depressions between separate ranges were green and leafy, and small streams often tumbled through them to the valley below. The men had no trouble finding ample forage for their mounts when they made camp or paused to rest here, for it was an area of beauty, peace, and verdant plenty, with colorful birds calling to each other across the sound of the torrents and many-hued flowers growing everywhere.

For several days now Michael and his troops had been overtaking groups of stragglers, men who had fallen out from the lines of march because of blistered feet, minor injuries, or simply lack of stamina. There had also been a number of minor casualties of equipment, for, though the way was now fairly broad, it was still rocky in places, particularly across the small freshets that poured down from the mountain heights. Even the iron-shod chariot wheels were not always able to take the punishment of the rocky stream beds, and wrecked vehicles lay beside the roadway in the rougher stretches. All in all, however, there seemed to have been remarkably little trouble for a force numbering almost two thousand chariots in addition to as many horsemen and nearly ten thousand foot soldiers —a tribute, Michael was sure, to the organizing ability of the Israelite king.

Finally a day came when Michael and his party rode around a projecting shoulder of rock and saw stretching before them a low rolling plain forming the main part of the Arantu Valley. In the distance was the small caravan junction point of Quatna, with the tents of the hosts mustered by the confederation of twelve kings guarding the banks of the steam that furnished water for the camp. Men, horses, and vehicles were moving along the caravan trails leading to this point, stirring up clouds of dust to mark their passage.

To the north, the road Michael and his troops were following continued along the course of the Arantu, crossing the river by means of a shallow ford on the way to Hamath and the rallying point of the Assyrian forces near Karkar. Eastward a road led to the famous Oasis of Tadmor or Palmyra, a junction point on the way to the Euphrates and to what had long ago been the fabulous kingdom of the Mari.

Just ahead was a junction with a road crossing the Arantu and leading southwestward to a pass in the Lebanon range. Michael was sure it must lead to the thriving Phoenician city of Arvad, which, unlike most of the southern cities of Phoenicia who had chosen to remain neutral, had joined forces with the confederation to fight against the Assyrians.

Michael and his troop paused only for a few moments to let their horses rest before riding down into the valley and across the plain toward the distant encampment of Ahab and his allies.

Chapter 14

As he rode through the camp, Michael compared it with the encampment of the Assyrian forces he had seen on his visit to Nineveh. Both showed the same varied assortment of nationalities: swarthy fighters from Damascus were bivouacked beside the desert people with their camels and flowing garments; the inevitable Hittite mercenaries strolled along, contemptuous of what they obviously considered only a rabble; and the small wiry Phoenicians of Arvad, half seamen and half husbandmen, busied themselves repairing military equipment.

It was a colorful place with the banners of the twelve nations fluttering above the tents and the babble of tongues in a dozen dialects assailing one's ears. With these sounds went the mournful protest of a camel being loaded and the rattle of chariots moving to and from the open field where they were being drilled in the discipline of fighting as a body rather than as individuals. Interspersed with these sounds was the clatter of horses' hoofs as courier after courier rode up to the great tent that served as the headquarters for the entire operation.

Sending Aaron and his lieutenat, a young nobleman

of Judah named Jehu, to seek forage for the horses and a place where the soldiers might find shelter, Michael proceeded through the camp to the great tent. Before it he was stopped by a tall mercenary, but an officer recognized him almost immediately and let him pass without question. The flap of the main tent was open, so he walked in.

Ahab was seated at a low table made from carved ivory panels, with several of the Phoenician maps which Michael had only seen once or twice before spread out before him. The use of maps marked a considerable innovation in warfare, Michael was sure, for heretofore military commanders in the field had been forced to rely upon knowledge of the unfamiliar terrain gained from the people of the country who were supposed to be familiar with it. Often these were captured enemies, who could be expected to try to deceive their captors wherever possible, so they were often deliberately misinformed and led into ambush.

Sitting beside Ahab was a broad-shouldered, very ugly man of about Michael's own age. Though almost repulsive in appearance, his rich robes and the jewels blazing in the golden chaplet he wore upon his head marked him as a person of considerable importance —at least in his own mind. Compared to the other's showy finery, Ahab's simple tunic and leather harness appeared almost shabby. A small man with the swarthy complexion of the Phoenician traders and seamen sat on the other side of the table. All were busy studying the maps which the smaller man was explaining in quick, terse sentences. Michael did not call attention to his presence until Ahab looked up and saw him.

"Michael!" the Israelite king cried warmly, getting up to put his arm about the younger man's shoulders and lead him to the table. "I am glad you have finally come."

Turning to the others, Ahab spoke in a somewhat

more formal tone. "Prince Michael of Judah, King Hadad-Ezer of Damascus."

The Syrian monarch acknowledged the introduction with a curt nod and Michael saw a smoldering glare begin to burn in his eyes, as if he were in a chronic state of anger. "Why is King Jehoshaphat not with us instead of hiding in Jerusalem?" Hadad-Ezer demanded.

Michael curbed his irritation at the other's tone. "My father sends his wishes that the venture here will be successful," he answered coolly. "Meanwhile—as we agreed upon with King Ahab—he guards the southern approaches to Judah and Israel."

Hadad-Ezer shrugged. "You would be expected to defend him, I suppose."

The Phoenician had not spoken. Now he turned to Michael with a warm smile. "I am King Matten of Arvad," he said. "Welcome to Quatna, Prince Michael. I hope you brought fighting men with you."

"Only a troop of about a hundred," Michael said. "But they are all completely equipped and ready for battle."

"By the fires of Chemosh!" Hadad-Ezer spat contemptuously upon the floor. "What are a hundred men when we need thousands?"

Michael did not reply, since there seemed to be no point in doing so. "King Jehoshaphat and I are in complete accord concerning the necessity of his remaining behind to defend the southern entrances into our country," Ahab said curtly. "But for him, a small force of Shalmaneser's army could easily penetrate Israel and come at us from the rear."

The king of Arvad smiled again. "We all have a part in this effort wherever we are. No one has a right to criticize the other for doing what it has been decided he should do."

"You have only a few men to lose but I have twelve hundred cavalry and twenty thousand foot soldiers,"

Hadad-Ezer said heavily. "If Shalmaneser destroys us here, I shall have to defend Damascus with tailors and women."

Ahab ignored the king of Syria and spread the map they had been examining out again. It was drawn upon a sheet of calfskin split into its thinnest layer, like the fine writing materials used in the highest Egyptian circles. Places, rivers, roads, and mountains, Michael saw, had been marked in considerable detail, giving a picture of the terrain that could only have been gained, he was sure, by actually seeing it.

"King Matten here has provided us with these maps showing what the country is like," Ahab explained. "Our spies tell us the forces of Shalmaneser are not very far from Karkar." He pointed to a spot upon the map. "It is a strongly fortified town guarding a ford and a narrow spot forming the chief entrance to this particular section of the Arantu Valley."

Michael had been studying the chart; it was the first time he had seen a map of this whole area. "I take it you plan to defend Karkar then?"

"We have no choice," Ahab agreed. "It is the key to this portion of the valley."

"How strong are its fortifications?"

"King Irhuleni says the troops there can hold out for some time but not for a long siege such as the Assyrians would mount against the city."

"As we came into camp, I noticed a road leading westward," Michael said. "Where does it go?"

The king of Arvad answered, "To the seacoast. It joins a coastal road a little south of my own city."

"Is it passable for horses?"

The Phoenician gave him a keen look. "Not to chariots; much of it follows the shore and they might become mired in the sand. But to horsemen, yes."

"Then why not send a flanking force around to the enemy's rear by way of the coastal route? They could

166

wait there until you are ready to attack from the south."

"Attack?" Hadad-Ezer demanded heavily. "Does a flea put an elephant to flight?"

"When I traveled in Egypt, I heard it said that even an elephant fears a mouse," Michael told him. "I have in mind making this mouse appear to be an elephant."

"What do you mean?" Ahab asked.

"With a force of perhaps two thousand men launching quick raids at dawn and dusk and hiding in the hills by day, the Assyrian generals might be led to believe a much larger force was in the rear of their army."

"By the fires of Malkarth!" Matten exclaimed. "It is a daring plan."

"And a foolhardy one," Hadad-Ezer said heavily. "Why risk two thousand men when we need them here to keep the Assyrians from moving south and taking Damascus?"

"If we sit here and wait for Shalmaneser to attack he will probably overrun us by sheer weight of numbers," Ahab pointed out. "What Michael has proposed might make the Assyrians so fearful of a force at their rear that they will hesitate to launch their entire army at us in this direction. In that way only two thousand men might make the Assyrians divide their forces so we would not have to fight more than half the army at a time."

"That is exactly what I have in mind," Michael agreed. "Of course someone who knows the area very thoroughly will be needed to guide the troops making the flanking movement."

"I know the region between here and the mouth of the Arantu like my own face in a mirror," King Matten said. "I would be glad to guide the troops, provided the one who leads them is the one who conceived this daring foray."

"Prince Michael will lead the force," Ahab said. "I will call a meeting of the twelve kings at once so the plan may be presented to them."

Hadad-Ezer lumbered to his feet. "I for one am against it. No troops of mine will ride on any such foolhardy expedition."

"Michael's own men and cavalry from my command and King Matten's will form the force," Ahab told him curtly.

An aide was sent to inform the other kings that a meeting of the members of the confederation would be held at the time of the evening meal, which they usually took together. Hadad-Ezer and Matten went out, leaving Michael and Ahab alone.

When the Israelite monarch got up and went to the open flap of the tent to look out across the camp, Michael saw that his forehead had become creased with worry in the few short weeks since he had last seen him. For a long moment Ahab stood there, his shoulders slumped in a gesture more eloquent of weariness and defeat than Michael had ever seen in him. Finally he turned back to his guest.

"Your coming is the first good thing that has happened to me in a week, Michael," he said. "I hope it is a good omen for the future."

"Haven't things been going well?"

"I suppose I should expect no more than we have accomplished," Ahab admitted. "At least we have gathered an army here in the Arantu Valley only a day's march from the enemy. I thought for a while we would not even get Hadad-Ezer to come this far."

"Surely he is intelligent enough to realize that the only chance of defeating the Assyrians lies in maintaining a united front and selecting the most favorable spot to defend?"

"Hadad-Ezer thinks only of Damascus," Ahab told

him. "I will wager that at the first taste of defeat he will run squalling back to his capital."

"What about the forces gathered here? Are they anywhere near equal to the Assyrians'?"

"From what my spies tell me Shalmaneser's army does not outweigh us too much now, unless he has been joined by troops from some of the kingdoms he conquered on the way from the Euphrates to the Arantu. If you succeed in carrying out this maneuver, we may be able to lure him into dividing his forces and bring those opposing us to about the same number as our own."

"Then you should have a good chance of stopping the Assyrians at Karkar."

"If the battle does not go too much against us in the beginning."

"What about the other kings?"

"Except for Irhuleni and a few Hittites from the north among the Musri tribes, the others brought only small numbers of troops with them. More than half of King Irhuleni's forces are guarding the walls of Karkar, so my own army and Hadad-Ezer's will have to bear the brunt of the attack if the Assyrians break through there." Picking up a wineskin from the table, Ahab drank deeply, letting the stream of ruby-colored fluid flow into his open mouth. "Was Ahaziah happy in Jerusalem when you left?" he asked, handing the skin to Michael.

"Very much so. He and Miriam have begun to study the ancient scrolls of the law together."

"The boy will make Israel a good king, probably better than I have been able to do."

"Your kingdom already covers almost as much territory as Solomon's did at the height of his reign."

"I have done well in material things, perhaps because they are all I really know," Ahab admitted. "But Elijah is right in saying I sinned when I permitted

169

people to drift away from Yahweh. My father before me was a soldier, Michael, and so am I. Perhaps when this is settled and we have regained Ramoth-Gilead, I can journey to Jerusalem and renew my own faith at the temple."

"How does Hadad-Ezer feel about your taking Ramoth-Gilead?"

Ahab shrugged. "When his father, Ben-Hadad, besieged Samaria and forced me to join the confederation, I agreed only upon the condition that Ramoth-Gilead would be returned to Israel. If Hadad-Ezer does not choose to honor his father's promise, my armies and your father's will make him do it."

The capacity of the large tent where Ahab had his center of command was taxed when eleven kings and their immediate lieutenants gathered there for the evening meal. While the meal was in progress, Michael subjected each to as close a scrutiny as he could without being discourteous.

Concerning Matten, the Phoenician, he had no doubts. King Irhuleni was not there, but he had always heard that the king of Hamath was a man of his word, as well as a warrior of great courage. Besides, the entire campaign so far was being fought in Irhuleni's own country, so he had nothing to gain by defaulting. Aside from the three rulers of Hamath, Israel, and Syria, however, the other kings were small fry, some of them no doubt valuable, like Matten of Arvad, because of their personal qualities, but none bringing any large amount of troops into the confederation.

The meal was a luxurious one and the evening was far advanced when finally the plates and viands were cleared away, leaving only wineskins strategically placed where all could reach them. King Ahab now rose to his feet at the head of the group of several low tables upon which the food had been served. At his nod an aide unrolled one of the calfskin maps and held it up for the others to see.

"You have all met my guest, Prince Michael of Judah," Ahab said. "He is a daring and experienced young commander who has visited Nineveh and is familiar with the Assyrians and their way of fighting. This afternoon he suggested a move which, I believe, will materially increase our chances of defeating the enemy at Karkar."

Ahab had his audience now. Even the gross Hadad-Ezer did not appear so contemptuous of the plan as he had been earlier that afternoon and Michael decided that the king of Syria must have been talking to his own military leaders.

"I am going to ask Prince Michael to explain what he has in mind to you," Ahab added.

Michael took a position beside the calfskin map and described the swift flanking foray he had envisioned as a means of sowing uncertainty and fear behind the Assyrian lines. "With a large army in the Arantu Valley, Shalmaneser no doubt has had to organize large caravans to supply them," Michael pointed out in conclusion. "We can harass those lines while moving southward toward the main part of his forces."

"How long do you think all of this will take, Michael?" Ahab asked.

"Less than a week, if we are able to find plenty of forage for the horses."

"The towns of my region along the coast will furnish that," Matten volunteered. "And we should be able to capture enough grain from the Assyrians in the Arantu Valley to take care of our needs thereafter."

"I still think it is foolhardy to draw off two thousand of our horsemen on such a wild venture," Hadad-Ezer said heavily. "They could be better used to defend our own capitals."

171

"We in Judah have as much to lose as any of you," Michael reminded the group. "Unless the Assyrians are stopped here in the Valley of the Arantu, they will sweep southward. Then my father will have no kingdom and most of my people will be dead."

When the vote was taken on placing Michael in command of the two thousand horsemen selected for the swift foray behind the Assyrian lines, everyone voted in his favor except Hadad-Ezer, who only grunted and did not vote at all. And, with the matter decided, Michael started immediately upon preparations for departure.

True to his promise, Ahab furnished the major portion of the cavalry placed under Michael's command. King Matten, Michael learned, was not only ruler of the city-state of Arvad, located upon a great rock a few miles off the northern coast of Phoenicia, but also controlled a wide area of the mainland lying opposite his capital. This area, populated by a fierce warrior people called the Zahi, furnished several hundred horsemen mounted upon small wiry ponies. When finally the expedition rode out of Quatna on the second day after the conference of the kings, Michael found himself in command of almost twenty-five hundred men.

He had offered to place King Matten in charge of half the troops, but the Phoenician ruler had demurred. Not primarily a soldier and with little training in the methods of cavalry warfare, Matten insisted that someone more skilled in the field command the second body, comprising roughly half of the expedition. For this important captaincy, Michael chose Jehu, who had been in command of the cavalry and chariot forces of Judah for some time. The two were very close friends, having grown up together as youths, and Michael knew he could depend upon Jehu to follow his orders yet assume full responsibility for the troops under his direction in case the two became separated.

Two days later, by riding fast through the domain of King Matten, they made camp near the ancient city of Ugarit, well beyond the northern limits of Phoenician territory. Here and there along the way Matten had pointed out the ruins of dwellings and other buildings erected by earlier inhabitants of this area, including the Hyxos people who had swept down along the coast in the time of Abraham and the so-called "Sea People," ancestors of the Philistines to the south, who had always been bitter enemies of the Israelites. Around them as they made camp were the moldy ruins of what had once been, according to King Matten, the largest and most populous center in this part of the world.

Michael felt no immediate need to sleep after the others had gone to improvised beds made from broken branches and piles of leaves. With his heavy cloak wrapped about him against the chill of the night, he sat before the dying embers of the fire watching the interplay of color as the tiny flames rose and fell from each glowing coal. And as he watched, pictures began to take shape in the dancing flames, very much as they had formed in his brain from the effects of the "Flower of Dreams" Jezebel had given him in Jezreel.

First came Abraham, the father of the Hebrew people, leading his flocks and herds as they moved southward toward the pasture lands of Judah and the lush flat delta region of the Nile. Soon that picture faded and he saw hordes of people rolling southward along this coast, driving wheeled vehicles which had never before been known in that region, chariots which identified them as the Hyxos invaders who had conquered the rich Nile delta and held it for so many years. It was during these years, he knew, that an Israelite, a grandson of Abraham's named Joseph, had

173

become second only to the Pharaoh in Egypt and had saved the Egyptians, as well as his own family, from famine.

Now the scene changed once again and long lines of men appeared, some bearing heavy burdens while others fashioned bricks of clay and straw, their backs bowed under the whips of the overseers. One, a prince of Egypt named Ahmose, dared to resist the whip and in a short but desperate struggle killed a brutal overseer, only to be forced to flee to save his own life.

Now, the pictures dancing in the coals of fire showed Michael the same long line of people, but this time they were carrying their possessions upon their backs or dragging them behind them on rude sleds and carts as they followed a much older Ahmose, now called Moses. Stumbling through a rocky wilderness, they came finally to stand before a great mountain whose cloud-wreathed summit was invisible save for tendrils of smoke rising into the sky from the eternal fires burning within it. As they watched, Moses came down from the mountain height bearing stone tablets upon which had been engraved by the hand of God the laws which had strengthened the people and kept them apart through the centuries.

A coal in the fire popped, and in the sudden flare of brightness Michael saw fires raging in a powerful city whose walls had been tumbled by a great cataclysm which destroyed it. And barely had the ashes cooled when a conquering horde of jubilant fighting men poured through breaches in the walls to complete the destruction of every living thing within it, as directed under the curse God had leveled upon Jericho.

Just so—Michael thought as his musing gave way to the present—would the Assyrians level the walls of the cities in Israel and Judah, if they were able to

174

break through the defenses at Karkar and spread out into the valleys of the Arantu and Litani, routes of invasion which would afford them almost unimpeded access to northern Israel.

Chapter 15

By the afternoon of the fourth day following their departure from Quatna, Michael's party was riding through the foothills of Karkar. It was about mid-afternoon when one of the outriders, who stayed constantly ahead of the party to detect any sign of the enemy, came riding back with news that a large encampment was visible only a few miles away to the south. Leaving the main force behind, Michael, Jehu, and Matten rode ahead to look over the situation. At what they saw, King Matten, who was not familiar with the extent of the Assyrian forces, gasped with disbelief.

An open section of the valley had been selected as a marshaling point for the Assyrian chariots, as well as a supply base for the main army ahead. Ranged row on row, with lanes between each double file so they could be driven out quickly once the horses were hitched, the vehicles covered a large area where dry grass had been trampled down. The horses had been turned into improvised pastures in the heavy green grass along the riverbank where they could forage. At one side of the group of chariots, and about halfway between them and the horses, were several of the large catapults which the Assyrians used in breaching the walls of fortified cities that resisted their onslaughts.

As the three watchers reined in their horses in the hills well above the area, a plan began to take form in Michael's mind, a plan which, if they could carry it into effect, would cause considerably more consternation in the rear of the main Assyrian army than he had possibly hoped to achieve.

"There must be two thousand chariots on that field and horses for them in the pasture beside the river," Jehu said in a tone of awe. "And look how few guards have been left to watch them,"

"Think what a blaze would do if it were set in the dry grass where the chariots stand," Michael suggested.

"The wooden parts would be consumed before anyone could stop the fire," King Matten cried, catching the idea.

"And the flames would terrify the horses so they would break out of the pasture by the river," Jehu added, the possibilities of the situation stirring his imagination as well.

"We will attack at dawn tomorrow," Michael decided. "The moon rises early and we can move our men into position during the first hours of the night. Then as soon as it is light enough for us to see, we will fire the grass around the chariots and make a foray upon the camp and the pasture. By the time the guards realize what has happened, we should be finished and far away, driving at least a thousand horses before us."

"It is a daring plan," Matten agreed. "But if we are going to set the grass afire to burn the chariots we will need torches. How will you be able to hide the fires while we wait to attack?"

It was a thorny question, until on the way back to camp Michael remembered Miriam's story of how Gideon's men, in preparing for the attack upon the

Midianites in the Vale of Jezreel, had hidden torches under jars. The method he proposed to use was somewhat different, but the principle was the same.

The men had built cooking fires to prepare the meat the hunters had brought in. When the cooking was finished, Michael instructed each squadron to fill one of the small copper pots they carried with coals which could be taken to the place from which he planned to launch the attack. He had decided that Jehu and his troops, along with about a hundred of the Phoenician cavalrymen—whose job it would be to drive the horses of the Assyrians northward—would cross the valley in the darkness some hours before the expected attack and launch a foray from that direction in order to increase the confusion in the Assyrian camp.

Getting a thousand horsemen into position in the hills without giving any warning of their presence was a slow and tedious process. Fortunately it did not seem to have occurred to the enemy that an attack from the rear was possible and no pickets were posted outside their camp to give warning. For the last portion of the route he had selected, Michael had the Israelite and Phoenician cavalrymen walk their mounts along a narrow hillside trail, the same tactic Joshua had used centuries before in a daring surprise attack upon the Canaanite city of Ai. By two hours before sunrise the entire force was in position, waiting only for the first rays of dawn to launch the attack.

Michael had no way of knowing how Jehu was faring on the other side of the valley. But since there had been no outcry in the Assyrian camp, he was sure their presence had not been detected during the wide sweep which the other troop had taken in approaching the eastern side of the valley.

Each of the Israelite cavalrymen carried a heavy cloak of thick woolen material which served him as a blanket at night, as well as for protection against cold during winter. Now, Michael put into effect the stratagem he had devised to enable them to light torches without making the enemy cognizant of their presence in the hills.

Each captain of a squadron was instructed to hang several of these cloaks on sections of saplings cut from the underbrush of the hillside. The coals carried in the copper pots quickly enabled them to start brisk fires burning behind these improvised curtains. Michael lay down to rest and, to his surprise, slept almost immediately. He did not awaken until Aaron shook his shoulder and pointed silently toward the valley below where the first glow of dawn was beginning to lighten the mantle of darkness which had covered it since the setting of the moon.

"The men are almost ready, master," the servant said in a whisper. "They are lighting torches at the fires now."

As Michael mounted his horse, his gaze swept the hillside, taking in the ranks of silent horsemen, their bodies forming shields that for the moment hid the torches in the hands of the bearers at the back of the line. It took perhaps ten minutes to reach the open ground of the valley below, but only then did Michael signal for the trumpeter who rode just behind him to sound a blast warning Jehu and his horsemen across the valley that the attack from the west had begun. As the clear sharp notes of the trumpet floated across the valley, Michael shouted the order to charge.

The Assyrian chariot commander had unwittingly done the attackers a great favor by placing his vehicles in orderly rows with room between for them to be turned into columns. Through these open lanes the attackers swept, spears lowered at the ready as the hoofs of a thousand horses thundered upon the dry turf of the valley floor. Michael saw the startled faces of several Assyrian soldiers loom up before him and read the stark terror in their eyes as they scrambled to keep from being ridden down by the first line of horsemen. The hoofs of his own horse scattered the embers of a fire beside which the Assyrian guards had been sleeping, and he saw with a surge of satisfaction that they had not even troubled to keep their weapons beside them in the night, so sure had they been that there was no danger of attack.

To the east, Michael heard the clear blast of a ram's horn trumpet and knew that Jehu had launched his own attack, trapping the enemy between the two charging columns. Then the immediate necessity of fighting for his own life outweighed any questions of strategy as he found himself engaged in a sword battle with a huge man bearing a weapon at least half again as long as his own.

The Assyrian was a doughty fighter and Michael was hard put to keep from being cut from his saddle, but his horse was trained to assist him in just such an emergency. Rearing, it struck at the Assyrian with its hoofs, forcing the man to step back and deflect his shield in order to protect himself. Taking advantage of the opening, Michael was able to drive forward with his spear and smash through the enemy's defenses, delivering a mortal wound.

Finding himself no longer under immediate attack, Michael turned in his saddle and took stock of the situation. Behind him the roar of flames and the almost solid wall of fire sweeping across the grassy area where the chariots had been located told him the torch bearers had done their job well. Several of them rode past, still bearing their flaming torches.

"Rally the others," Michael ordered them. "And fire the supply stations." There would be no time to utilize any of the supplies except what food and forage for the horses they could carry.

The men went racing off to plunge their torches into

180

piles of dry fodder waiting to be carried forward to where the main part of the Assyrian army was located before Karkar. The fighting here on the west side of the valley had ended almost as soon as it had begun. Only to the east, where Jehu's troops were just now going into battle, was there still some resistance. The chariot area was a raging inferno as the flames swept rapidly through the dry grass and attacked the wood of the vehicles.

The enclosure by the riverbank had been smashed by the frantic horses and the animals were racing northward away from the flames, with the wiry Phoenician horsemen hard put to keep up with them. King Matten's men had been instructed to drive the animals out of the valley toward the coast through one of several passes. There they could be kept in the area around Arvad until their disposition was decided by Ahab.

From the east, where Jehu and his men were locked in combat with the remainder of the camp's defenders, the sound of battle was dominated by the exultant shouts of the Israelite cavalry as they went about what was now only a mopping-up operation.

Matten joined Michael as he rode to meet Jehu. The Phoenician's sword was red and his eyes were bright with excitement. "Shalmaneser will think the whole army of the confederation is behind him," he cried exultantly.

"Our job is not to let him know how few we really are," Michael said. "As soon as we finish here, we must be on our way."

Jehu was joyously draining an Assyrian wineskin he had picked up at the edge of the camp. Blood was trickling down his cheek from a scratch that he had not even bothered to bandage.

"You left nothing for us to do, Michael," he complained.

"When Shalmaneser hears of this, we'll all have

enough fighting to suit us," Michael assured him. "Right now our task is to take what supplies we can and be away quickly."

"I'd say almost the whole two thousand horses were captured," Jehu said.

"And a fine prize they are," Michael approved. "Have the trumpeter sound a call for the captains to join us here. The men can take care of the few stragglers that are left."

One of Jehu's captains approached with a small worried-looking man dressed in ragged clothes. The prisoner prostrated himself upon the ground before Matten and Michael, whose armor and harness identified them as being of noble birth.

"I am called Ahmen, noble princes," he said. "A merchant of Damascus, captured and cruelly treated by the cursed Assyrians."

"What were you doing here when the Assyrians are at war with your king?" Michael demanded.

"I left Damascus weeks ago with a load of goods for sale in the towns along the way and in Hamath," Ahmen explained. "How was I to know the enemy had already captured this whole country?"

"Where is the main Assyrian army?"

"Before Karkar," Ahmen said without hesitation. "Once they break through there, Hamath will lie before them and can be taken easily."

"Hamath will be defended by fifty thousand men," Michael said sharply.

The merchant shrugged. "The numbers of the Assyrians are like the sands of the sea. No one could stand against them."

"Did you hear them name the number?"

"Some say eighty thousand, some a hundred."

It was disquieting news. If the merchant's figures were correct, Shalmaneser's forces outnumbered those of the confederation by almost two to one.

"Can you guide us through the hills to Karkar?" Michael asked the merchant.

"I can do better than that, noble prince," Ahmen said eagerly. "The Assyrians took all my goods and I would see them troubled as much as possible."

"Help us win the victory and you can take any loot you wish in place of your own possessions," Michael assured him. "But hold nothing back."

"I will tell you the whole truth," Ahmen promised. "The valley narrows at Karkar and the city has very strong battlements, but who can say how long King Irhuleni will be able to hold out? You would be foolish to try and help defend the city. Instead I can show you a way through the foothills to the east so you can lie in wait near Karkar and destroy both men and supplies behind the Assyrian lines."

If what the Syrian said was true, they could accomplish far more by following his direction than by trying to join the defenders of Karkar. On the other hand, if he were leading them into a trap, they might find themselves hopelessly outnumbered with no chance to fight their way clear. As commander of the expedition, only Michael could make that decision.

"You will serve as our guide," he told the Syrian merchant. "If you succeed and we win the battle, great riches will be yours. But if you betray us, be sure that I will kill you before I die."

"What reason would I have to betray you, noble prince?" Ahmen protested. "I have everything to gain if you live and my own life to lose if you die."

"Can we reach this hiding place you spoke of by nightfall?"

"Yes—by riding hard. Once there you could defend yourselves against a hundred thousand."

All that day, with Ahmen as their guide, the raiding party rode southward through the foothills overlooking the Arantu. The valley was fairly wide here but narrowed steadily as it approached the region of Karkar. At nightfall they paused to rest and eat while the horses munched grain captured in the highly successful foray against the Assyrian supply camp. When the moon rose, the journey was resumed.

An area of brightness on the skyline ahead had been apparent since sunset and as they rode southward it grew steadily stronger in intensity. When they paused for a rest after the second hour, Jehu rode forward to where Michael and Matten were standing, looking toward the distant glow.

"What could that be?" he inquired. "The Assyrians would hardly have such large campfires burning all night."

"Before I was captured, I saw great loads of logs and brush being hauled toward the city of Karkar," Ahmen told them. "The enemy must be burning the city and the inhabitants in it."

"Then Karkar has already fallen," Jehu said.

"Not necessarily," Michael interposed. "One of the Assyrians' favorite methods of siege is to pile wood against the walls of a city and fire it so the heat drives back the inhabitants. By leaving spaces between the fires, their men are able to approach and dig beneath the walls."

"Then we have no time to lose," Jehu said. "King Ahab must be warned so he can come up to Karkar before it is taken and the Assyrians break out into the valley below it."

"I plan to send couriers to Ahab as soon as we come near enough to Karkar to see what has happened," Michael agreed.

The moon was low upon the horizon and the glow of the Assyrian fires was almost opposite them to the west when Ahmen finally called a halt. In the half darkness ahead Michael could see a narrow pass that was partially hidden by the shadows of the hills rising abruptly on either side.

"There lies the entrance to the valley I told you of, Prince Michael," the Syrian said. "But some of us should ride ahead first to make sure the cursed Assyrians have not fortified it."

"Jehu," Michael called, "take ten men and scout the valley. Ahmen will lead you."

In less than an hour, Jehu and ten men of the exploring party rode out of the darkness. There was no sign of their guide.

"Where is the Syrian?" Michael demanded.

"He gave us the slip in the dark," Jehu admitted wryly. "He knew the land well and we did not."

"What about the valley?"

"It appears to be all Ahmen said it was," Jehu reported. "There is plenty of room for us to hide without being detected, and with only a few men we could defend the entrance here against the whole Assyrian army."

"If the opposite end does not lead directly into the Assyrian camp."

"Do you think Ahmen would have gone to Shalmaneser's camp to warn them?" Matten asked.

Michael looked at the moon, which was now hanging just above the Lebanon range to the west. "Whether he did or not, we have no choice except to go into the valley. We will leave a hundred men here at the pass to defend it in case we are attacked. The rest of us will see what we can discover."

Beyond the narrow defile through which a stream emerged from the foothills, the valley widened out quickly to where it could easily hide an entire army. They did not pause, even after the moon sank beyond the Lebanon range to the west, but rode on southward, picking their way as best they could in the darkness along the banks of the small stream which ran through the center of the valley.

After about another hour of riding, the valley began to close in and, since the stream had grown steadily smaller as they proceeded deeper into the valley, Michael decided that they were approaching its end. When it narrowed to what was only a small pocket, he ordered the troops to halt and picket the horses alongside the stream where they could graze on the lush grass. With Jehu, Matten, and Aaron, he climbed the side of the steep ridge that formed one wall of the secluded area in which they were hidden.

It was a stiff climb in the darkness and by the time they reached the top all of them were panting. But when they topped the crest of the ridge that hid the Arantu Valley from view and came out upon a small ledge overlooking the lowlands, they saw a sight that made them catch their breath in wonder and apprehension.

A number of great fires were burning around the small city, whose walls were outlined in stark silhouette by the flames. The ledge on which they stood was roughly opposite Karkar, which—they could see from the illumination of the flames—was a fairly heavily defended strong point, with tall battlements rising from the rocky mound where the main valley of the Arantu appeared to be narrower than at any point they had seen so far. They were too far away to be able to tell much in the darkness about the condition of the city itself, but it was hard to believe any fortified area could hold out long under the terrible heat generated by the fires burning against its very walls.

"Do you suppose they have already taken Karkar?" Jehu asked.

"Hardly," Michael said. "Else they would let the fires die down and drive through into the valley beyond. But I don't see how anyone could hold out very long under those circumstances."

In the east behind the watchers upon the hilltop, red streamers heralding the dawn were already beginning to spread through the sky. It was still too dark to tell very much about the country between them and Karkar, but while they watched from their vantage point, wrapped in their cloaks against the coolness of the night, a scene such as Michael was sure he would never witness again began to take form below them.

The camp of the Assyrian army stretched as far as they could see across the valley and Michael was sure now that Ahmen had not been exaggerating when he estimated the number of enemy troops at close to eighty thousand men. Two huge catapults operated by specially trained men who handled the mechanism were in place before the city. As they watched, a giant boulder was tossed through the air to crash against the walls. Several of the portable siege towers developed by the Assyrians were also in place, ready to be pushed against the wall as soon as the heat from the flames drove the defenders back and a breach of the fortification was achieved.

Michael needed to see no more; the whole picture was clear. With Karkar destroyed and the way southward open, Shalmaneser would be able to throw an overwhelming force against Ahab and destroy all protection that remained for both Judah and Israel. The most important thing now was to warn Ahab while there was still time.

"Do you think you can find your way to Quatna through the hills?" he asked Aaron.

The servant shaded his eyes with his hand and studied the region to the south. "Several of the ridges seem to parallel the Arantu Valley," he said. "I should be able to hide behind them until I am safely

187

beyond the Assyrian lines. Then I can turn westward toward our own camp."

"Go to King Ahab and describe to him exactly what you saw here," Michael directed. "Tell him he must bring his armies up before Karkar as quickly as possible, else the Assyrians will break through the defenses of the city and spill out upon the plains below it toward Hamath. Be sure and tell him he must throw his full strength close to the walls from the south, if he is going to keep the Assyrians from putting their whole army through Karkar."

Aaron nodded and started down the slope to where his horse was tethered with the others. "Be careful, old one," Michael called after him. "I would hate to lose you."

"Don't wait here too long." The gruffness in Aaron's voice betrayed his emotion. "The Syrian may have gone to Shalmaneser after all."

All day long the raiding party remained hidden in the valley. Only after night had fallen again did Michael ascend the ridge with Jehu and Matten to view the doomed city of Karkar. What he saw made his heart fall, for already the fires were beginning to die down, a sure sign that the Assyrians had begun to launch the final assault.

"Karkar has been taken," Matten said. "It could be the beginning of the end."

"Unless Aaron got through to Ahab and he started moving northward at once," Michael agreed gloomily.

"Will he be in time, even then?" Jehu asked.

"The fires are still burning," Michael said. "That means the enemy can probably not put many troops through Karkar before tomorrow morning. Ahab should be here by that time."

None of them answered; there was nothing to do but hope.

"I will stay here and watch," Michael told the others.

188

"If Ahab and the army fail to arrive by tomorrow morning, we will have to ride out of this pocket and hope to make our way southward to Hamath or Quatna."

"More likely to Damascus," Jehu said gloomily. "If Hadad-Ezer could see the Assyrian army, he would turn tail and scuttle back home."

Chapter 16

MICHAEL REMAINED AT THE LOOKOUT POINT THROUGH-
out the day, watching while the Assyrians methodically
went about reducing what remained of Karkar. As yet
he had seen no sign of Ahab or the armies of the
confederation, and when darkness approached he sent
Jehu and Matten down the slope with orders that, as
soon as dawn afforded enough light, the men and
horses were to be brought up to a point just below
the brow of the ridge, where they would be ready for
a swift dash southward when daylight revealed the
situation.

Michael wrapped himself in his cloak and lay down
for a few hours of sleep. When he awakened just before daylight, he found Matten and Jehu standing beside him. While he munched the bread and meat they
had brought him, he studied the stirring scene revealed
by the rising rays of the morning sun.

To the west the already crumbling walls of Karkar
still partially blocked the narrow part of the valley for
which the city had been guardian. They did not form
enough of a barrier, however, to stop a stream of men,
cavalry, and chariots from pouring through Karkar to

fan out below the city on the south and take up their positions across the valley.

As yet, Michael estimated, hardly more than a quarter of Shalmaneser's army could possibly have come through the gap. But at the rate they were pouring through, he was sure the Assyrian commander fully appreciated the danger of his situation, with the smoking ruins of Karkar narrowing his forces in the center very much as an hourglass restricts the flow of sand.

To the south, the forces of the twelve kings were moving toward Karkar in a broad line extending from one side of the narrow valley to another. At the front rode the cavalry, interspersed with squadrons of chariots. Behind them, Michael could see from his elevated position upon the crest of the hill, marched rank after rank of foot soldiers, each carrying a spear, a bow, a quiver filled with arrows, and a short sword.

It was a thrilling sight, for Ahab had obviously taken Michael's advice and risked everything by throwing his entire force against the Assyrians before they could break through into the plain. If the maneuver succeeded, he would be able to drive the enemy back and perhaps recapture Karkar. With that done and the armies of the confederation controlling the narrowest portion of the valley, Ahab would then be able to concentrate his forces in such a small area that he would largely overcome the inequality of numbers which so heavily weighted the battle in favor of the Assyrians. The main question in Michael's mind—and he did not doubt in Ahab's also—was whether the approaching army of the twelve kings could make contact with the Assyrians before a large enough section of Shalmaneser's forces broke through the bottleneck at Karkar to equal them in strength.

At the moment the advantage appeared to be with King Ahab and his army, for the Assyrians were handicapped by the fact that, whereas they could send a large number of men on foot through the narrow region which Karkar had formerly guarded, getting chariots through the ruined city would take more time. As a result, the forces drawn up so far to face the confederation were largely composed of foot soldiers and spear-bearers. The latter could fight against a cavalry attack by driving the butts of their long spears into the ground and steadying them so that approaching horsemen or charioteers would be impaled upon the point. Behind them, rows of archers would lift their arrows over the heads of both men and horses to strike those behind the more mobile mounted forces. But it was a game that two could play and the way Ahab was deploying his men showed that he fully understood that fact.

As Michael and his lieutenants watched, a troop of about a thousand horsemen broke free at the western end of Ahab's line and launched a furious sweeping attack against the front ranks of the enemy soldiers, throwing them out of position and keeping them from forming the solid line of spears that could do so much damage to chariots by killing the horses before the men in the vehicles had a chance to fight.

Ahab had organized the attack exactly as he would have done had he been in charge, Michael decided. The only question now was whether the Israelite king had the strength, and could depend upon the troops and their leaders, to drive the Assyrians back and destroy them when they tried to retreat through the narrowed section of the valley at Karkar.

The Assyrian commanders were not fools either, Michael saw from his elevated observation point. As soon as the horsemen from Ahab's command started their sweep across the front of the foot soldiers' ranks, a squadron of enemy cavalry, mounted upon the beautiful horses bred in the oases of the desert region lying between Israel and the valleys of the Tigris and Euphrates rivers, broke loose from the main body of the Assyrian army and rode to meet the attackers. A furious battle quickly ensued in which, Michael estimated, the odds appeared about even, for the number of men and horses involved was approximately the same. The Assyrian forces were superbly trained and mounted, however, and this advantage soon outweighed whatever gain Ahab's men had obtained by having launched the attack first. For a brief period the battle raged furiously, then a trumpet blast from Ahab's line recalled his own cavalry and, breaking off the engagement, they raced back to the relative safety of their own line.

Ahab's daring use of a flying cavalry squadron had accomplished its aim for the moment, however. even though they had been forced to break off the engagement. The foot soldiers and spearmen who had been seeking to form a solid line at the front of the Assyrian army had been thrown into confusion and much valuable time had been lost while their commanders worked to restore order in the ranks. On that ground, Michael decided, Ahab had come off the victor in the brief engagement, in spite of the fact that he had ordered his cavalry to withdraw.

Michael had so far not been able to distinguish Ahab in the long line of advancing men. From the banners fluttering above the heads of the troops, he recognized that the eastern flank nearest him was made up of troops under the command of King Hadad-Ezer of Damascus, a fact that made him somewhat uneasy. The justification for his fear was shortly apparent.

The brief foray by cavalry from the western flank of Ahab's army had been merely a diversionary operation, designed to throw the enemy off balance. And even the brief encounter with the Assyrian cavalry had not been in any sense a defeat for the Israelite troops. Unfortunately, however, the commander of the eastern flank—whom Michael judged to be King Hadad-Ezer himself—chose to regard it as just that. And as he watched what quickly began to happen upon the plain below, Michael felt a rising sense of dismay.

Until now the line maintained by Ahab's army had been relatively straight, formed by a solid mass of cavalry and chariots backed by bowmen ready to launch a hail of lethal missiles upon the Assyrians. Meanwhile the enemy was at a disadvantage because they must defend the city they had just captured, their hope of success depending entirely upon being able to hold a line until enough troops could be put through the bottleneck at Karkar to turn the tide of battle in their favor.

And since the Israelite forces and their allies were the attackers, the advantage of momentum was on their side.

As Michael watched now, a trumpet blew on the eastern end of the line and, to his horror, he saw that section begin to slow down and waver in its advance. The western and central sections were still moving toward the Assyrian forces, but someone in charge of the eastern flank had obviously decided that the brief cavalry encounter represented a major defeat for the forces of Ahab. Acting on that assumption, he had ordered the Syrian troops to draw back and, in the confusion, the eastern end of the line now began to curve in a reverse flanking movement that was just as effective as if it had been carried out by the enemy.

Michael did not wait to see what would happen. There were only two possible ways to prevent the debacle now developing with such frightening rapidity upon the field below, and he could further neither of them by remaining as an observer upon the ridge. Either Ahab must take command of the eastern flank himself, countermand the order to retreat, and try to rally the disorganized forces, or help must come to prevent the Assyrians from turning them back.

That Ahab would do his best, Michael was sure. But whether or not this could prevail in the face of the Syrian king's reluctance to continue the attack, he did not stop to discover. Shouting orders that sent every man of his force into the saddle, Michael mounted his own horse and urged it over the top of the ridge that had hidden the waiting cavalry from the field below. Behind him he could hear Jehu shouting orders to his own command and, as Michael topped the ridge and plunged down the opposite side, the stirring blasts of ram's horn trumpets sounded the order to charge.

What Michael saw as he sent his horse down the slope verified his worst misgivings about the effect of the Syrian withdrawal. Enemy cavalry and charioteers were already being directed against the eastern flank of Ahab's forces by their alert commanders. The foremost of these had engaged the troops under Hadad-Ezer's command and, since the latter were confused by the order to fall back, a rout was already in the making.

Michael saw a familiar chariot with a tall figure in shining armor standing in it racing eastward behind the confederation line but doubted that even Ahab would be able to rally the rapidly disorganizing Syrian forces quickly enough to prevent disaster now. The only hope lay in a sudden and unexpected attack by his own force of some two thousand mounted men upon the Assyrian cavalry who had been sent against the wavering eastern flank of Ahab's army.

With trumpets blowing the charge and the men shouting their battle cries, Michael's force came over the low ridge and rolled down into the valley like a tidal wave. Two thousand men on horseback charged the mass of Assyrian foot soldiers who were now streaming in the wake of their chariots and horsemen

195

to attack the flank of Ahab's army. Jabbing with his spear and—when it was gone—slashing with his sword, Michael rode into the masses of Assyrian foot men followed by his own troops and those under Jehu's command.

The screams of foot soldiers dying under the hoofs of the plunging horses added to the deafening pandemonium. At the moment, however, Michael was not concerned with the cavalry and chariots between him and Ahab's forces. The most important thing was to cut off the stream of reinforcements being poured against the eastern flank of Ahab's army. Riding completely through the stream of troops, Michael shouted in exultation when he saw the Assyrian foot men turn in the face of this unexpected attack by mounted men and race toward their own lines. Wheeling in his saddle, he shouted to Jehu to continue the attack from the rear upon the Assyrian horse and chariot forces which had now come in contact with the fleeing troops of King Hadad-Ezer.

Trumpets were blowing frantically in the ranks of the Syrian army. As Michael swung his horse to lead a charge against a dozen Assyrian chariots that were wreaking havoc among the troops of the eastern flank, he saw Ahab riding through the ranks of the fleeing troops in his chariot, driving them back into battle with the flat of his sword.

A chariot loomed up in front of Michael, with a spearman beside the driver raising the long-hafted weapon to hurl it at him. He swung low in his saddle and swept past the chariot, slashing with his sword and decapitating the enemy fighter with one blow. Around him horses and men were screaming in agony, and shouts and curses filled the air as the enemy's horse and chariot corps were locked in furious conflict with Michael's own mounted cavalry. Busy hacking a path through the enemy ranks, Michael had no time to see whether Ahab had succeeded in stiffening the lines and putting Hadad-Ezer's forces back into battle. He refused to yield to panic at the possibility that their eastern flank would be turned by the enemy.

Fighting furiously to destroy the remainder of the Assyrian troops whose retreat to their own lines had been cut off by his daring charge across the rear to break up the ranks of the supporting foot soldiers, Michael heard a sudden crash of metal upon metal indicating that the two main lines of both sides had at last met in combat. At the moment he could not look, being engaged in a furious bit of swordplay with an Assyrian officer in a chariot. Fighting desperately for his life, Michael's right hand and arm were suddenly numbed when the Assyrian struck a blow against the hilt of his sword, knocking it from his grasp. He tried desperately to pull his horse away as he reached for the bow at his back, now his only weapon, but at such close quarters it was a very unhandy weapon indeed.

Ahead of him, almost as if all motion had been stopped and he were watching a scene painted upon a wall or chiseled in stone, Michael saw the Assyrian officer raise his sword for the lethal blow and knew he had no chance to avoid it. Then another chariot crashed into the enemy vehicle, a spear in the hand of a tall man wearing the polished silver armor of a king drove through the Assyrian's heart, and Michael found himself staring into the grim face of King Ahab of Israel. "I owe you my life," he gasped when finally he found his tongue.

"Pick up your sword." Ahab wrenched his spear from the Assyrian's body. "There is work yet to be done."

The death of the enemy officer had removed one of the last of the attackers. The chariot driver, knocked from his stand by the impact of Ahab's vehicle, had been trampled to death by his own horses, and for a moment there was an island of relative quiet around them. Michael swung from his horse and picked up his sword, settling it in the sheath. He also took a spear from the rack in the Assyrian's chariot before mounting again.

"What happened here?" he asked Ahab. "It looked as if an order was given for retreat."

"The king of Syria is a coward," Ahab snapped. "When the trumpet sounded the order to withdraw our cavalry after the charge, he took it as a defeat and ordered a retreat."

"Where is he now?"

"At the back of the lines, cringing with terror." Ahab wiped his face with a muscular forearm. "If you and your men had not come riding over that hill when you did, the Assyrians would have turned our flank. You saved my army twice, Michael."

"Then we are even. If you had not caught that Assyrian on your spear he would have split me in twain."

"I am placing you in command of the troops of the eastern flank in place of Hadad-Ezer," Ahab told him. "We must hold at any cost and push forward where we can."

"Will the Syrian commanders obey me?"

"They will obey or be executed," Ahab said grimly. "Your first task is to achieve some order from the chaos their king wrought by being a craven fool." He spoke to his driver and the chariot sped away, toward the center of the line.

Michael quickly surveyed the troops that were now under his command. Cavalry, chariots, and men-at-arms were in a muddle, milling around without leadership. Not far away, Jehu was busy mopping up the last of the Assyrian mounted men.

"Jehu!" Michael shouted. "Over here."

The Israelite lieutenant obeyed immediately. His

eyes were shining with excitement and his sword was dripping blood.

"King Ahab has put me in command at this end of the line, but I need time to restore order," Michael told him. "Can you give it to me?"

Jehu's nod told him he understood the meaning of the question. "I will attack Shalmaneser's eastern flank," he said. "They will be too busy for a while to trouble you here."

He wheeled and rode off, blowing upon the ram's horn trumpet that hung at his back a call for the Israelite cavalry to come together into a unified fighting force once again. Certain that Jehu would give him all the protection possible while he restored his new command to some semblance of order, Michael turned and rode along the line, picking out the Syrian officers as he went and instructing each one to turn the men and start moving forward.

At the moment there was little fighting and, after their brief period of panic following the order to retreat and the sudden slashing attack by the mobile forces of the Assyrians, the troops seemed ready enough to obey. Riding back and forth along the front, Michael encouraged them and urged them forward. In addition, they now had the example of his own command which, with Jehu in the lead, had raced across the short distance between the lines and was slashing into the Assyrian forces, disrupting their attempts to launch another attack.

Jehu was fighting in the traditional manner of cavalry warfare, sweeping in to jab and slash at the infantry, smashing foot soldiers beneath the hoofs of the horses or impaling them upon the murderously sharp spear points, then wheeling to ride back. Each new charge bowled over many of the enemy by its mere momentum and kept them from getting set to launch another offensive.

In throwing all the chariots and horsemen available to him against the eastern flank of Ahab's army when Hadad-Ezer had given the order to withdraw, the Assyrian commander had risked everything in the hope of a quick victory. Only the charge of Michael's command had foiled him, and now, with almost no mounted troops to oppose Jehu and his men in the savage attack they had launched, the situation began to change with startling rapidity.

Now the Assyrian east flank was in danger of being turned and the enemy was forced to retreat in some confusion toward the bottleneck of Karkar. At the same time, the enemy troops being pushed through the still smoking city found themselves in difficulty when those ahead were not able to move forward and make room in front of Karkar itself.

From one end of the long line to the other the sound of battle filled the air, the sharp blast of trumpets, the clash of shield upon shield and sword upon sword, the screams of dying horses and wounded men.

Hadad-Ezer was still nowhere to be seen but his fighting men were well trained and brave. Once the confusion of the retreat had been corrected, their officers led them valiantly against the enemy, sweeping across the narrow space that separated the two armies to seize the advantage given them by Jehu's cavalry raid.

For hours the battle raged on the plain before Karkar, seesawing back and forth as Shalmaneser poured reinforcements out upon the plain to take the place of those killed and wounded in the fray. Ahab was everywhere in his chariot, a majestic, fearless figure who fired his men with courage as he moved to whatever section of the line seemed to need bolstering at that particular time.

For a while it seemed that the Assyrians would be able to put enough men through Karkar to drive the forces of the confederation back. And once this was accomplished the considerable reinforcements still available to them north of the city could be brought into play and the battle would shortly be over. But Ahab's forces realized this danger, too. Driven by the knowledge that what was accomplished here today would decide not only their own fate but that of their countries as well, they fought like men possessed by demons. And as the hours passed, the area of intense fighting where the lines came together began to move slowly back toward the blackened shell of the once fortified city.

By nightfall, both sides were so exhausted from the long day's battle that an unspoken truce went into effect. Neither sought to cross the narrow hiatus between the lines and men fell to the ground where they stopped fighting, panting for breath or moaning as they sought to improvise dressings for their wounds and stop the flow of blood. Michael was overjoyed to find Aaron unharmed among the men who had fought in the center of the battle line under Ahab's direct command. The two busied themselves carrying water from the river to the wounded and bandaging them as best they could upon the field until a courier came for Michael, ordering him to report to King Ahab, behind the lines, immediately.

He found Ahab, King Irhuleni of Hamath, Matten of Arvad, and several others of the confederation together. Hadad-Ezer was there also, as sulky and unpleasant-looking as ever.

Ahab's face was stern as he called the council of war together. "I need not tell you we have not yet won a victory," he said. "In fact the best we can hope for is to hold the Assyrians here before Karkar until they become discouraged and give up trying to move southward along the Arantu Valley."

"Will you be able to do it?" Hadad-Ezer demanded

201

churlishly. "Half my own men are either dead or wounded."

"They would all be dead if I had not countermanded your order to retreat," Ahab snapped.

"The order was to attack. Someone misunderstood it."

Ahab shrugged and did not answer. Michael did not reveal what he had learned from the Syrian captains, namely that Hadad-Ezer had given a personal order to withdraw as soon as the first skirmish occurred. Furthermore, the king had been the first to obey his own command.

"Whether or not the order was given," Ahab said, "the fact remains that the eastern flank retreated before they met the enemy. If Prince Michael and his troops had not come riding down from the hills at just that moment, our whole flank would have been turned and we would probably have been destroyed before the battle really began."

Hadad-Ezer shrugged and said no more; obviously he was going to brazen out the lie.

"You have surveyed the situation north of Karkar, Prince Michael," Ahab said. 'What would you say should be done now?"

"I believe the Assyrians lost more men, horses, and chariots today than we did," Michael said. "But they still have a large number of troops who have not yet been thrown into the fight. Only the fact that the city of Karkar is acting like the neck of a bottle and limiting the flow through it prevents them from throwing their whole army against us."

"Then neither side can win," Hadad-Ezer said.

"I do not agree," Ahab said sharply. "Because Prince Michael recognized the danger to us once the Assyrians broke through into the valley south of Karkar and warned us, we are able to keep the enemy penned up in the valley north of Karkar."

"Unless he attacks around our flank," one of the kings said.

"We secured the only valley on the east large enough for such an attack," Michael said. "A small body of my own men are holding the entrance to it."

"What of the west, King Matten?" Ahab asked. "You know that region better than any of us."

"It is all rough country," Matten said. "They could put only small bodies of men through the mountain passes there."

"Then we have only to keep them pressed back into the narrowest part of the valley so the number that can get through Karkar is kept as small as possible," Ahab said.

"Would you order these men to attack again?" Hadad-Ezer demanded. "How do you know they will not refuse?"

"Your troops fought bravely after the order to retreat was canceled," Michael told him. "I am sure they will see that what King Ahab proposes is our only wise course."

"When will the attack begin?" King Irhuleni asked. He was a solid-appearing man with a cut over his right eye. His clothing was still smeared with blood from the day's battle.

"Early in the morning. If we give them time to reinforce the troops facing us, we are lost." Ahab looked around the circle and found no objection. "It is settled then. At the first rays of dawn, I will sound the trumpet for the attack."

"If you tell the bowmen to concentrate their arrows into the narrow space before Karkar," Michael suggested, "the dead will pile up and interfere with any reinforcements Shalmaneser tries to send through the city."

"An excellent suggestion," Ahab approved. "We will do it."

The council broke up and each leader went to the section of the line occupied by his troops to issue the necessary orders for tomorrow's battle. When Michael started to leave, Ahab signaled him to remain.

"You saved me from a terrible defeat today, Michael," he said. "I wanted to thank you personally and alone."

"Any experienced commander would have seen the danger and done the same," Michael protested.

"That may or may not be true, but one thing is certain. Hadad-Ezer will one day pay for his treachery. As soon as this affair is finished, I shall demand that he fulfill his part of the bargain and return Ramoth-Gilead to us. If he refuses, the armies of Israel and Judah will teach him a lesson he has needed to learn for a long time."

Dawn had barely begun to break when the army under Ahab's command started to move forward in response to a trumpet blast from his own chariot. As the light increased, Michael saw that Shalmaneser's commanders had acted as he would have done in their place. They had pushed a large number of their mounted troops through the partially destroyed city of Karkar during the night in order to strengthen their forces on the plain south of the city. The armies met with a crash of weapons and shouted curses just as the sun appeared above the esatern ridge over which Michael and his troops had ridden that morning to turn almost certain defeat into a possible victory.

This was close-quarter fighting—slogging, stabbing, thrusting, pulling, tearing, seeking to disable the opponent in every possible way. Even more than the day before the Assyrians were hampered by the restricted space in which they operated, a fact Michael had counted upon to give the advantage to the armies of the twelve kings.

For most of the day the battle raged back and forth,

204

but as evening approached, the Assyrian forces gradually began to retreat, jamming the narrowed area of Karkar as they sought to escape. By the time darkness fell, Ahab's army had managed for the second day to keep Shalmaneser from putting an effective force out upon the plain where they could have roamed at will, harrying the troops of the confederation.

It was a night of tense waiting. When, in the morning, the Assyrian troops did not launch an attack, Ahab still kept his own forces drawn up in readiness while the exhausted soldiers and horses and the wounded were carried back to improvised shelters under the trees along the riverbank south of the fighting line.

Around noon an observer Michael had posted on the eastern ridge to keep watch on the enemy's actions rode down to report that the major part of the Assyrian army appeared to be moving northward along the Arantu Valley. Michael climbed the ridge to see for himself before reporting to a hurriedly called council of war.

"Shalmaneser has given up the attack!" Hadad-Ezer cried when Michael finished describing what he saw. "The victory is ours."

Ahab's eyes had brightened at Michael's words, but he did not let himself be carried away. "What part of the Assyrian army is leaving?" he asked.

"About two thirds," Michael told him. "They left enough troops behind to hold here at Karkar. The rest appear to be moving elsewhere, perhaps to attack in another direction."

"Damascus!" Hadad-Ezer squealed. "It is practically defenseless!"

"We have as much reason to believe Shalmaneser is returning to Nineveh as that he is going to attack Damascus," Ahab pointed out. "His losses have been heavy here and he will need time to recruit and build up another large army. The Assyrians rarely attack unless they are in overwhelming strength."

"But we cannot leave Damascus undefended," Hadad-Ezer protested. "If the Assyrians take the city, I will be without a kingdom."

"If they had been able to put their army through Karkar all of us would have been without kingdoms," King Irhuleni reminded him shortly. "We still could lose—if we withdraw and let the Assyrian forces in Karkar escape to the plain where they can attack us freely."

"Obviously we must protect our Syrian ally," Ahab said. "And that means a sizable portion of our forces must be diverted eastward, where they will be in a position to defend Damascus in case Shalmaneser moves against it."

"What about our position here?" King Irhuleni asked.

"We must hold it, too, until all possibility of the Assyrians returning to the attack has been removed."

Hadad-Ezer purpled. 'Unless you agree to protect Damascus, I shall remove my army tomorrow."

"I have no more desire to see Damascus fall than you do," Ahab said wearily. "The road from your capital leads directly into Israel, so you and I have more reason to fight in that area than any of the others."

"If the enemy is leaving no more than a third of his army at Karkar," King Irhuleni of Hamath interposed, "the rest of us should be able to hold him at bay."

"That is my thinking," Ahab agreed. "This is your homeland; it would not be fair to ask you to leave it and go elsewhere."

"But will you have enough troops to hold the region of Damascus against Shalmaneser if he should attack in that direction?" Matten inquired.

206

"We should—if we are there and ready for him."

Ahab looked around the half circle of men. "King Irhuleni should have the right to command here at Karkar, since it is his own territory."

"I relinquish my claim in favor of Prince Michael of Judah," the King of Hamath said at once. "He has proved his worth twice over since the fighting began."

Michael started to protest, but a chorus of assent from the others drowned out his words. "If you wish me to serve, sires," he said, "I shall not shirk the responsibility."

"Then it is settled," Ahab said with evident relief. "We will leave for Damascus as soon as the troops can be ready to march."

Two days after Ahab's departure, one of the observers Michael had posted in the hills to the eastward to follow the Assyrians reported that Shalmaneser had now withdrawn most of his army along the Arantu Valley northward and appeared to be heading toward his own capital of Nineveh. Michael and King Irhuleni had decided that nothing was to be gained from the further carnage that would result if they tried to attack the fortified city—whose walls, though partially burned out and destroyed, would still afford considerable shelter to the defenders—so the situation at Karkar remained static.

It was almost a month after the major fighting at Karkar had stopped before spies reported that the remainder of the Assyrian forces at Karkar were being withdrawn. Michael made no move to pursue them and a few days later the troops of King Irhuleni marched into a deserted Karkar.

Ahab had sent couriers with news that the Assyrians had made no attempt to attack Damascus and had apparently given up the spring offensive against the land of Canaan. And with Irhuleni now able to defend his own realm, Michael bade farewell to Matten and the squat, capable king of Hamath. At the head of the Israelite troops left under his command by Ahab, he moved southward along the way they had come about two months before.

In evaluating what had happened at Karkar, Michael could only judge that it could not be called a true victory for either side. The forces of the confederation had met a vastly superior Assyrian army and had stopped it at Karkar, but both sides had suffered serious losses in men, weapons, horses, and vehicles. Meanwhile King Hadad-Ezer of Syria had revealed himself as the weakest link in the union of the twelve kings, and Michael doubted that Ahab would ever trust his entire army again in a situation where another defection like the one the Syrian monarch had almost managed to accomplish with his order to retreat could expose the remaining troops to destruction. Nevertheless, for a brief period at least, something that had never happened before in this region had taken place. A large number of people of disparate nationalities and loyalties had joined together to face a common threat.

Forced to move slowly because the major part of the wounded had been left to him when Ahab began the swift march to Damascus, Michael was almost another month in reaching Israel. Summer was already at its height when he rode once again into the Vale of Jezreel and climbed the hillside to where Naboth's villa nestled beside King Ahab's vineyard and palace.

Jehu had been sent on to Jerusalem with the remainder of Michael's original hundred horsemen, and only Aaron was with him when he rode up to the gate of Naboth's villa. To his surprise, an armed mercenary of King Ahab's guard stood at the gate. When the man lowered his spear to bar their entrance, Michael reined in his horse.

"What is the meaning of this?" he demanded brusquely, but could not still the cold feeling of apprehension that was already rising within him. "Where is my lord Naboth?"

"This villa is the property of King Ahab," the mercenary said. "I know nothing of Naboth."

"He was the owner a few months ago."

"You must mean the blasphemer."

"Blasphemer! Naboth was no blasphemer."

"The man who owned this palace was stoned to death in Jezreel by its people for blasphemy. His property was taken by the king because of his guilt."

Michael could not believe his ears. And yet there was no denying the reality of the man's presence or the spear he held.

"Is Queen Jezebel at the palace here?"

"She is in Megiddo," the mercenary told him. "The people of that city have chosen to honor King Ahab tomorrow for his great victory over the Assyrians. The queen will be at his side."

"Did King Ahab agree to this—this taking of another man's property?"

The mercenary shrugged. "As you can see, it belongs to the king."

"If Naboth was really stoned to death by the people of Jezreel, the property would go to the king under our law," Aaron reminded Michael.

"But no man in Israel was more pious than Naboth. He would no more blaspheme against the Lord than I would turn upon you and kill you with my bare hands."

"You have forgotten one thing, master," Aaron said.

"What is that?"

"The queen hated Naboth. She must have arranged this."

Michael turned to the mercenary. "Did you say the people of Jezreel stoned Naboth to death?"

"At the edge of the city," the man confirmed. "You can still see the blasphemer's blood upon the clay of the wall by the gate."

Blasphemy was the most serious crime a Hebrew could commit; the prescribed punishment was stoning to death by his fellows. Once the cry was raised, the passions of the people would have been excited quickly; Michael had seen it happen before. But a man still could not be executed for blasphemy until he had been tried by a court of his peers, in this case the elders of his tribe, who must sit in judgment upon him and pass sentence. And it was unbelievable that the elders of Jezreel, respected men among whose number Naboth himself had been listed, would have conspired to destroy one who fought to preserve the worship of Yahweh against even the queen herself.

The thought reminded him of something. "Was Queen Jezebel here at the time?" he asked the mercenary.

"She was in Samaria. I was sent here with several others on her orders to guard the property when it was taken in the name of King Ahab after the execution."

"Then this happened before King Ahab returned?"

"Yes. About six weeks ago."

At least Miriam was safe in Jerusalem, so there was something to be thankful for, Michael thought. He must go to her as soon as possible, but he must also find out the truth of what had happened here and see that whoever was responsible was properly punished. In this endeavor he knew he could count on Ahab's support, for both of them had counted Naboth as a friend.

"What are you going to do, master?" Aaron asked.

"We will go to Megiddo tomorrow, and hear from

King Ahab's own lips what he thinks of this affair. But first I must talk to the elders of Jezreel."

In small Hebrew cities and villages, the respected old men called the elders, who were both the religious and civil leaders of the community, spent most of the day beside the main gate leading into the city. Thus their advice and counsel, as well as their judicial help in settling disputes, were available to everyone. As Michael had expected, he found the elders of Jezreel beside the gate—four old men with long beards and palsied, shaking hands, sitting in the sun near the well that was the center of the town's social and political life.

"I am Prince Michael of Judah," he said courteously. "A friend of Naboth."

"I recognize you, noble prince," one of the men said. "But it would be better if you did not name yourself the friend of a blasphemer."

"I am here to give the lie to those who say they heard Naboth blaspheme against the Lord."

One of the old men looked up at him. Michael saw that his eyes were kind and gentle, certainly not the sort of person who would condemn his neighbor to death without just cause. "It is natural for a man to come to the defense of a friend," he said. "My name is Amram and I knew Naboth for, lo, these many years as a true worshiper of the Lord God. It pained me, too, when he was found guilty of such a crime."

"Did you hear him blaspheme?"

"Not with my own ears."

"Then why did you let him be stoned?"

Amram's lined face grew stern. "Because the provisions of the law were fulfilled when two men swore they heard Naboth blaspheme against the name of the Lord God of Israel. The punishment for one who commits such a crime is well known; he shall be stoned with stones until he is dead."

211

"Did it ever occur to you that these men might be lying?" Michael demanded heatedly. "And that they were hired to perjure themselves in order to destroy him?"

"The witnesses took an oath before the Council of Elders as the law requires," another of the men interposed. "They swore their testimony was true."

"We found it hard to believe such a thing of our brother Naboth," Amram admitted. "But when the pestilence came—"

"What pestilence?"

"It was a little while after King Ahab went north to the region of Hamath with the army. A pestilence broke out in the city and our children were dying. We sought its cause but found nothing until we asked Zedekiah, the High Priest at Samaria, for help. He said Jezreel had sinned against God and the pestilence was a punishment. We ordained a fast as he suggested and prayed to the Lord that whoever had sinned would be revealed. It was then that the two men testified they heard Naboth blaspheme against the name of the Lord."

"And you brought him to trial on no more evidence than that?"

"Our people were dying and two witnesses swore to the crime," Amram insisted. "We had no choice under the law save to order him stoned."

"What of the pestilence? Did it end summarily?"

"No," Amram admitted. "It continued to kill our children for another month, then finally died away."

"So Naboth was killed for nothing," Michael said bitterly.

Amram's eyes blazed and his withered cheeks flushed. "We treated Naboth according to our law, as he would have treated one of us. Without the law, all of Israel would quickly perish."

There was no point in questioning the old men further. With a pestilence killing the children of Jezreel and witnesses testifying under oath that one of its leading citizens had blasphemed against the Lord, bringing the disease upon them, Michael could easily understand how the passions of the city had been aroused. The Council of Elders, adhering strictly to the sacred law which said that when two witnesses swore to any charge, the accused was considered guilty, had acted as similar councils had acted through the centuries.

"Where is Naboth buried?" Michael inquired.

"In his vineyard," Amram said. "The one that now belongs to King Ahab."

"And what of the sons of Belial who testified against him?" It was a contemptuous phrase, used ordinarily to designate those known to be liars.

"The witnesses cast the first stone as our law provides."

"Are they still in the village?"

Amram did not answer and Michael saw that the old man's face was troubled, as if he had doubts. But another of the elders spoke up. "They remained here for a while, eating and drinking and living in luxury. Lately, though, they have moved away from Jezreel."

"Had they lived in luxury before?" Michael asked.

"No."

"Then where did they get the money, unless someone hired them to perjure themselves?"

There was no answer and he turned away, for nothing else could be learned in Jezreel. As they rode out of the city, Aaron said, "You know who really killed my lord Naboth, don't you, master?"

Michael nodded. Only Jezebel desired his death enough to carry out such a clever plot.

"What will you do now?" Aaron asked.

"Go to Megiddo and face Ahab and Jezebel. If she

213

admits her guilt, he must punish her, even though she is the queen."

"And if she does not?"

"Then I shall not rest until I have proved her guilty—and seen her punished."

Chapter 17

As Michael and Aaron approached Megiddo the next day, they found the roads almost choked with happy Israelites on the way to honor their king for saving them from the Assyrians. Progress was reduced to a walk, and it was time for the celebration to take place when finally they managed to enter the city. The affair, they were told, would be held upon the stone-paved esplanade or plaza in front of a large building that served as headquarters for the chariot corps. Tethering their horses in the yard of an inn, they proceeded on foot.

In sharp contrast to the contest between Elijah and the priests of Baal on nearby Mount Carmel, the scene today was one of merriment and celebration. The threat of the Assyrians had been removed, at least for a year and perhaps longer. And the drought had been broken, turning the Vale of Jezreel into a sea of rich grain fields and green vineyards.

As he walked toward the esplanade, Michael could not help comparing the scene today with one he'd left about a month ago: the burned-out walls of Kar-kar, the streets littered with rubbish, and the stones still slippery with the blood of those who had died while holding the Assyrian hordes in check until Ahab and his allies could bring up forces to stop the enemy advance at that point. Megiddo might well have been in the same position, he knew, for had the battle been fought here instead of at Karkar—an eventuality which was the main reason for Ahab's strengthening the fortifications protecting Megiddo—these same people might now be the victims of Assyrian butchery.

Michael was walking along, lost in thought, when Aaron said, "Look, master! The prophet Micaiah is here with my lord Elijah!"

Farther up the slope, Michael could see Micaiah now, easily recognizable by his great height and his golden beard; Elijah, a smaller and slighter figure, stood beside him. The two were hurrying toward the esplanade, now visible only a little distance away.

Michael quickened his own pace, but the press of the crowd kept him from catching up with the others before they reached the open space. There, Ahab was already sitting upon an ivory throne chair, with Jezebel beside him, surrounded by his captains in splendid new uniforms and a number of priests arrayed in rich vestments.

Ahab wore the shining armor that marked him in battle, while Jezebel was arrayed in magnificent royal robes and a jeweled golden crown. And even though he was certain now that she was a murderess, Michael could not completely suppress a sudden surge of desire at the sight of her radiant beauty and the memory of the hours they had spent together.

The ceremony had already begun. A short, heavy-set priest in rich vestments was finishing a long and sonorously voiced prayer, thanking the Most High for giving Ahab the victory and bringing Israel's king safely back to his own land. The prayer finished, the priest stepped back and Ahab rose to his feet.

Before the king could begin his address to the people,

however, a familiar figure appeared in the open space of the esplanade where the ivory throne stood. It was Elijah and, as usual, the old prophet had made no concession to the splendor of the occasion. His robe was of the same rough homespun fabric he always wore; his sandals were travel-worn; his hair and beard uncombed. Nevertheless, there was an awe-inspiring majesty about him as he faced Ahab and his queen.

At the blaze of condemnation in the old prophet's eyes, Jezebel seemed to cringe. Ahab's hand gripped the elaborately carved arm of the throne chair beside which he was standing, as if to steady himself against the impact of Elijah's gaze. In the silence that ensued Elijah's voice could be heard clearly by the great crowd; the sonorous tones, it seemed to Michael as he listened, were like the voice of doom itself.

"Have you killed and also taken possession of that which was once owned by Naboth?" Elijah demanded, speaking directly to the king.

"What is this talk of killing?" Ahab demanded. "Naboth was stoned to death by the people of his own city because he blasphemed. His vineyard is now royal property according to our law."

"Thus saith the Lord," Elijah said sternly. " 'As the dogs licked the blood of Naboth, so shall dogs lick thy blood by the pool of Samaria!' "

Ahab stared at the old prophet as if he were seeing his own ghost. When he spoke there was a note almost of resignation in his voice that startled Michael.

"Have you found me, my enemy?" he asked.

"I have found you," Elijah answered. "Because you have sold yourself to work evil in the sight of the Lord, behold, the Lord will bring evil upon you and will take away your prosperity."

Jezebel had finally broken free of the spell created by the old prophet's sudden appearance and his dramatic condemnation of Ahab. "Kill him!" she screamed.

"He cannot thus threaten the king who has saved Israel from destruction and live!"

There was a surge of people toward the old man, but Ahab spoke sharply, stopping them as if he had put out his hand. "Harm him not," he commanded. "He speaks not his own words but with the voice of God."

The richly garbed priest who had given the prayer started to voice a protest. Michael could not hear what he was saying, but there was no doubting the meaning of the peremptory gesture with which Ahab silenced him. A babble of voices rose from the crowd, startled by this unexpected bit of drama, but when Elijah began to speak again, it quickly died away.

The prophet had turned to Jezebel. Now he lifted a bony forefinger to point it accusingly at her as he thundered: "Of Jezebel the Lord also said, 'The dogs shall eat Jezebel by the wall of Jezreel.'"

It was a terrible curse and Jezebel blanched visibly, shrinking back into her chair. Elijah did not say more but, turning abruptly, started through the crowd followed by the tall form of Micaiah. And the people, who a few moments before had been ready to attack him in answer to Jezebel's cry, now parted silently, letting him through unimpeded.

For a long moment after Elijah's voice had died away, Ahab stood with his shoulders almost slumped, as if the terrible curse of the old prophet was a burden too heavy for him to bear. When Jezebel whispered urgently to him, he finally shook himself as if to rid himself of the weight and spoke once again.

"My people," he said, "it is good of you to come here to honor me. But I would rather you honored instead our soldiers, who fought so bravely at Karkar to keep the Assyrians from our land, and those who lie dead there. Because of their courage the enemy was stopped long before he reached our borders. I do not tell you the enemy will not come again, for I am certain that he will. But we have proved to all the world that even the might of Assyria is not invincible when we fight in the name of the Most High. Enjoy yourselves now in celebration of our deliverance from the hand of the Assyrians and give God the praise for his favor to us."

He turned away and, almost stumbling, moved across the stone pavement of the esplanade toward the building behind it, followed by Jezebel and the members of the court. Michael hesitated a moment, torn between the desire to follow Elijah and Micaiah and his determination to face Ahab and learn the truth about the king's connection with what had happened to Naboth. Elijah's curse would seem to indicate that Ahab himself had participated in the death of Naboth, but this Michael found very hard to believe of his old comrade-in-arms.

"Follow Micaiah and Elijah and bring news of them to the inn where we left the horses," he told Aaron. "I will go and speak with the king."

Aaron nodded and left at once, pushing his way through the crowd toward where Micaiah's golden beard and head marked the progress of the two. Michael followed Ahab's entourage into the building, where refreshments for the royal party had been set out upon elaborate tables. Two more of the ivory chairs had been placed as thrones at the end of a long assembly room in the center of the building and the king and queen had already seated themselves there. Hamul stood just behind Jezebel, with the richly robed priest who had spoken the prayer at Ahab's elbow.

The people were milling around before Ahab and Jezebel, flattering their king with congratulations, but Ahab seemed almost morose, and for the most part it was Jezebel who answered them. She, however, appeared not at all depressed by the curse Elijah had put upon her outside the building.

Michael made his way to a place before the throne. When Ahab saw him, he rose immediately and stepped forward to embrace him. "Prince Michael!" he cried. "I was wondering why you had not come to report on conditions when you left Karkar."

"My own men went on from Chinnereth to Jerusalem," Michael explained. "I came to Jezreel first instead of going to Samaria."

"My husband has told me of your bravery at Karkar, Prince Michael," Jezebel said graciously. "We owe you a great deal."

"Did he tell you that he saved my life?"

She shook her head. "King Ahab is always modest when it comes to his own deeds of valor. It is his greatest weakness."

"What about Karkar?" Ahab asked impatiently. "Do you think King Irhuleni will be able to control that region with his own forces, Michael?"

"All the Assyrians had withdrawn before we left," Michael assured him. "Until Shalmaneser launches another invasion, I am sure the city is safe."

"The journey to Damascus was a fool's errand," Ahab growled. "Hadad-Ezer is afraid of his shadow; I shall not league myself with him again."

Michael decided to go directly to the point. "I was very much saddened to learn of the death of Naboth when I reached Jezreel."

"So were we all," Ahab agreed. "Naboth and I did not always see alike, but each of us respected the other."

"Since his vineyard is now yours, you will have no need to build the wheel for lifting water."

"The vineyard is mine by right of our law," Ahab said morosely. "But I find no pleasure in it now."

"My husband is overly sentimental, Prince Michael,"

Jezebel interposed. "Of course he will keep the vineyard, along with all of Naboth's property that fell to the Crown according to the law of Israel."

"Was Naboth given all the rights that were his under the law?" Michael asked, speaking now directly to Jezebel.

He saw a startled look in her eyes. For a moment her hand contracted upon the arm of the chair, looking for all the world, he thought, like the claws of a predatory bird ready to tear the flesh from its prey.

"What is this?" Ahab demanded. "Are you implying that there is any truth to what Elijah has accused me of?"

"Neither you nor I were here when Naboth was stoned," Michael reminded him. "Perhaps Queen Jezebel knows the true story of what happened. After all, Naboth was a member of the Council of Elders and a prince of Israel. She must surely have sent someone to Jezreel to investigate."

Jezebel had recovered her composure now, but for a single moment Michael had been allowed to see the light of guilt in her eyes that damned her as the murderer of Naboth. "What Prince Michael implies is an insult that should not go unavenged, my lord," she said angrily. "I sent the High Priest Zedekiah to investigate. He will tell you what happened."

Ahab turned to the plump man who had offered the prayer. "What is the story, Zedekiah?" he demanded.

The priest spoke in a soothing, unctuous voice. "Prince Michael was Naboth's friend as we all were, so his concern is understandable. Shortly after the armies moved northward a pestilence broke out in Jezreel. Naboth had gone there some time before to look after his vineyard. When word of the pestilence reached Samaria, Queen Jezebel sent me to Jezreel to see if I could discover why the favor of the Most High had been withdrawn from the city. When I found

221

no reason for it, I ordered a fast—as is our custom—so the people might beg forgiveness for their sins. During this time, two men came forward and swore they heard Naboth blaspheme against the name of the Most High because his vines were not bearing as he thought they should. The matter was investigated by the Council of Elders at Jezreel and Naboth was judged guilty by them of blasphemy. Many families in Jezreel had lost loved ones because of the pestilence and naturally the people were angry that Naboth's sin had brought the disfavor of the Lord upon the place."

Ahab had been listening intently to Zedekiah's story. "These men who testified against Naboth," he said. "Were they from Jezreel?"

"Not only from Jezreel, sire. One of them was Naboth's own servant, who kept the vineyard for him when he was away."

This was news to Michael, for the elders in Jezreel had not mentioned it. It appeared to make the evidence against Naboth seem more damning, but he could not bring himself to believe that the whole affair could possibly have happened as Zedekiah described.

"You have made serious charges here, Prince Michael," Ahab said severely. "Knowing your love for Naboth, I am prepared to overlook them if you are now convinced there was no wrong in his death and withdraw your accusation."

Michael glanced from Ahab's serious, concerned face to Jezebel. The look of triumph in her eyes convinced him more than anything else could have done that Zedekiah had been her agent. Between them they had experienced little difficulty in utilizing the fortuitous occurrence of an epidemic in Jezreel to bring about the death of the man who, after Elijah, had served as the strongest rallying point for the forces opposing Jezebel in her determination to stamp out the worship of Yahweh in Israel.

"I do not blame Prince Michael for being distraught, my lord," Jezebel interposed sweetly. "It is rumored that Naboth's daughter Miriam will become his wife and naturally he is concerned that now she can bring him no dowry."

Michael had the feeling that the king of Israel was urging him to admit he was wrong, thereby assuaging Ahab's own conscience. But however much he admired his former comrade-in-arms, he would not lie merely to retain Ahab's favor.

"What I have heard here merely confirms my belief that false testimony was given against Naboth," he said firmly.

"But why?" Ahab protested. "I had long since given up my desire for the vineyard."

"The vineyard did not cause Naboth's death, my lord King, but rather his support of Elijah and the Most High God."

Ahab stiffened. "Are you accusing Queen Jezebel of bringing it about?"

"It is well known that your queen sought Naboth's death," Michael said quietly. "Ask her how it was accomplished, since I have no proof at the moment. She will no doubt deny it, but I swear to one day lay the proof before you."

A dead silence filled the room as Michael turned upon his heel and started toward the door. Suddenly Jezebel's voice, taut with rage, broke the silence. "Hamul!" she cried, but Michael turned and cut short whatever else she had been going to say.

"Do not send your lackey to kill me by stealth as you tried to kill Elijah or I will cut him in pieces for your watchdogs to feed upon," he warned. "And the same holds for your assassin priest, Zedekiah."

Jezebel was too convulsed by rage to answer, but Ahab's voice arrested Michael at the door of the chamber. "Send Ahaziah back to Samaria at once," he ordered. "A troop of cavalry will meet him at the border crossing a week from today."

In his anger and grief at the death of Naboth, Michael had not stopped to consider that his charge against Jezebel might put Ahaziah in danger. He had no choice except to leave Israel, but he could not do it without making one last attempt to save the crippled prince.

"You will be signing the order for Prince Ahaziah's death if you bring him back to Israel now," he warned Ahab.

"I am king in Israel," Ahab thundered. "Obey my order, unless you want warfare between our kingdoms."

Michael bowed his head. "Prince Ahaziah will be at the border crossing a week from today," he promised and left the room. Outside he wasted no time in reaching the inn where they had left the horses stabled. Fortunately Aaron had already returned.

"What did you learn from Elijah and Micaiah?" Michael asked him as they rode out of the city.

"They are sure Jezebel plotted the death of Naboth."

"Do they have any more proof than we have found already?"

"My lord Elijah says they need no more proof. You heard the curse he put upon both Jezebel and King Ahab this afternoon. He says you must not risk your life trying to punish them for their sin, since God has already revealed their fate."

Remembering the look upon Ahab's face that afternoon when Elijah had uttered the curse, Michael could not help feeling sorry for the king, even though Ahab had just driven him from his court. For no greater degradation could come to anyone in Israel than that dogs should lick his blood and eat his flesh.

Chapter 18

MIRIAM HAD KNOWN ABOUT NABOTH'S DEATH FOR several weeks, Michael discovered when he reached Jerusalem a few days later, word of it having been sent to her by Micaiah. With Ahaziah and King Jehoshaphat, the two of them met together after the evening meal that same night to hear his story of what had happened at Karkar and what he had learned about the tragedy at Jezreel.

Jehu had already given an account of the battle at some length, embellishing Michael's role in it, but Michael now told the story as he had seen it, giving credit mainly to Ahab for forcing Hadad-Ezer to give up command of his troops in time to save the battle. When he finished, Ahaziah's eyes were shining with excitement.

"It was a great victory to turn back almost twice your number!" the boy cried.

"In that sense, yes," Michael agreed. "But the Assyrians inflicted heavy casualties that we could ill afford to lose, so Shalmaneser could even consider it a victory for himself."

"He will no doubt do just that," Jehoshaphat agreed. "The Assyrians were ever a boastful people and fond of chiseling exaggerated reports of their victories on tablets of stone."

"You have every reason to be proud of your father," Michael assured Ahaziah. "Not only did he direct the battle masterfully, but he was in the forefront of the fighting all the while."

"And yet he allowed Jezebel to kill Naboth," the youth said bitterly. "I could never forgive him for that."

"I found nothing to prove it did not happen just as the priest Zedekiah said," Michael pointed out.

"Not even from the elders at Jezreel?" Miriam asked.

"No. Their story agrees in every detail."

"What about those who testified against him?"

"They had already left the city, but I learned that they were men of Jezreel. In fact one of them was in charge of your father's vineyard."

"Maon!' Miriam cried. "Of course he would be the one! Father caught him stealing money he had received for selling wine and discharged him last year. Before Maon left, he swore to get back at my father some day."

Here was the first concrete evidence Michael had heard to prove that Naboth had been killed as a result of a plot. But unless they could find Maon and force him to confess, there was still no hope of proving Jezebel's perfidy.

"When Zedekiah went to Jezreel, he must have sought out Maon and paid him to swear falsely against my father," Miriam continued. "Jezebel arranged for Zedekiah to become High Priest while Ahab was away, so the people would think she had turned to Yahweh. He repaid her by having my father killed."

Michael had not yet told Ahaziah about Ahab's orders concerning him but there seemed to be no point in delaying any longer. "Your father wants you to return to Israel," Michael told the young prince.

"A troop of cavalry will meet you at the border two days from now."

"But why?" Miriam protested. "Ahaziah is happy here."

"I practically accused Jezebel in Ahab's presence of murdering Naboth," Michael explained. "Since I did not know then that the vineyard-keeper had sworn to do your father harm, Miriam, I could bring no proof, but King Ahab was magnanimous and gave me an opportunity to retract the accusation. When I refused, he could not overlook what must have appeared to be an unjustified affront to the queen."

"Were you ordered to leave Israel?" Jehoshaphat asked.

"I forestalled that by announcing my departure, so there would be no hard feelings between you and Ahab," Michael told him. "It was then that he ordered Ahaziah's return."

"I will go back to Samaria with you," Miriam told Ahaziah, but the crippled prince shook his head.

"The queen hates you already. If you go back, she will only plot to destroy you as she killed your father."

"But you will be in danger there."

"I am no longer a child," Ahaziah reminded her with simple dignity. "Jezebel cannot harm me so long as my father is in Israel. If I pretend to be angered by Prince Michael's action, no one will suspect that I know the truth and I can seek the proof we need that she plotted your father's death."

Michael could see that Ahaziah had matured considerably during his stay in Jerusalem. He possessed a good deal more self-assurance and seemed to be much less conscious of his deformity. The danger to Ahaziah lay, as Miriam had pointed out, in Jezebel's desire to see her own son, Joram, reign after Ahab. But, as the young prince had said, it did not seem likely that she would dare harm Ahaziah as long as his father was in Israel.

Since Miriam was remaining in Judah, Michael could see no obstacle now to their marriage. On that score, however, he discovered that he was wrong.

Miriam was very devoted to her faith, obeying the laws strictly. She insisted upon the prescribed period of mourning for her father extending over many months and, although the weeks of absence from her had increased a hundredfold Michael's longing to have her as his wife, he did not press her.

Prince Ahaziah was delivered to the cavalry troop from Israel at the border near Bethel a few days later. Confident that Shalmaneser of Assyria would not idly accept the repulse by a considerably smaller force at Karkar, Michael busied himself during the winter months training and equipping the largest army Judah had ever marshaled in peacetime.

Miriam remained in the palace as a guest and as the affianced bride of Michael, so they saw each other every evening. During the daytime, while Michael was working with the soldiers, she busied herself at a task she loved, exploring the ancient records of the Hebrew people which were stored in the temple and in the archives of the scholars. There she unearthed details concerning the once fabulously profitable trade with Ophir and the almost legendary mines of Solomon in Africa from whence had come vast quantities of gold. As she and Michael discussed these exciting events of the past in the evening, a project began to materialize in his mind. He did not tell either Miriam or his father, however, that the idea had first been given him by Jezebel.

Since the time of Solomon the Edomites inhabiting the region south of the Salt Sea had gradually assumed control of the southernmost part of Judah, including the seaports of Ezion-Geber and Elath, which had been neglected and allowed to become silted up. As soon as they could be sure that the Assyrians would not attack again in the spring, Michael proposed to launch an expedition against the Edomites and retake all of the lands southwest of Judah as far as the port of Ezion-Geber on the Gulf of Akaba.

Jezebel had held out to him, in return for joining in her scheme to put all of Canaan under Ahab's rule, the lure of furnishing Phoenician shipbuilders and seamen from Tyre and Sidon to help regain the trade with the rich eastern lands. But now Michael knew that once the ports were retaken from the Edomites he could obtain shipbuilders and mariners from King Matten of Arvad to build the great ships of Tarshish and sail them eastward to the fabled lands from whence had come such great riches. And this time it would not be necessary to divide the profits of the voyages with another, as Solomon had done with King Hiram of Tyre, because the ships would be built and sailed for Judah by the skilled Phoenician seamen of Arvad. Most important of all, Jezebel would have no part in it.

The heat of summer waned, bringing the coolness of fall. Soon frost lay in the morning upon the hilltops of Jerusalem. Miriam and Michael had set their wedding date for the spring, after the celebration of the Passover, almost exactly a year since they had pledged their troth while all of Jerusalem sang the lovely hymn signifying the end of its most sacred religious festival. A month before the date they had set, Michael came in one afternoon from a busy day of drilling the soldiers on the hills outside Jerusalem and found his father and Miriam talking with a tall man who wore the uniform of the Israelite army.

"Rakkon!" he cried, embracing the other warmly. The Israelite was captain of Ahab's largest chariot

229

squadron. During the battle of Karkar he and Michael had fought together and become close friends.

"What is the news from Prince Ahaziah?" Michael asked the newcomer.

"He is well and sends greetings to you and the lady Miriam. King Ahab is more than pleased with what you did for Ahaziah here in Jerusalem," Rakkon told Jehoshaphat. "The boy is wise beyond his years and is no longer troubled in his mind because of his limp."

"Miriam deserves the credit," Jehoshaphat said. "We learned to love the boy while he was here. He will make Israel a good king some day."

"Let us pray that he is allowed to sit upon the throne," Rakkon said.

"Is anything wrong?" Miriam asked quickly.

"Queen Jezebel plots to have her son, Joram, reign in Prince Ahaziah's stead. But that is no news to any of you."

"Israel has not changed then," Miriam said sadly. "I am glad not to be there."

"Do you know anything about Elijah?" Michael asked.

Rakkon shook his head. "The prophet has not been seen in Israel since he cursed King Ahab and Jezebel at Megiddo. Some say he went eastward across the Jordan to the land around Tishbeh."

"And Micaiah?"

"He teaches and heals in the villages. And prophesies in the name of the Most High."

"Then the worship of Yahweh is not restricted any more?" King Jehoshaphat inquired.

"The priests are allowed to sacrifice to the Most High without harm," Rakkon confirmed. "But Queen Jezebel hates Micaiah because he is a disciple of Elijah and she plots to destroy him. That is why he no longer comes into Samaria, except by stealth."

"Rakkon brought a message from King Ahab that we all need to hear," King Jehoshaphat told Michael. "It will especially interest you."

"Is Shalmaneser preparing to launch another attack?" Michael asked quickly.

Rakkon shook his head. "As far as our spies have been able to tell, the Assyrians will make no move against us this year at least. But King Ahab has demanded that Syria return Ramoth-Gilead to Israel as was promised, and Hadad-Ezer has refused."

"Then there will be war."

"We are preparing for it now," Rakkon confirmed. "King Ahab sent me here to bid your father join him with the armies of Judah to free the land that once was ours from the hand of the Syrian."

Michael looked at his father; the decision would, of course, have to come from him. "I have been expecting this," Jehoshaphat said. "And you, Michael, have been preparing for it, so it is not exactly news to us."

"Then we will go against the Syrians?" Michael asked.

"As Rakkon says, Ramoth-Gilead is a part of our ancient heritage from Moses and Joshua. We cannot let it remain in the hands of a usurper."

"May I take that message back to King Ahab?" Rakkon asked.

"I will have the scribes write a letter to my brother Ahab telling him our armies will march northward soon to join him at Samaria," Jehoshaphat said. "Michael has been readying our forces. We may not equal the armies of Israel in numbers, but I am sure you will not find us lacking in courage."

A week later Michael and his father rode out of Jerusalem at the head of a large army of horsemen, chariots, and foot soldiers. His older brother Jehoram, the heir, stayed behind to govern in Jerusalem during their absence. This assignment the rather indolent crown prince did not find at all disappointing, since he was much fonder of his harem and the pleasures of the table and the winecup than of martial activity.

Following the central highway across the hilltops of Canaan, the army of Judah reached the plains before the Israelite capital of Samaria and camped there, since their numbers greatly exceeded the ability of the city to house them. About half of Ahab's army was already in the capital or camped on the slopes nearby. The rest, they were told, would move eastward directly from the headquarters at Megiddo for the attack upon Ramoth-Gilead.

Samaria had not changed since he was here last, Michael saw. The grove of Ashtoreth where he had first seen Jezebel was still green and cool, with the temple of the goddess visible through the trees. The walls of the city were stronger than ever, for Ahab was constantly fortifying it. But even the magnificence of Ahab's new palace was dominated by the massive fortifications of the tower that rose from the older section, called the "Wall of Jezreel" because money for it had come from that city when Ahab's father had decided to build this massive capital upon Watch Mountain in the center of his kingdom. From his tent Michael could hear the constant growling and barking of the ferocious dogs that were kept in the enclosure at the foot of the tower because of Jezebel's fear that some of the Israelites who hated her might climb it and reach her private quarters.

The army of Judah had reached Samaria in the early afternoon and Jehoshaphat rode into the city to take up quarters in Ahab's palace. Remembering the harsh words that had passed between him, Ahab, and Jezebel at their last meeting, Michael did not accompany his father, remaining instead with the troops in their camp on the hillside near the wall. But there were too many memories here for him to be really comfortable in Samaria—or anywhere else that was near Jezebel.

He had told himself that, because he had forcibly put her out of his thoughts, she was also out of his feelings and senses. And as long as he had been far away from her, he had been able to maintain that illusion. Now, with everything around him reminding him of Jezebel, he faced the truth that not even his love for Miriam had been able to exorcise completely the demon of desire which had been lying dormant in his soul. At all costs, he knew, he must keep himself aloof, lest he yield to the strange fever that even the thought of the days and nights he had spent with Jezebel in Jezreel started burning again in his blood.

Sitting alone in his tent after the evening meal while he wrestled with his thoughts—as Jacob had wrestled long ago with an angel on the shore of a brook at the place called Peniel—Michael at first thought the familiar perfume that struck his nostrils was an illusion, part of his remembered consciousness of Jezebel's allure even when she was far away. But when he looked up and saw a woman standing inside the flap of the tent he could not deny the evidence of his eyes —or his suddenly racing pulse.

It was Jezebel!

Chapter 19

Israel's queen was as vital and as alluring as Michael remembered her from the first time he had seen her in the grove of Ashtoreth. The same circlet was upon her forehead with the glowing jewel in its center, and her eyes glowed with the warmth which he knew so well could suddenly turn into a flame of overpowering desire. She was wrapped in a heavy cloak and had thrown a piece of *byssus* over her head as a veil, holding the end across her face just beneath the eyes to hide her identity. When she removed it and let her hair fall upon her shoulders, every angle and plane of her face and the slender column of her neck, as well as the outlines of her figure, were just as they had been etched idelibly in his memory. She did not loosen the long cloak, but he was sure that beneath it her robe would be like gossamer and her loins enclosed only by the tiny golden girdle she wore so often, her breasts gold-tipped as they had been on the night they had spent in Jezreel.

"A year ago you would have been gracious enough to rise and greet a visitor, Michael," she said, her voice light and mocking.

As he stumbled to his feet he experienced once

again the strange feeling that he was actually two people, one watching the other. And when she gave him her hand, he saw himself lift it to his lips and kiss it, then carry it to his forehead in the same instinctive gesture of fealty he had made on the night when Naboth had taken him to the reception in the palace nearby.

It was a strange experience indeed, this sense of watching himself do something he had sworn he would never do again. But the watching self had no power over the other and he knew he would not be able to keep what was happening from going on to its inevitable conclusion.

"I can only stay a little while," Jezebel said. He had not released her hand and now she moved nearer, until their bodies were almost touching. "It hurt me when you did not come to the palace with your father tonight, Michael. Surely you cannot believe me responsible for Naboth's death, when you could not have found any evidence to convince you I was involved—because none exists."

"No," he admitted. "I did not find any."

"Ahab had no need for the vineyard, once you had devised the way of lifting water from the spring to keep his garden alive. And I have not fought any more against the worship of Yahweh in Israel since Elijah's triumph on Mount Carmel turned Ahab back to the ways of his father.

"I loved you deeply once, Michael, and I still do," she said before he could answer. "And I can read in your eyes that you have not forgotten me and the 'Flower of Dreams.'"

He no longer heard the small voice in the watching part of himself insisting that she would have murdered Elijah on Mount Carmel if her plan had succeeded and that she must certainly have destroyed Naboth. It had been stilled by the beat of his pulse,

235

throbbing like the sound of the timbrels used to urge men into battle.

"When Ahab defeats Hadad-Ezer at Ramoth-Gilead, the people of Canaan will know he is strong enough to protect them against Assyria," Jezebel continued. "We still have time to build a great confederation of nations here and your part in it can be very important. Ahab often says he would be proud to follow you into battle, and the kings of the confederation trust you. Admit that your accusations against me were unfounded and you can be comrades-in-arms with Ahab again. And even if you will not be king of Judah, you might one day be warlord of Canaan, with the kings of the individual countries under your control."

A rational part of his being knew she was seeking to mold him to her own purpose as a part of her ambition to rule all of Canaan and, one day perhaps, the world. But a stronger part of him was only conscious of her beauty and the fact that she was offering herself to him in return for agreeing to her plan. When he reached out to draw her to him, she did not resist, and he knew in a moment of supreme elation that the woman in Jezebel desired him fully as much as he desired her. As his hands roved down her body and began to draw away the folds of the heavy cloak, both were oblivious to anything outside the tent, until Jehu's voice snapped a sharp command, breaking the spell that held them. Michael involuntarily loosened his embrace and Jezebel stepped out of it quickly. With deft fingers she arranged the cloth about her hair and across her face so as to hide it.

"Come to me when the battle for Ramoth-Gilead is over," she said—and with the words was gone, through the flap of the tent.

Michael moved outside to find Jehu tongue-lashing the guard who had been posted before the tent. From the tenor of Jehu's remarks, Michael judged that the soldier had been found sleeping at his post, but he was quite sure the man had actually been bribed to let Jezebel pass unaccosted into the tent. And since he was himself partially responsible for the whole thing, he could not let the sentry bear all the blame.

"Let him be," he told his lieutenant. "Surely I can be in no danger in the camp of friends."

"A guard is a guard," Jehu said angrily. "If he sleeps here at his post, he would do the same on the battlefield."

"It has been a long day and we are all tired," Michael said. "Come into the tent and have a drink of wine."

Jehu stopped in the open flap, his nostrils flaring. "That scent. A woman has been here."

Michael shrugged. "Someone I knew when I was in Samaria once before."

"And rich surely, by the smell of the perfume. That means the guard was bribed to let her pass."

"Leave him be. I was in no danger."

Jehu shrugged. "From the look in your eyes, I wonder if the lady wasn't in danger—of losing her virtue. That is if she had any to lose." He picked up a wineskin and tilted it to pour a stream into his mouth. "So the bridegroom-to-be is sampling the pleasures of the flesh one last time before locking on the shackles of marriage."

"There was no time for what you are thinking," Michael said shortly.

"No time, perhaps—but desire, yes. You have the look of a rutting goat, my friend."

"If you have nothing better to tell me than that," Michael said, "drink your wine and go to your tent."

"A man is asking for you," Jehu said. "But if you are too tired after your—"

"Who is it?"

"A priest."

"A tall man with a golden beard?"

"Yes."

"That is Micaiah. Bring him here at once; we are old friends."

Jehu shortly ushered Micaiah into the tent and departed to his own quarters. The two men embraced warmly.

"Rakkon told me you were well," Michael said. "Are you sure it is safe for you to be here now?"

"When I heard you were coming to Samaria to join Ahab in the attack upon Ramoth-Gilead," Micaiah told him, "I had to come and warn you."

"Against what?"

"Ahab may be destroyed and perhaps Israel with him, if he fights Hadad-Ezer for the city."

"How do you know this?"

"Do you remember the prophecy of Elijah at Megiddo when you returned from the battle of Karkar? He said then that the dogs would lick the blood of Ahab by the Pool of Samaria."

"I remember the words, yes. But what did he mean by the Pool of Samaria?"

"What else but the large pool in the courtyard between the old home of Omri and Ahab's new palace."

"Surely that doesn't sound as if Ahab would die on the field of battle at Ramoth-Gilead," Michael protested. "The city is several days' journey away."

"I only know that Ahab will one day die according to the curse Elijah put upon him," Micaiah said. "And I have no wish to see you lose your life at the same time."

"So you risked your own life to warn me against going with him? It was a brave thing to do, my friend."

"That is only part of it," Micaiah admitted. "In our youth, Ahab and I were friends; we once swore blood brotherhood by pricking our fingers and mixing our blood as boys will do. Since he returned from Karkar, Ahab has served the Lord; if he does not go to Ramoth-Gilead, the curse may be delayed. Or the Most High might even relent."

"You know Ahab will not listen to me—after I accused Jezebel of having Naboth murdered."

"He will not attack the Syrians unless your father's armies support him," Micaiah insisted. "If you persuade Jehoshaphat to return to Jerusalem, the affair will be ended."

"I cannot do it, Micaiah. Ramoth-Gilead would still be in the hands of Hadad-Ezer and Ahab would feel that both my father and I had failed him."

"I saw a woman pass through the camp just a few minutes ago," the priest said. "Did Jezebel visit you?"

There was no point in denying what was obviously true. Besides, Michael knew Micaiah was concerned only with his welfare and Miriam's. "She was here just now but only for a moment," he admitted.

"Why?"

"Apparently she cannot believe any man who ever desired her could put her away."

"Can you?" Micaiah asked directly.

Michael hesitated. "I had thought she could not hold me any longer—"

"But now you are not sure?"

"No."

"Once before by being with Jezebel, you learned of the plot to kill Elijah in time to save him," Micaiah said thoughtfully. "There may be a purpose behind her coming tonight that we cannot see at the moment."

"You are letting me off too easy, old friend. The truth is that just now I was on the point of being unfaithful to the girl I love more than anyone else on earth. Surely no good could possibly come from that."

"You were not unfaithful?"

239

"No, but only because Jehu came to tell me you were in the camp asking for me."

Micaiah put his hand upon Michael's shoulder. "That, too, may be a part of God's will. The fate of Jezebel has already been decided; the dogs shall one day eat her flesh by the Wall of Jezreel, as Elijah foretold. I was wrong in trying to influence you, for if Ahab is to die at Ramoth-Gilead, nothing you or I can do will really stop it. We can only carry out whatever part of the plan God has set for us."

"When will I see you again?" Michael asked.

"I am lodging at the house of the priest, Nahom, but I cannot stay in Samaria long. Zedekiah is afraid I may persuade Ahab to make me the chief priest again in his stead. If he learns that I am in Samaria, he will surely try to have me killed."

"I need to know one thing more," Michael told him. "Was Jezebel really responsible for the death of Naboth?"

"Yes."

"How did she accomplish it?"

"When the pestilence struck in Jezreel, she found the pretext she needed. Naboth happened to be there at the time and Jezbel sent Zedekiah to hire perjurers to accuse him of blaspheming against the Lord. The people were naturally distraught from the pestilence, and when two men swore to the charge before the Council of Elders, as is required by our law, their terror drove them to destroy Naboth."

"Was one of them Maon, the vineyard keeper Naboth had discharged?"

"Yes."

"Then why not bring charges against Jezebel before Ahab?"

"The men who swore to the lies about Naboth have left Jezreel. They were well paid and will no doubt stay away a long time, spending the money they earned by perjury. But you need not concern yourself about Jezebel; her fate is already settled."

"And Ahab's, too?"

"Who can say whether or not the same hand will strike both of them down? I can only pray that Ahab will realize how he has sinned and beg the Lord humbly for forgiveness, before it is too late."

As Michael watched the tall figure of the priest disappear down the slope he was remembering the day he had first met Micaiah on the road to Jerusalem and the attack by the thieves. From the way the paths of their lives had crossed and recrossed since that day, it did indeed seem that both of them were part of some plan whose end they could not yet foresee. And somehow, Michael could not throw off the ominous feeling that the terminal events of that plan were already in the process of working themselves out and that before very much longer its ultimate purpose would be revealed.

In the morning Michael sent Jehu to his father in the city asking him to come to the camp some time that day. Shortly before noon King Jehoshaphat entered Michael's tent; the younger man dropped the flap together behind him so they would be alone.

"Last night I was visited by Micaiah the prophet," he told his father. "He wants me to persuade you not to go against Ramoth-Gilead with Ahab."

"On what grounds?"

"At Megiddo Elijah prophesied the death of Ahab in punishment for the murder of Naboth."

"But you yourself said there was no connection."

"Not directly with Ahab," Michael agreed. "Micaiah says Jezebel sent the High Priest Zedekiah to Jezreel to hire the witnesses to swear Naboth had blasphemed and stir up the people to kill him."

"Does he have proof of this?"

"Apparently he could find no more proof than I

was able to discover, but he is certain of what happened."

"We cannot bring charges against the queen on such flimsy evidence," Jehoshaphat protested.

"Micaiah says there is no need. Jezebel's fate is already sealed and Ahab's with her."

Jehoshaphat frowned. "Has the Lord revealed to him that Ahab will be stricken down at Ramoth-Gilead?"

"Not the place," Michael explained. "But he fears it might happen there and seeks to keep Ahab from going."

Jehoshaphat stroked his beard thoughtfully. "I know Elijah thinks very highly of Micaiah, but even prophets do not always understand the meaning of what other prophets say. It could be that this disaster to Ahab may take place many, many years in the future."

"Even Micaiah admits that."

"We can't break off our aid to Ahab on such trivial grounds," Jehoshaphat decided. "Nevertheless I will insist that tomorrow the priests and prophets gather before the army to bless our attack upon Ramoth-Gilead and seek the will of the Lord concerning it."

"We can do no more than that," Michael agreed. "I only hope the omens are favorable."

Chapter 20

AHAB DID NOT OBJECT TO JEHOSHAPHAT'S SUGGESTION that the armies be blessed before the expedition began to move eastward against the area on the other side of the Jordan which had been taken over by the Syrians. The sun was high in the southern sky, warming the hilltop with the promise of good weather for the coming attack, when the two kings and their armies gathered on the slope before the gate of Samaria for the ceremony of blessing and invoking God's favor in the coming battle.

Two carved ivory throne chairs had been brought out for Jehoshaphat and Ahab. Behind them stood the nobles of Israel and the officers of the armies in their rich uniforms, highly polished armor, and long cloaks of luxurious fabric. Before the two kings were massed the ranks of their troops, the foot men in front, the chariots behind them, and the horsemen in the saddle behind the vehicles. Thus all could see and hear what was taking place.

As commander of the armies of Judah, Michael stood beside his father. Ahab nodded civilly to him but there were no other words of greeting between them. The king of Israel was the first to speak.

"You know that Ramoth and Gilead belong to us," he told the troops massed before him. "And yet we keep still and do not take them out of the hand of the king of Syria."

"Let us go and wrest what is ours from the hands of Hadad-Ezer," an officer in the front ranks shouted, and a great roar of approval rose from both armies.

Ahab allowed the shouting to continue for a few moments before raising his hand to stop it. Then, turning to Jehoshaphat, he asked formally, "Will you go with me to battle at Ramoth-Gilead?"

"I am as you are," Jehoshaphat answered solemnly. "My people are as your people and my horses are as your horses."

"Then we will fight and take what is ours together."

"I beg you inquire concerning the word of the Lord," Jehoshaphat said. "Whether or not he looks with favor upon this venture."

Ahab looked at the richly garbed priests who stood to one side, ranked behind Zedekiah. "Shall I go against Ramoth-Gilead or shall I forbear?" he asked.

One of the priests gave Zedekiah a massive pair of iron horns. Carrying them, the portly High Priest approached Ahab's throne and knelt before it, placing the horns with their sharp-pointed tips upon the carpet that had been rolled out before the two kings.

"Thus saith the Lord," he said. " 'With these you shall punish the Syrians until you have consumed them.' Go up to Ramoth-Gilead and prosper, for the Lord shall deliver it into the king's hands."

Another shout of approval went up from the troops massed before the throne. Once again Ahab made no motion to quell it, apparently in the hope that this sign of approval for the venture would serve to allay any misgivings King Jehoshaphat might have about the expedition.

Jehoshaphat, however, was still not convinced. "Is

there not a prophet of the Lord here besides these others of whom we might inquire?" he asked.

"There is Micaiah, the son of Imleh," Ahab admitted, reluctantly. "But I hate him because he does not prophesy good concerning me, but evil."

"If Micaiah prophesies the word of God, then we should hear it," Jehoshaphat insisted.

"Is Micaiah here?" Ahab inquired.

When there was no answer, Michael said, "I know where Micaiah can be found; he lodges with a priest called Nahom."

"Do you know this Nahom, Zedekiah?" Ahab asked.

"His house is not far away," Zedekiah admitted with some reluctance. "If Micaiah is there, he can be brought here quickly."

"Send for him then. We will listen to what he has to say."

It was not long before Micaiah came striding through the ranks of the troops, his golden beard shining in the sunlight. He did not wear the rich robe of a priest, although he had every right to do so as a former High Priest of Yahweh. Instead he was dressed in the same homespun type of robe and rough sandals that Elijah always wore. Before the two kings he stopped and bowed in homage.

"The words of the prophets declare good to the king with one mouth," Zedekiah said haughtily to Micaiah. "Let your word be like one of them and speak that which is good."

"As the Lord lives," the tall prophet said simply. "What the Lord says to me, that I will speak."

"Shall we go against Ramoth-Gilead to battle or shall we forbear?" Ahab demanded.

Micaiah did not speak immediately and, looking into his eyes, Michael was sure the tall priest had received some sort of a revelation since they had talked together the night before. But when he spoke, his words did not bear out that assumption.

"Go and prosper," Micaiah said. "For the Lord shall deliver it into the hands of the king."

Ahab, too, had been watching Micaiah closely and Michael sensed that some indefinable something had passed between the two men, an unspoken message perhaps from the days of their childhood when they had been boys together.

"How many times shall I adjure you to tell me nothing but that which is true in the name of the Lord?" Ahab demanded almost angrily.

Micaiah faced him then and spoke to the king alone. "I saw all Israel scattered upon the hills as sheep that have not a shepherd," he said. "And the Lord said, 'These have no master; let them return every man to his house in peace.'"

Ahab's face darkened still more with anger as he turned to Jehoshaphat. "Did I not tell you he would prophesy no good concerning me, but evil?"

Micaiah appeared not to have heard Ahab's words. "Hear therefore the word af the Lord," he said, his voice rolling sonorously down the hill across the heads of the waiting troops. "I saw the Lord sitting on his throne and all the hosts of heaven by his right hand and on his left. And the Lord said, 'Who shall persuade Ahab, that he may go up and fall at Ramoth-Gilead?'

"Then one said on this manner and another said on that manner until a spirit came forth and stood before the Lord saying, 'I will persuade him.'

"The Lord said unto this spirit, 'With what will you persuade him?' And the spirit said, 'I will go forth and I will be a lying spirit in the mouth of all his prophets.' Then the Lord said, 'You shall persuade him and prevail also. Go forth and do so.'"

Micaiah's eyes now blazed at Zedekiah and the

ranks of priests behind him. "Behold the Lord has put a lying spirit in the mouth of all these your prophets," he said to Ahab. "And the Lord has spoken evil concerning you."

The portly Zedekiah was livid with rage. Before Micaiah could lift his hand to protect himself, the High Priest stepped forward and struck him sharply upon the cheek.

"Which way did the spirit of the Lord go from me to speak to you?" Zedekiah demanded.

"Behold you shall see when you go into an inner chamber to hide yourself," Micaiah answered contemptuously.

"Joash!" Ahab called.

From the front rank of Israel's nobility a plump man stepped forward. "Yes, my lord King," he said.

"I am placing Micaiah in your care as governor of Samaria," Ahab said. "Take him and carry him to the prison. Feed him with bread and water until I come in peace, but do not harm him."

"If you return at all in peace, the Lord has not spoken by me," Micaiah said quietly. Then he turned to the people. "Listen, O people, every one of you. Listen to the words which I have spoken."

At a sign from the governor of the city two officers stepped forward to take Micaiah away to prison. Michael started to protest, but when his father shook his head he held his tongue.

Ahab's face was still suffused with anger. "The prophet lied because he hates me," he said to Jehoshaphat. "If you and your armies will not accompany me, I will go against Ramoth-Gilead alone."

"I am as you are and my people are as your people, my horses as your horses," Jehoshaphat said once again. "Let us go against the Syrians and what will happen will happen."

Two days later, the combined armies of Israel and

Judah began to move eastward for the attack upon Ramoth-Gilead.

When the children of Israel, wandering in the wilderness southwest of the Salt Sea, had considered entering Canaan in the region around Hebron to the south—Abraham's old home—spies sent out by Moses had returned with stories of fortified cities and great giants. Terrified, the Israelites had taken a route east of the Salt Sea skirting the kingdom of Moab. Moving northward, they had begun their conquest upon the east bank of the Jordan. There the fertile plains leading up to the eastern range of mountains and the vast endless desert beyond had been conquered in a series of lightning campaigns under Joshua's leadership. The campaigns had carried them northward almost to Damascus, and while that most ancient of cities had not fallen to them, the great city of Ramoth located in the borderland of this frontier region in the district of Gilead had become a pearl in the crown of Israel, a treasure desired by the kings of Syria who also claimed it as their own.

Ben-Hadad, father of the present occupant of the throne of Syria, had fought against Israel and taken Ramoth-Gilead. But the agreement under which Ahab had contributed to the defense at Karkar and helped turn back the Assyrians had included the return of the city to Israel. This agreement Hadad-Ezer, with his customary talent for duplicity, had failed to honor.

Ahab could not long allow such an insult to go unrevenged and, besides, Ramoth-Gilead was an important outpost for the protection of Israel itself, as well as Judah. In case war was resumed with Damascus, or the Assyrians chose to attack by the eastern route, the enemy could move down the east side of the Jordan along the ancient caravan trail known as the King's Highway, crossing into Judah at any of several fords, including the traditional route of invasion by way of Jericho.

Guarding the great tablelands of the mountain range and the rich fields of Moab and Ammon, now under the rule of King Jehoshaphat, Ramoth-Gilead was therefore a prize of great value and must be returned to Israel if the prosperity of both the northern and southern kingdoms were to continue. The city was especially important to Jehoshaphat because an enemy in control of Ramoth-Gilead would be free to launch raids southward against Judah or to enlist the allegiance of subject kings in the lands on the eastern bank of the Jordan—men like Mesha of Moab, who paid tribute to Judah. It was for this reason that King Jehoshaphat had decided to go into battle with Ahab in spite of Micaiah's prediction that the Israelite leader would be killed.

Having crossed the Jordan a little northeast of Bethshan, the invading army entered a beautiful rolling mountainous region with Ramoth-Gilead, Mahanaim, Peniel, Succoth, Tishbeh, and Jabesh-Gilead among its most prosperous cities. The chariot corps from Megiddo traveled about a day behind the combined forces of Israel and Judah, and when Ramoth-Gilead came into sight upon the hilltop across a broad valley, Ahab called a halt and ordered a camp made while the vehicles caught up with them and the attack was being organized.

Ramoth did not have heavy defensive walls like Samaria and the cities of Canaan, so Ahab expected the decisive struggle to take place in the valley before the city instead of inside it. Hadad-Ezer's forces were already drawn up in considerable strength both in and around Ramoth-Gilead, so the Israelite camp was made a few miles away across the valley out of contact with the enemy.

By common consent, Ahab was in command of the

entire expedition, not only because of his considerable military experience but also because he was actually the ruler of Judah as well as Israel, with King Jehoshaphat holding the throne at Jerusalem as friend and vassal. So far Michael had not been called upon to attend the daily conferences between Ahab and his father, by which he judged that his accusations concerning the death of Naboth still rankled in the mind of the Israelite monarch.

It had been a long journey from Samaria and Michael was pleased when Ahab deferred the attack for several days. His men and horses needed rest and the opportunity to get their equipment in the proper condition for battle. Besides, with the cares of looking after an army on the march no longer resting upon his shoulders, he could think about what had happened in his camp before Samaria when Jezebel had visited his tent.

He did not seriously consider her suggestion that he might eventually become general of the armies of Canaan, a warlord who could impress his will upon any individual king by virtue of the power he wielded. Such a thing would be possible only if he betrayed his father and the others who trusted him. What did concern him was the tremendous surge of desire that had swept through him again at the sight of Jezebel, a demon he had hoped was exorcised long ago but which, he realized now, possessed him still in spite of his love for Miriam.

The two forces in his life—his love for Miriam and the desire for Jezebel—could not coexist much longer, Michael realized. Inevitably, one would be destroyed and he was under little illusion about which that would be as things stood now. Once again he found himself in somewhat the same position in which he had been in the tent with Jezebel, that of an observer forced to watch another part of himself moving along a path that could only destroy all chance of happiness, yet totally unable to keep the tragedy from happening.

Aaron prepared a particularly tasty meal the first night they made camp before Ramoth-Gilead. Michael ate and drank leisurely, half lost in his own thoughts while listening to the continuous flow of gossip that was Aaron's habit under such circumstances. Suddenly something the servant was saying struck a bell in his mind and he became alert.

"I recognized a fellow from Jezreel in the army of Ahab today," Aaron had said. "He boasts of having been the vineyard keeper of my lord Naboth, but I believe he lies. My lord Naboth would never have had such a scoundrel in his employ; all the man does is drink and boast that he will soon be an officer because he knows something King Ahab does not want to be revealed."

"What is his name?" Michael demanded excitedly, wondering if at last the thing he needed to unravel the puzzle of Naboth's tragic death finally was dropping into his lap.

Aaron rubbed his chin. "Let me see. It was a short name, that much I remember."

"Maon?"

The servant looked at him in surprise. "That was it. But how did you know?"

"He is one of the two who swore Naboth was a blasphemer and caused the Council of Jezreel to sentence him to death."

"What kind of a man would perjure himself to bring about the death of a fine and generous master?"

"One who hated that master," Michael said crisply. "And who was paid well for the task of destroying him."

Aaron loosened the knife at his belt and started out of the tent. "He will not boast much longer. My knife will find his throat before cockcrow."

"Wait!" Michael ordered. "We must wring the truth from the man first. Is he with Ahab's troops?"

"Yes."

"Then we must figure a way to get him into our own camp."

"Leave that to me." Aaron picked up the wineskin from which he had filled Michael's cup for the evening meal. "If there is one thing this fellow Maon loves more than boasting, it is wine. I will bring him here before midnight."

"See that he is still able to talk," Michael warned. "We must have the whole story."

It was a little more than an hour before Aaron returned with a small raw-boned man in tow. Though he was already drunk, his small shifty eyes showed alarm when he saw Michael, and he started to edge toward the tent opening. Aaron had already drawn the flap, however; he stood before it now, idly whetting the blade of his dagger with his thumb.

"You said we would find women," Maon squealed.

"Where you are going, my friend," Aaron said grimly, "women will do you no good."

"Don't touch me!" Maon backed away. "I am under the protection of Queen Jezebel herself."

"In return for swearing to the lie that Naboth was a blasphemer?" Michael demanded.

"You cannot prove it. Let me out of here or I will go to King Ahab."

"That is just where you *are* going," Michael told him grimly. "But only after you tell me the truth about the death of Naboth."

"I will tell nothing. The queen will protect me. Zede—" He stopped, his eyes suddenly wary.

"So the priest Zedekiah promised you protection if you swore to a lie and condemned Naboth?"

Maon stubbornly shut his lips and did not answer.

"And I suppose he paid you and your confederate well into the bargain?"

"You cannot prove anything!" Maon shouted, but the look of guilt in his eyes condemned him.

Michael unsheathed the dagger he always wore at his belt. It was razor-sharp, with a point like a needle. "Hold him, Aaron," he ordered.

The slave stepped forward and seized Maon, pinning his arms behind him. The man tried to struggle, but he might as well have sought to move the rock upon which the Israelite capital at Samaria was built. Dagger in hand, Michael approached him and set the point against his cheek.

"Naboth died a terrible death and so shall you," he promised Maon. "I shall begin with your eyes."

The knife shifted until the point was pressed against Maon's lower eyelid. "I learned this trick in Nineveh," Michael told him. "The Assyrians are skilled in such things. Only a little pressure and the point enters the eyeball."

Maon was staring at him with pupils dilated by terror. His skin was like bleached parchment and his mouth was slack with fear.

"The king will protect me," he babbled. "I only did it because Zedekiah said Ahab had every right to the vineyard but Naboth would not sell it to him."

"The king is in another part of the camp," Michael told him. "We are surrounded by the forces of Judah, and I command here. You will neither be heard nor heeded if you call for Ahab."

He pressed the point of the stiletto a trifle harder and Maon screamed with pain. "Take the knife away," he begged. "I will tell you everything."

Michael relieved the pressure upon the point a little but did not remove it. "Speak and speak truly," he ordered. "Remember I already know enough about

253

what really happened to tell whether or not you are lying."

"I will tell the whole truth," Maon promised eagerly. "The priest Zedekiah came to Jezreel and said the pestilence had come upon the town because Naboth sinned in not selling the vineyard to the Lord's anointed king of Israel."

"Whose idea was it that you swear to a charge of blasphemy against Naboth before the council?"

"Zedekiah's," Maon insisted. "He even told us what to say."

"And paid you well, no doubt."

"With gold. He said the queen wanted to give the vineyard to King Ahab as a present when he returned from the great victory in the north. He swore she would see to it that we were protected."

"Who is the other man?"

"My brother-in-law, but you cannot reach him. He died during the winter."

Michael reached for his cloak. "Where are you going?" Maon demanded apprehensively.

"To King Ahab, so he can learn the truth before you decide to start lying again."

"But I did it for him," Maon protested. "Zedekiah said the queen was worried because King Ahab had been sick with desire for the vineyard—"

"Tell him that and maybe he will let you off with your life," Michael told the cringing prisoner. "Bring him along, Aaron."

They were challenged by the sentry before Ahab's tent, but Michael could see that the king was inside. While he was talking to the guard, Ahab came to the flap.

"Is that Prince Michael of Judah, sentry?" he asked.

"Yes, my lord," the soldier answered. "And two others with him. I said your rest should not be disturbed so late—"

"Let them in."

Ahab spoke first when the three were inside the tent. "What is the cause of this intrusion, Prince Michael?" he demanded frostily.

"I think you should hear this man's story," Michael told him.

"Is he a spy?"

"A traitor and perjurer."

Ahab's eyes clouded with displeasure. For a moment Michael was afraid they might be ejected from the tent before Maon's story could be heard. Then the king nodded slightly and said, "Let him speak."

"His name is Maon."

"It means nothing to me."

Michael felt the burden upon his heart lift a little. He had come to love Ahab like a brother during the campaign at Karkar and still admired him as a great soldier and a fair-minded ruler. But his faith had been shaken when Ahab had refused to believe Naboth's death had been brought about by Jezebel through trickery. The fact that Ahab did not know Maon seemed to indicate that the Israelite king had played no part in the murder of Naboth.

"Your words lift a heavy burden from my heart," Michael told him sincerely.

Ahab turned to the cringing Maon. "Speak," he ordered.

"My lord, I know nothing——" Maon tried to bluster, but when Michael took his dagger from the scabbard with a casual gesture the man's momentary bravado collapsed.

"I once worked as a keeper in the vineyard of my lord Naboth in Jezreel," he whined. "He discharged me for stealing the money I received from selling wine."

Ahab stiffened, and Michael knew he was beginning

to realize why the man had been brought before him. "Go on," the king ordered, his voice harsh.

"I knew how my lord the King pined for the vineyard of my master Naboth," Maon said. "And how my master sinned against the Most High in withholding it from the Lord's Anointed."

"No man can be forced to sell his inheritance," Ahab said harshly. "Not even to the king."

"When the pestilence came, the priest Zedekiah said it was a punishment from the Most High for Naboth's sin," Maon protested. "He is the High Priest and—"

"Did Zedekiah hire you to swear falsely against Naboth before the Council of Elders at Jezreel?" Ahab demanded.

"He said it was for you—and that Naboth was blaspheming against the Lord's Anointed when he refused to sell the vineyard."

"Who else swore to that lie?"

"My brother-in-law. He died last winter."

"Did the priest tell you I had sent him to you?"

"It was the queen who sent him. Zedekiah said she wanted to give you the vineyard as a present when you returned from fighting the Assyrians. He promised me more gold and said the queen would always protect me if I did not reveal the secret."

Ahab slumped back in his chair. "Take him away," he directed. "But do not kill him. He was only the tool of others."

Unable to believe his good luck in escaping death, the perjurer scuttled from the tent, followed by Aaron. As Michael also turned to leave, Ahab spoke.

"Please stay awhile, Michael." he said. "You and I have much to discuss."

"I am sorry this news had to come to you," Michael said with genuine regret in his voice. "But I thought you should know it."

"I think I have known it in my heart for a long time," Ahab admitted. "Ever since you spoke the truth in Megiddo. But I was reluctant to admit I could be so wrong. Naboth was my friend, yet I allowed him to be murdered."

"You were in Hamath at the time," Michael reminded him. "Preparing for the battle of Karkar."

"The responsibility is still mine, I suppose . . . my guilt began long ago, when I let my desire to be called Israel's greatest king lead me into the marriage with Jezebel. I could have stopped her when she tried to massacre the priests of Yahweh, but I told myself I needed the good will of Tyre and Sidon, so they would remain neutral in the war with Assyria."

"The leader of a nation must always do what he thinks is best for his people."

"It is easy to convince yourself that what you wish for yourself is also best for the people, Michael. You heard Maon say just now that I am the Lord's Anointed. That also means obeying the will of the Lord as set down in the tablets of stone upon the mountain in the wilderness. On them the Most High said, 'Thou shalt have no other gods before me,' but I still let Jezebel bring in the worship of Ashtoreth and Baal and allowed sacrifices to them in the High Places of the land. For this great sin, Elijah cursed me with death, and now it is too late to undo the harm I have done."

"Micaiah did not say you would die at Ramoth-Gilead. Neither did Elijah."

"Death will come when the Lord wills, but I do not think it will be much longer before Elijah's prophecy is fulfilled. The burden of my guilt condemns me and I must set my house in order. That is where you can help me."

"Ask whatever you will."

"Ahaziah is growing into a fine young man, largely

257

because of what you, Miriam, and Naboth taught him and the influence of your father while he was in Jerusalem. He alone among my sons is fit to rule Israel after me, but unless he is supported by powerful forces he will never be able to take the throne."

"You talk as if you were already dead," Michael protested.

"I really died the day Elijah put the curse upon me at Megiddo," Ahab said somberly. "The only thing that remains before the memory of Ahab begins to fade from the face of the earth is for the dogs to lick my blood in the Pool of Samaria as he predicted. The most I can do for my people now is to be sure they will have a just ruler after me. For that I am depending upon you and your father."

"We will carry out your orders," Michael assured him. "Whether you die tomorrow or twenty years from now."

"It may not be easy," Ahab warned. "Jezebel wants Joram to reign after me, so what is done must be done swiftly—and ruthlessly. You will be opposing people who are more ruthless than you can ever be."

Michael knew that what Ahab said was true. And yet he could not help wondering whether he would have the strength to destroy Jezebel, if it came to a final struggle between them.

"I know Jezebel once sought to bewitch you, Michael, as she has bewitched many another," Ahab continued, almost as if he had been reading the younger man's thoughts. "But I am counting upon you to be stronger than she is. If you fail, Israel will be torn by a religious conflict between the followers of Yahweh and Baal and the country will be left prostrate with the heel of Assyria upon its neck. Hadad-Ezer would never be able to stand alone against Shalmaneser, and all of Canaan would become subject to Nineveh."

258

"But would the people of Israel follow my father and me without question?"

"They will follow Ahaziah—if he is backed by strength. The army will obey you because they already know you as a great leader in battle."

"My father gave you our answer at Samaria," Michael told him simply. "We are as you are, our people as your people, our horses as your horses."

"I still want your personal oath to me that you will let nothing stop you in putting Ahaziah upon the throne of Israel," Ahab insisted. "Swear by the God we both worship and I will be content."

"I swear in the name of Yahweh," Michael said. "It is the least I can do for one to whom I owe my life."

"Tomorrow I will have a scribe draw up a decree, naming Ahaziah as my successor with you and Jehoshaphat as joint regents," Ahab told him. "That will give you the authority you need to use the army in enforcing my decision."

Michael got to his feet. "I still say you have no assurance the curse will destroy you during the coming battle. If I did I would insist that you not go into it."

"Ramoth-Gilead was a part of Israel when I inherited the throne from my father," Ahab reminded him. "I cannot die and leave it unrestored, so I must fight and face whatever fate awaits me."

"Hadad-Ezer is sure to tell his men to seek you out when the battle begins."

"That, too, is a risk I must take."

"Then go into battle wearing simple armor, like any other officer," Michael pleaded. "If you wear no insignia of royalty, even those ordered to kill you will not be able to find you out in the heat of the battle."

Ahab's face brightened a little at the suggestion. "It is a wise precaution," he said. "My own men know me, so nothing will be lost."

Chapter 21

HAD HE BEEN ABLE TO SELECT THE GROUND FOR THE
battle to regain Ramoth-Gilead, Michael would have
chosen other than the shallow valley before the city,
with the necessity of crossing a stream and storming
the massed ranks of the defenders drawn up before
the wall. But Hadad-Ezer's commanders had selected
the field and Ahab had no choice except to fight there,
or give up the attack.

On his way to take command of the right flank
where, under Jehu as captain, the horsemen of Judah
waited, Michael stopped by the tent where he and
Ahab had talked the night before. As he had expected,
the king had already left to inspect the battle lines
before giving the order to attack the ranks of the Syrian forces, a custom he rigidly carried out before
every battle. He had taken Michael's suggestion, however, and the highly polished royal armor Ahab usually
wore in battle now hung upon its rack in the corner
of the tent.

"Come and help me arm," Michael called to Aaron,
who rode just behind him.

"You are already armed, master," the servant protested.

Michael was removing his gear, unbuckling the strap that held it in place. "Hurry," he said. "We have no time to lose."

Aaron dismounted and helped Michael put on Ahab's armor. It was a little large but not enough to interfere with his movements. In the heat of battle, with the plumed helmet partially hiding his face, he was sure the enemy would not be able to tell that he was not the Israelite king.

"You must be mad, master," Aaron grumbled as he was buckling the last greave into place. "The enemy always tries to cut down the leaders in battle."

"I intend to draw their attack," Michael explained as he mounted his horse once again. He had retained his own spear and sword, since he was accustomed to their feel and weight in battle. "King Ahab believes the curse of Elijah will strike him down today."

"Would you divert the curse to yourself?"

"If the Most High plans to destroy Ahab and fulfill Elijah's curse, he will surely know who is wearing the king's armor. I am counting only on deluding the Syrians."

Aaron struck his head with his hand in an eloquent gesture. "Truly I have a fool for a master," he said. "To risk your life to save another, even one so important as the king of Israel, is madness."

"Stay away from me," Michael warned. "Else they may strike you down when they attack me."

Aaron shook his head dourly. "One of us at least has to be sensible," he said. "I will ride just behind to guard you and I will tell my lord Jehu to send horsemen to protect you from your own folly."

"That might be wise," Michael agreed. "I only want to be mistaken for King Ahab, not to fight the whole Syrian army alone."

Michael and Aaron had barely reached their place in the battle line when Ahab ordered the trumpets to sound the attack. The line moved forward as it had before Karkar, the chariots in front with the horse and the foot men behind, ready to send a hail of arrows over the heads of the front ranks. They splashed through the shallow stream without event and began to move up the slope toward the waiting Syrian forces. Even from his elevated position on horseback, Michael could see no sign of Hadad-Ezer and judged that the corpulent king of Syria was keeping behind the wall of Ramoth-Gilead, where he would be in no danger during the battle.

King Jehoshaphat was riding in a chariot in the van of the right wing where Michael commanded, but Michael spurred his own horse forward to the front lines so that his polished silver harness and armor, gleaming in the morning sunlight, would be immediately visible to the enemy. At the sight of him, a shout went up from the ranks of the Syrians across the narrow stretch of greensward.

"It is Ahab!" an enemy officer cried. "A bounty awaits him who kills the Israelite king."

Ahab had been right, Michael realized. Hadad-Ezer had indeed singled him out for destruction as he expected, which made it all the more important that Ahab maintain the anonymity given him by not wearing his royal arms.

Jehu spurred up beside Michael. "Aaron says you are deliberately drawing their attack to save Ahab. I can't believe he would let you risk your life that way."

"Ahab doesn't know I took his armor," Michael explained. "The battle will be engaged before he can do anything about it."

"I shall not wait idly for you to be killed, even though you probably deserve it for being such a fool." Jehu turned and rode down the line, shouting orders as he went. Immediately a squadron of ten horsemen wheeled out of their place and came to surround Michael.

"Keep the front clear," Michael told the officer in charge. "I want the enemy to see me."

The officer gave the order and those assigned to guard Michael quickly formed a square with one side open, facing the enemy troops. The order was barely executed before the two lines met in a tremendous clash of metal and the fighting began. For a while Michael had no time to wonder what Ahab or anyone else was doing, for the spearhead of the enemy attack upon the flank he commanded was launched directly at the area where he was fighting. He and the ten men assigned to guard him fought like demons and finally blunted the attack, but the ranks of his guards were very much thinner when, during the first lull of the battle, they drew back to regain their breath.

Michael did not know Ahab was near until the square suddenly opened to admit the king's chariot.

"Jehu told me just now why you took my armor, Michael," Ahab said. "You did not need to expose yourself so freely just to save me."

Michael smiled wearily. "We are even now. Besides, it was a good move. In trying to win the bounty by killing me, the Syrians took chances. You can see how many are piled up there before the place where we were fighting." Then his face sobered. "How does the battle go? I was so busy here I could not tell."

"We won the first skirmish, but the second is about to begin. Take care of yourself and keep these guards about you." At Ahab's order, the guards surrounded Michael once more, after making an opening in the line so the chariot could pass through and return to the center, where Israel's king had established his post of command.

Ahab had been right about the beginning of the second part of the engagement. The fighting was quickly renewed around Michael, keeping him busy jabbing and thrusting at a constant stream of the enemy who sought to attack him and win the reward. The horsemen assigned to his defense were being cut down one by one, but Michael did not turn back. Then suddenly a horse went down just in front of him and he saw something he had not faced so far in the battle.

It was a bowman, standing not ten paces away, his bowstring already drawn and the arrow aimed at Michael's body at point-blank range. Driven by the full power of the bowstring and traveling such a short distance, the iron-pointed arrow could easily penetrate Michael's armor and inflict a fatal wound. In the emergency he acted instinctively, doing the only thing left to him in such a desperate situation. His spear was in his hand and—without taking time to draw it back—he hurled the weapon directly at the bowman.

The spear struck the enemy in the chest, just below the right shoulder, the point driving deep into his body. Mortally wounded, the man was toppled back by the force of the impact and, as he started to fall, his nerveless right hand loosened the drawn bowstring.

Since the bowman was already falling backward, the arrow cleared Michael's head in an arching path. As it rose, some impulse he could not name made him twist in his saddle to follow its flight. Rising in a long arc, the arrow flew over the heads of the troops toward the center of the line and then began to descend. But even before it struck, Michael was sure of the target toward which the missile had been sent winging by the dying hand of the enemy bowman.

It was Ahab!

Wheeling his horse through the line, Michael rode rapidly to where Ahab's chariot driver had brought the vehicle to a halt. The arrow had struck the king above the shoulder, in an unprotected area between the upper rim of his corselet, or chest piece, and the lower part of the helmet, which did not extend quite close enough to the chest to afford complete protection for the lower part of his neck.

Ahab was in the act of pulling out the arrow point when Michael arrived. His face was white with pain, but when Michael started to dismount and help him he waved him away. "Go back to the troops," he ordered. "It is only a small wound."

"There may be bleeding; you should go to the physicians at the back of the line."

"My driver here will staunch the flow. Take command in my place. I will stay on the field lest our forces think I have been killed."

Michael rode away and was immediately occupied with his duties as the battle seesawed back and forth. He had no opportunity during the rest of the afternoon to see how Ahab was faring but could not rid himself of the premonition that all was not well with the Israelite king.

The fact that an arrow launched by chance from a bow in the hands of a dying man had chosen the king of Israel as its target somehow seemed to be more than a happenstance and Michael could not help believing it was actually the working out of the curse Elijah had put upon Ahab. And yet, as he had reminded Micaiah in Samaria, the words Elijah had used seemed to indicate that the dogs would lick the blood of Ahab in the Pool of Samaria, not here before Ramoth-Gilead far to the east.

It was almost dark and the forces of Hadad-Ezer had been driven to the very walls of the city, when Michael heard a dread cry behind him.

"King Ahab is dead!" the shout arose. "Every man to his city and every man to his own country!"

The cry was taken up at once by a thousand voices. When Michael wheeled his horse and rode back through the lines to where Ahab's chariot had stood during most of the fighting, he saw the fear of the curse that had found Ahab out even here, far away from Samaria, already beginning to show in the eyes of the men.

He could do nothing for Ahab, Michael saw as soon as he dismounted. The king had somehow managed to remain upright through the afternoon while blood seeped from his wound and dripped beneath his armor to form a pool upon the floor of the chariot in which he was standing. Michael could imagine what fortitude it had taken for Ahab to hold himself erect, even while dying, and knew he had been driven by the need to encourage the army with his presence during the close battle and assure them that no curse could stop their victory at Ramoth-Gilead.

Now, with Ahab dead, the chill grip of terror in the face of something they could neither see nor understand was settling upon the hearts of the fighting men. The conviction of defeat by a supernatural force could easily turn them—tired, wounded, and worn out from the day's conflict—into a fleeing rabble, destroying everything that had been accomplished by the day's battle and through Ahab's dying act of courage in remaining upon the field.

"Men of Judah, keep your places!" Michael shouted to his own troops as he rode along the lines. He saw his father's chariot with Jehoshaphat standing upright in it and, pulling up momentarily beside it. quickly told the king of Judah what had happened.

"If Judah holds firm, we may yet save the day," Michael urged. "Take command here at this end of the line while I rally the forces of Israel. Most of them know me from the battle of Karkar."

The fighting had almost stopped and if he could possibly keep the army intact for another day, Michael knew, Hadad-Ezer's troops would have to withdraw from Ramoth-Gilead because the fortifications of the

266

city were not strong enough to allow them to defend it. But unless he could stave off the wave of terror that had swept over the men of Israel at the realization that Ahab was dead as Elijah had predicted, all they had fought for that day would be lost.

As he rode through the ranks of the Israelite army, Michael picked out officers he knew and spoke directly to them by name. He told them the truth—that Ahab had been wounded in the course of battle, an event that could happen to anyone, and had died from loss of blood because he insisted upon remaining in his chariot so the battle would proceed. Instructing each one to rally the forces under his command and keep them intact while massing them beside the army of Judah which his father and Jehu commanded, Michael moved along the whole length of the line. Then, turning, he rode back behind it, driving forward any stragglers he saw trying to leave the ranks.

When he heard the commanders to whom he had spoken shouting to their troops and saw the line begin to stiffen in the center and upon the left where the Israelite forces had been stationed, Michael knew Ahab had not died in vain and the incipient rout had been stopped, for a while at least. By nightfall, the army had gone into bivouac between the river and the walls of Ramoth-Gilead. Only then could Michael draw a deep sigh of relief at the assurance that, barring any other complications, the day appeared to have been saved.

While they ate the evening meal of meat and bread brought to the front by men sent to forage behind the lines, Michael, Jehoshaphat, and Jehu conferred with Rakkon and some of the other leading members of Ahab's officer corps concerning what should be done.

A disquieting piece of news was brought by one of Ahab's officers, who reported that most of the Hittite mercenaries who had been with his section had broken ranks and ridden westward as soon as word of Ahab's death was announced. Knowing that the troops left to garrison Samaria were composed largely of these same Hittite mercenaries, Michael did not doubt that they had gone to report to Jezebel the death of Israel's king and to bargain with her for their services at a price higher than Ahab had been paying them. Such a custom was almost universal among mercenary troops and Michael did not doubt that this explanation suited the present situation. His face was grave as he spoke to the officers gathered around the campfire just back of the lines.

"King Ahab had a premonition that he would die today," Michael told them. "Only this morning he issued a decree naming Prince Ahaziah king in his stead in case he was killed during the battle. My father and I are named regents in the decree to insure that Prince Ahaziah takes the throne."

"He will have to wrest it from Queen Jezebel and her son Joram," Rakkon said. "The mercenaries who fled are in the pay of Hamul. They will tell what has happened here long before we can reach Samaria."

"You must go to the capital at once, Michael," Jehoshaphat said. "Prince Ahaziah will be in danger as soon as the mercenaries reach there with word of Ahab's death."

"It is the only way to save the young prince," Rakkon agreed.

Michael knew the advice was sound. Yet they must hold here, too, else all they had gained would be lost.

"How many troops will be needed to hold before Ramoth-Gilead, father?" he asked.

"The forces of Israel and half those from Judah should be enough."

"Then Jehu and I will leave for Samaria with a

268

troop of horses and chariots tomorrow morning," Michael said.

"What of King Ahab's body?" Rakkon asked.

"It must go to Samaria with us," Michael said. "Else Jezebel may claim he is still alive and refuse to honor our commission to name Ahaziah king."

"You can cover the bier and bind it across Ahab's own chariot," Rakkon agreed. "Ahab's chariot horses are the fastest in Israel."

"Before you go we should read the decree naming Prince Ahaziah king to the armies and have them swear allegiance to him," Jehoshaphat suggested. "In that way, we will have forestalled Jezebel if she seeks to divide the country through the army."

It was a wise move and they decided to adopt it, even though it meant a delay of an hour or more in the morning. At dawn, the trumpets blew for the army to assemble. From Ramoth-Gilead there was no sign of any enemy action and the pickets Michael had posted reported that most of the Syrian troops had withdrawn from the city during the night, leaving it largely undefended. With such evidence of Hadad-Ezer's lack of intention to reinforce Ramoth-Gilead, Michael felt quite safe in taking a sizable number of horsemen and chariots with him on the trip to Samaria.

Before the assembled armies, King Jehoshaphat mounted a platform erected upon two chariots and read the decree by Ahab naming Ahaziah as his heir in case of his death.

"Men of Israel," he said when the reading was finished, "your king gave his life here yesterday that this territory might be restored to our land. As king of Judah, I hereby swear allegiance for myself and all my people to King Ahaziah of Israel. And I call upon all of you in tribute to the memory of your great King Ahab to swear with me."

With one voice the massed ranks of men repeated

the oath of allegiance to Ahaziah as the new king of Israel. And with the ceremony of swearing allegiance completed, Michael and Jehu started westward toward the Jordan with a thousand horsemen and five hundred chariots. Just behind the leaders, the body of the fallen king rode upon a bier lashed to his chariot. It, in turn, was drawn by Ahab's own fiery team with his personal driver at the reins.

Three days later, shortly after noon, the funeral procession reached the gate of Samaria. Their march westward had been unopposed, and Michael dared to hope his forebodings might not be correct and that Ahaziah would be accepted as king in Samaria without question.

A considerable portion of the population of the capital city had gathered outside the walls when word reached Samaria that the funeral cortege of King Ahab was approaching. Michael had been half expecting Jezebel to deny them entrance through the main gate of the city, but she made no move to bar the procession as it filed through. Joash, the governor of the city, met them at the gate with the information that the queen desired the body to be taken to the old palace of Omri.

Included within the ancient defensive wall of the town, the palace of Omri was still outside the powerful fortifications built by Ahab around the newer palace, of which the tower erected by him as a place of last defense was the most prominent feature. The broad courtyard and pool separated the two structures.

Michael had been informed by Joash that it was Jezebel's wish for his troops to be quartered outside the city so the sound of martial activities and the sight of men in uniform would not disturb her grief over the death of the king. Privately he was sure the reasons given were not the actual ones, but since the spies he sent to learn of activities inside the royal palace reported that Ahaziah was alive and well, he made no move to proclaim the young prince king until after his father was buried in the tomb. He did, however, take the precaution of investing the main gate of the city—so there would be no question of Jezebel's being able to shut it against him later on—and of moving his own headquarters into the old palace of Omri.

The following day Ahab was laid to rest beside his father Omri in a cave sepulcher located in the side of a hill overlooking the surrounding countryside. Heavily veiled, Jezebel appeared and walked behind the coffin until it was properly interred with the usual ceremonies. Of Ahaziah there was no sign and only her own son Joram walked beside her, wearing regal robes and a crown. To Michael, all this was a portent of trouble to come, but he still sought to avoid a clash with Jezebel which might result in further danger to Ahaziah.

The day after the funeral, Michael made a formal request through Joash for an audience with Jezebel and the Council of Elders, in order to present them Ahab's will concerning the succession of the kingdom. The governor of the city put him off again, however, on the grounds that the queen was distraught from grief. And when he demanded to see Ahaziah, that request, too, was refused by Joash in her name.

"Obviously she intends to displace Ahaziah and not let him assume the throne," Jehu said grimly when the conference with Joash ended.

"There's not much question of it now," Michael admitted. "I held off hoping to free Ahaziah or at least insure his safety. Perhaps I made a mistake in delaying so long."

"One of our spies reported to me as I was leaving to come here," Jehu told him. "I hate to bring you bad news, Micheal, but Ahaziah is not the only one in danger. Miriam is inside those walls, too."

"But that is impossible! She is in Jerusalem."

271

"Not any more. Jezebel somehow lured her here, probably with a message pretending to be from you. She is holding them both as hostages."

Michael went to the door of the large room in Omri's old palace that now served as his headquarters. The grim walls of Ahab's palace fortress were plainly visible only a few hundred paces away across the courtyard from the main gate. Ever since he had found Ahab dead in his chariot on the battlefield before Ramoth-Gilead, Michael had been oppressed by an ominous feeling that the death of the Israelite king was only the first in a series of connected events and that perhaps the worst was yet to come. Now he knew his misgivings had been all too true, for with Miriam a prisoner of Jezebel within those walls, everything he held dear in life was in the balance.

It would be simple to make a bargain with Jezebel, he knew—the bargain she was no doubt expecting to drive when he raised the question of Ahab's successor. Nor did he doubt that she would gladly exchange Miriam's life in return for naming her own son Joram as king of Israel, with herself as regent. But Jezebel was far too clever, and unscrupulous, to allow Ahaziah to go free also to form a rival government with the support of Judah. Thus, though he could have Miriam with such a bargain, Michael knew he would doom the lawful king of Israel at the same time.

He had sworn to Ahab the most sacred oath a worshiper of the Most High could swear—that he would not rest until Ahaziah was secure upon the throne of Israel. Anything less would be a betrayal not only of his oath to Ahab, but of his obligation to God himself. For with Jezebel ruling Israel, the worship of Yahweh would soon be stamped out and that of Baal and Ashtoreth substituted in its place.

"What are you going to do?" Jehu asked.

Michael turned toward him, his face bleak with pain. "Jezebel must be destroyed."

"What of Miriam and Ahaziah?"

"If we can save them, we will!"

"And if we cannot?"

"Miriam will understand, even though it is my own hand that sends her to her death."

"Storming the citadel will not be an easy task," Jehu warned. "We can only approach from one side, toward the main gate of Samaria. The other side of the fortifications, where the tower stands, is set upon solid rock with a sheer drop to the small area at the base where Jezebel has her dogs on guard."

"Is there no possibility of killing the dogs and scaling that part of the wall?"

Jehu shook his head. "Even if we silenced the dogs, a few bowmen on top of the tower could pick our men off before they got halfway up the side of the cliff."

"Then we must make a frontal assault upon the main fortifications of Ahab's palace."

"Without machines of war such as the Assyrians used at Karkar, that is impossible, too," Jehu said flatly. "Jezebel is in the most favorable position possible. By posting her mercenaries along the walls of the palace, she can shoot us down before we make contact with her forces."

"Shall we starve her out then?" He knew very well who Jezebel would allow to die first.

"I imagine she foresaw this possibility, too, and laid in a large supply of food. As for water, a well inside the palace runs straight down through the rock and forms a plenteous supply."

"Then we must take it somehow by a trick."

"My spies have searched for some weakness in the fortifications; they found none."

"Keep them at it," Michael instructed him. "And call all our forces together at once. We will present an

273

official demand that Ahaziah be elevated to the throne and see what answer Jezebel will give."

Michael put on his most splendid uniform while Jehu was marshaling the horsemen and charioteers they had brought from Ramoth-Gilead. As he was crossing the open area in front of the palace of Omri, he skirted the edge of the large pool that occupied a portion of the courtyard. A chariot was being washed at one side of the pool and a pack of curs were growling about it, eagerly licking up the bloodstained water that dripped from the vehicle. In his preoccupation with the task of trying to discover some way to save Miriam and Ahaziah, Michael would have passed by without noticing, until Aaron spoke.

"Look, master!" he cried. "At the chariot there."

Michael glanced at the chariot but could only see that the driver was washing it in the pool, kicking aside the curs that tried to drink the blood-tinged water flowing from it. "What is so unusual about a chariot being washed—"

He stopped with the question unfinished, for this was no ordinary chariot. It was the royal vehicle of Ahab. And the blood staining the water running from it as the driver scrubbed the floor could only be Ahab's. Michael remembered noticing how the blood had puddled upon the floor and dried while Ahab had stood that whole afternoon before Ramoth-Gilead, holding himself upright in his chariot so his army could see that he still led them and be encouraged to keep up the battle.

"The prophecy of Elijah is fulfilled," Michael said in an awestruck voice. "The dogs are licking the blood of Ahab in the Pool of Samaria."

"Let us pray the rest of it will follow," Aaron said. "But it is a long way to Jezreel and the curs that must eat the flesh of Jezebel by the wall before we can be rid of her."

Chapter 22

HEAVILY ARMED HITTITE MERCENARIES LOOKED DOWN from the protected tower above the gate of Ahab's palace as Michael came to a stop before it. Behind him his troops were massed rank on rank, with the people of Samaria on every side, watching the tense drama taking place in the courtyard.

Signaling the herald to blow a blast upon his trumpet, Michael stepped out in front of the troops and unrolled a small scroll upon which Ahab's decree naming Ahaziah king in his stead had been written.

"Let Joash, Governor of Samaria, and all who pledged fealty to Ahab, their king, hear the words of his royal will recorded in the presence of witnesses before the city of Ramoth-Gilead prior to his death," Michael announced.

He paused a moment and then read from the scroll:

"I, Ahab, son of Omri, by the grace of the Most High God, King of Israel and Judah, do hereby name my son, Ahaziah, as my heir, to rule in my place after my death. I further designate Prince Michael of Judah and King Jehoshaphat, his father, as regents to advise my son, Ahaziah, together with

the Council of Elders of Israel who sit in the city of Samaria. Let no person oppose this will under pain of death."

Michael rolled up the decree and handed it to Jehu, who stood just behind him. "People of Samaria, you have heard the will of your King Ahab," he said. "By the authority of this decree, I proclaim Ahaziah king in Israel."

A shout went up from the crowd, for Ahaziah was very much liked in Samaria. But there were murmurs of uneasiness, too, for it was common knowledge by now that Jezebel intended to defy the will of her husband.

"I call upon Joash, as Governor of Samaria," Michael continued. "Let him bring out the new king, so he may be crowned and may bless his people."

All eyes were raised to the place atop the gate where Joash, a weak-willed, corpulent man known to be under Jezebel's thumb, stood with the mercenaries behind him.

"What is your reply, O Joash?" Michael repeated.

He saw the governor draw back and was not surprised to see the stocky body and handsome scowling visage of Hamul behind him, talking earnestly. They conferred for several moments, then Joash stepped forward again.

"With King Ahab dead and no ruler in Israel," the governor quavered, "the decision as to who will succeed to the throne must rest with the queen and the Council of Elders."

"Where is the Council?" Michael demanded.

"They are in the palace, consulting with Queen Jezebel."

Beside Michael, Jehu muttered, "That is why we were never able to find any of them. Even their families have gone into hiding. No doubt they were warned by

Jezebel that they, too, will be killed unless they obey her will."

"The decree of succession set down by King Ahab before his death takes precedence over any other decision concerning who will reign in Israel," Michael told Joash. "As regent in the name of King Ahaziah, I give you the space of one day to deliver this city and all in it over to the new king."

Michael had been half expecting Joash to defy him then and there. To his surprise, however, the governor said, "You will receive my decision before tomorrow's dawn, Prince Michael. I must first consult with the queen and the Council of Elders."

Michael turned and went back to the line of horsemen and charioteers drawn up before the palace. "Set men to watch the palace everywhere," he warned Jehu. "I am sure they plan some trickery."

"Ahaziah must still be alive. Perhaps they hope to use him as a lever to force concessions from you."

"Keep the men within the city, and allow no exit from the palace. We will hold it under siege until we receive word from Joash."

"Or bury Prince Ahaziah beside his father." Jehu's face was grave. "If we could only storm that gate somehow, the field would be ours. Once in the palace we could easily defeat the mercenaries that guard Jezebel."

"As you say, they could cut us down before we could even reach the gate," Michael reminded him. "It would be futile to try."

"It is like the battle of Karkar," Jehu agreed. "Neither side can win a decisive victory."

"But we can lose without an arrow being fired if Jezebel destroys Ahaziah," Michael said soberly. He was turning toward his quarters when his gaze fell upon Ahab's chariot. Scrubbed free of the bloodstains, it now stood in the sunlight before the palace of Omri.

"Jehu," he said, excitement raising the pitch of his

voice. "We have overlooked the most important thing."

"What?"

"The curse of Elijah. Only part of it was fulfilled when the dogs licked the blood of Ahab at the Pool of Samaria. Jezebel's fate is yet to come."

"It is a slender prop," Jehu said doubtfully.

"But our only one. If only Micaiah were here to tell us the will of God."

"He is still a prisoner. Remember Ahab ordered him held while we carried out the attack upon Ramoth-Gilead."

"And Elijah is too far away to help us. This is a bad day for Israel—and for me."

Michael was eating the evening meal when Jehu appeared at the doorway. The captain's eyes were blazing with anger, and when he stepped aside to allow the men behind him to enter with the burden they were carrying, Michael saw the reason. He would have recognized the golden beard of Micaiah anywhere, even though stained and clotted now with blood.

"Jezebel has sent you her answer, Michael," Jehu said grimly. "Micaiah was thrown from the topmost tower of the palace a little while ago. We picked him up and brought him here."

"Is he still alive?"

"Barely."

The priest's body had been cruelly broken by the fall from the top of the tower to the stone pavement. Blood trickled from one side of his mouth and his breathing was shallow and hurried.

Michael knelt beside his friend, lifting his head gently as he held a cup of wine to the priest's lips. Micaiah managed to swallow a little of it and the stimulant seemed to strengthen him somewhat, for he opened his eyes and tried to speak. A spasm of coughing interrupted the words, however, and a fresh trickle of blood at the side of his mouth verified Michael's

278

suspicion that the stones upon which Micaiah had fallen had crushed his chest as well as other parts of his body.

"Don't try to talk," Michael advised him. "We will have a physician here in a moment to take care of you."

"No physician can help me now," Micaiah managed to gasp.

"Why did they throw you down?"

"I am Jezebel's answer to your demands," Micaiah told him between fits of coughing. "She has declared Joram king and the Council of Elders has approved."

"At the point of a sword no doubt," Jehu growled.

"She threatened them and their families with death if they did not agree."

"What of Ahaziah?" Michael asked. "And Miriam?"

"They are both still alive. As soon as you left Samaria for Ramoth-Gilead, Jezebel sent word to Miriam at Jerusalem saying you were gravely ill here. She hurried to Samaria and Jezebel imprisoned her immediately."

"Then the queen has plans to kill them both."

"I was to bring you that message," Micaiah confirmed. A spasm of coughing left him unable to continue for a moment. His breathing was much more hurried, being little more now than gasps between which blood gushed from his mouth, but he struggled to finish the message he had brought.

"Jezebel says you can only save Ahaziah and Miriam by tearing up the decree of Ahab and naming Joram king," Micaiah managed to say between the spasms that racked his broken body. "If you do this, she will let Ahaziah and Miriam return to Jerusalem with you."

"We already know how much her word is worth," Jehu objected. "Tear up the decree of Ahab, and you have no proof except your own words that he ever named Ahaziah to succeed him. Jezebel can then destroy the boy and Miriam in the name of Joram as king."

Michael knew Jehu spoke the truth; to Jezebel, Miriam was of no importance, except as an additional means of winning the concessions she desired. And Ahaziah alive would always be a threat to the rule of herself and her son, so she could hardly afford to let him live, whatever bargain Michael offered to make.

Micaiah echoed that thought. "If you try to storm the gates, she promises to kill both of them at once."

"And if we do not, both will die anyway." It was a bitter choice that was actually no choice at all.

"Why not pretend to agree to Jezebel's wishes and withdraw from Samaria?" Jehu suggested. "When King Jehoshaphat returns with the army from Ramoth-Gilead, we can storm the city and destroy the queen and her get. The army has heard the decree read before them; they will support you in proclaiming Ahaziah king."

"By then Ahaziah will be dead," Michael reminded him. "And Miriam with him."

Micaiah had apparently drifted into unconsciousness, for his eyes were closed. He was barely breathing and death was evidently only a few moments away. "At least we can let him die in peace," Michael said. "Say no more of this for the moment, Jehu."

To Michael's surprise, however, Micaiah opened his eyes once again. When he spoke, the words were barely a whisper and they had to lean close to understand them.

"I know a way to enter Ahab's palace secretly," the priest said. "A tunnel from a space under the courtyard leads into the inner part of the palace. Use it, if you would ever see Miriam and Ahaziah again alive."

The effort of speaking had taken the remainder of Micaiah's strength. His mouth went suddenly slack in death and his head rolled to one side. Michael stood looking down at him for a moment, remembering the day he had first seen the priest on the road to Jerusalem laying about him bravely against the robbers with a cudgel. Now he was dead and, unless Michael himself acted quickly, Miriam, whom he had first met and come to love that same day, would be dead too.

"Separate fifty men for me," he told Jehu. "We will try to get to the palace tonight and rescue Ahaziah and Miriam."

"Let me lead the party," Jehu begged.

Michael knew what was in his lieutenant's mind—the possibility that the fascination Jezebel held for him might make him spare her at the last moment. But he could not let anyone go in his stead on what could easily be a fatal errand. Unless the passage Micaiah had described was a large one—and that was hard to believe—they would be lucky to get the fifty men into the palace. And even then they must manage somehow to open the great gates to the inner court defended by the tower, or be cut to pieces by the Hittite mercenaries who, according to Jehu's informers, numbered several hundred men.

"This is my task," Michael said firmly. "Hold the rest of your men ready to attack as soon as we open the gate from within. But keep them quiet; we don't want the defenders to know what we are doing."

"How will you find the chamber Micaiah referred to?"

"I don't know. But find it we must, at all costs."

From the window of his chamber in the palace of Omri, Michael could see the stone slabs that made up the pavement of the courtyard. They appeared to be solidly sealed, indicating that they rested upon the rock which formed a foundation for the palace. The only chance that Micaiah could have been right about a chamber or passage beneath one or more of them, he decided, was that, when leveling the foundations of the city and the palace which crowned it, the workmen

281

had opened into a cave such as pocked the hillsides in the surrounding area.

He considered what might be the quickest way to discover the location of such an opening beneath the pavestones without chipping through the stone slabs or taking them up, a task that not only would take a great deal of time but would inevitably attract the attention of Jezebel's guards upon the palace tower. And then he thought of a simple maneuver for the first try. A rock not seated securely upon its base would move under a man's weight; if he could find such a stone in the courtyard, it might lead him to the passage. Suiting action to words, he left the palace and went outside.

"Walk beside me," Michael told Aaron, who had followed him out into the courtyard. "If you feel a stone move, speak at once."

Aaron caught his meaning immediately. Side by side, they began to pace the length of the courtyard, accommodating their steps so that their feet struck the stones at the same time. Once across the court they marched, and back, without detecting any movement.

"Are you sure of this?" Aaron asked in a low voice so the guards upon the tower by the main gate would not overhear. "After all the priest was dying when he spoke of the chamber."

"It is our only chance," Michael said grimly. "Keep walking."

Once more they moved across the court and back. By now they had covered half the stone-paved space and Michael's hopes were beginning to plummet. Then, on the third trip back, near the wall of Omri's palace, Michael felt a stone move beneath his feet. He did not speak at once, but waited to see whether Aaron had detected the same thing.

"Step back one pace, master," the servant said. "I believe one of them shifted."

They moved back and again felt the unmistakable

shifting of the stone slab beneath their feet, followed by a faint thud when they removed their weight and it fell back into place.

"Find Jehu and bring a lamp with something we can use to pry up the stone."

When Aaron was gone, Michael remained standing upon the stone so they would not lose its location in the darkness. Setting his feet apart, he rocked back and forth and felt a thrill surge through him when the slab unmistakably moved again beneath his weight. Best of all, it was located behind a corner of the older palace, outside the line of vision of the guards on the main tower.

Jehu and Aaron emerged from the darkness in the shadow of the palace wall a few moments later, followed by a line of men. The servant carried a short stave that could be used to pry up the stone and Jehu a long piece of iron. Several of the soldiers behind them carried burning lamps but, at Michael's whispered order, they remained in the shadow of the wall, well hidden from view.

Kneeling beside the loose stone, Michael worked the end of the iron bar into the crack separating it from the next slab and raised the edge gently. On the first try it slipped a little and fell away from the end of the metal bar, opening a space into which he was able to push the end of the lever a little deeper on the second try. This time the stone came up and they were able to insert the timber beneath it. With this additional leverage, they had no trouble in prying up the slab and slipping it to one side.

While the men grouped about him to shield the light from view, Michael lowered a lamp into the cavity revealed by the rectangular opening where the paving stone had lain. A small chamber in the solid rock was revealed, hardly large enough to allow two men to sit side by side. Opening into it from the direction of

283

Ahab's palace was what appeared to be a low-roofed tunnel or passage running through the foundations of the court and the buildings nearby.

Dropping into the small chamber, Michael held the lamp so he could see into the narrow passageway. He could tell nothing, however, except that it appeared to lead away from where he stood and was at least large enough to allow a man to travel through by crawling upon his hands and knees.

"I'd hate to be trapped in there," Jehu said at his shoulder, echoing Michael's own thoughts.

"It's a chance we must take," Michael said. "Micaiah was no doubt right about it leading into the palace. Once we get inside, perhaps we can cause enough confusion to get the gate open and allow you to enter with the rest of the troops."

Reaching inside the passageway, Michael set the lamp on the floor ahead of him and crawled into it. By moving the small lamp forward, he was able to make fairly good progress through the tunnel. It did not appear to have been used for some time. Nor did it grow smaller as he moved away from the entrance chamber, by which he judged that Micaiah had been correct in saying that the passage was open all the way into Ahab's palace. Behind him as he crawled, he could hear Aaron's breathing, the scraping of the iron bar he dragged with him, and the whispered injunctions of the men who followed.

For what seemed an eternity, Michael moved along the narrow passage. He was unable to tell which way they were going, for it changed directions several times in order to take advantage of softer areas in the rock from which it had originally been dug.

Michael's knees were bleeding from the rough stone chips lining the bottom of the passage, and each forward movement brought more pain. Nevertheless he managed to keep a mental count of the steps, so to speak, that he had taken upon his hands and knees. And by estimating the distance covered by each of them, he was able to calculate that they must already be under the newer palace of Ahab. Finally, when he lifted the small lamp to move it farther ahead, he saw what appeared to be an obstruction several paces in front of where he was crouching.

Passing a whispered command back to the others to wait, Michael moved forward carefully until he could touch the barrier. It appeared to be made of wood and, when he held the small lamp up, he could see that it had apparently been placed across the end of the tunnel at a point where the latter opened into a larger space of some kind.

"I am going to try to break through," Michael whispered to Aaron, who was just behind him. "If I am attacked when I open the barrier, it will mean they have discovered what we are doing and we will have no chance of succeeding. The rest of you return to the courtyard as quickly as you can and let Jehu know what happened."

Before Aaron could protest, Michael set the end of the bar between the edge of the rock at the end of the tunnel and shoved down, working the metal between the rocky wall and the wood. To his surprise, the barrier moved very easily and he decided that it was only a piece of furniture which had been pressed against the opening to hide it. Placing the bar upon the other side, he pried again and felt it move out farther. When he held up the lamp, he could see it was, as he had guessed, a heavy chair, and had no trouble in moving it forward and clearing the opening.

They found themselves in what appeared to be a storage chamber, and brief exploration revealed that several caves had been opened into during the course of constructing the newer palace. These had been utilized as storage space for furniture—perhaps that which was no longer needed when Jezebel had brought with her from Phoenicia the carved ivory pieces that had caused the people to name the building the "Palace of Ivory."

Moving carefully, stirring up clouds of dust indicating that the passageway had not been used for years, Michael explored the rooms and was delighted to find a stairway leading to the upper level. As they moved along the corridor into which the stairway opened, the odor of food grew stronger and stronger.

"We were lucky to come into the kitchens," Aaron said in a whisper behind Michael. "They will not be using them this late at night."

Michael was moving with infinite caution, for they were approaching the central part of the palace now and one false move could make their presence known. At the far side of the kitchen area they entered a corridor illuminated by several burning torches and at the end of it came upon a closed door beyond which Michael could hear the sound of men's voices.

They had seen no side passage through which they might bypass the chamber ahead, so there appeared to be no way to reach the main gate and open it except through the chamber from which the men's voices came. Warning the others—in a whisper passed back along the line—to get their weapons ready, Michael kicked open the doorway and plunged into the room, his naked sword in hand.

Six of the Hittite mercenaries who guarded the palace were lounging in the room; it was evidently an armory, for weapons and armor hung upon the wall. A door at the far side of the room was open and Michael's heart leaped when he saw that it gave access to the courtyard leading to the gate.

The men looked up in startled surprise at the sudden appearance of an armed man in the doorway. For an instant they did not realize he was not one of them. and

286

Michael took advantage of that moment to race across the room and slam the door leading to the outside, so the noise of fighting inside the palace would not be heard by those at the gate. As he turned to face the mercenaries, one of them recognized him and shouted, "It is the enemy!"

Seizing a weapon, the man lunged forward, and as the two swords clashed, Michael saw Aaron race into the room and run one of the mercenaries through before the man could deliver a blow in his defense. Behind Aaron, the other men came pouring through the door, and instantly the room was filled with fighting men, grunting and cursing as they thrust, jabbed, and struggled in the narrow space.

The fight lasted only a few moments; with the odds heavily against them, the Hittites were cut down almost immediately. The sight of a row of helmets hanging from pegs around the wall gave Michael an idea. Obviously the men they had killed belonged to a detail of the guard, perhaps one waiting to exchange places with those at the gate; by taking advantage of this fact, he saw that they might achieve their purpose through deception, without rousing the entire palace guard before they were able to open the gate and let Jehu's waiting forces inside.

"Replace your helmets with the Hittite ones," Michael told a dozen of the men in the forefront of his small group. "They will probably get you safely across the court to the gate without being recognized. But throw them away immediately afterward or our own men will cut you down."

The dozen who were to make the foray across the courtyard to open the gate quickly arrayed themselves in Hittite helmets. When they were ready, Michael opened the door and carefully surveyed the small length of corridor connecting it with the courtyard outside.

The court was very small here, he saw, actually little more than an opening between the palace itself and the gate with the tower guarding it. The royal apartments, he knew, were in the massive tower-fortress that was the most prominent feature of the palace. And since Jezebel no doubt had Miriam and Ahaziah under guard there, he must reach this area while the smaller detail was making its foray across the court.

Standing aside to let the dozen men start across the court as if to relieve the mercenaries at the gate, Michael and the rest of his group began to move toward the entrance into the royal quarters, keeping always in the shadows close to the building. They were almost there when a sudden uproar in the direction of the gate told them the men assigned to open it had been detected and were fighting with the guards. Moments later, he heard the groaning of hinges as the massive gate leading into the palace was opened, followed by the sound of a trumpet as Jehu led his men in a foray through the gate into the inner courtyard.

Without waiting to see how Jehu and the attackers were faring, Michael had continued to lead his group along the wall, seeking a way into the fortress tower. He reached the massive doorway guarding the entrance to the royal quarters, but when he tried to open it, found that it was locked. Wasting no time with the door—for now more than ever it was important to get inside the palace as quickly as possible—he continued along the side of the building, seeking another entrance that might have been left open. Around them, the shouts of officers and the blast of trumpets summoning the Hittite mercenaries indicated that the presence of Michael's attackers in the palace had already been discovered, but too late to save it from capture.

The third door Michael tried yielded to his pressure and, followed by Aaron and the rest of his small group, he started up a stairway, hoping it led to the tower where Jezebel's own quarters were located. Halfway up they met a group of mercenaries rushing down the stairway to join in the defense of the palace, leaving Michael and his group no choice except to fight it out there upon the stairs.

Always thinking of their own safety in battle, the mercenaries gave ground slowly, instead of attacking and spitting themselves upon the swords of Michael's men. Thus they were able to force the attackers to fight their way up the stairway toward the royal quarters at the next level, a procedure that took time Michael needed desperately for his own purposes.

Fighting every step as they backed toward the upper level, the guards resisted bravely. And since no more than two men could face them upon the stairway at once, the fact that Michael's men outnumbered them had very little effect. The Hittites were in a more favorable position, too, because they could thrust downward at the attackers.

The men with Michael had been especially chosen by Jehu from among his most skilled swordsmen, however, since sword and dagger were the only weapons they could carry through the shallow tunnel. In the end, their skill began to tell and the Hittites were forced up the stairway and back through a door at its head. Fortunately for Michael, one of the mercenaries was cut down in the open doorway, blocking it so the defenders could not close the door. As the few mercenaries remaining on their feet backed into the chamber at the stairhead, Michael followed them and leaped across the body of the fallen Hittite into the room. There, with the naked, bloody sword in his hand, he found himself facing Hamul.

The renegade captain was carrying a spear. He gave a shout of exultation when he saw that Michael was armed only with a sword and dagger, and lunged forward, stabbing with the longer weapon in the hope of catching Michael off balance and dispatching him at the first thrust. Fortunately Michael was able to leap aside so the spearpoint only glanced off the metal plate strengthening his harness. Behind him one of his own men sliced down with his sword upon the end of Hamul's spear, severing the head from the shaft and rendering the weapon useless. With a curse, Hamul flung it away and moved in to attack Michael with his sword.

They were fighting at the very entrance of the room, so there was no opportunity for any of Michael's men to enter the open doorway and come to his aid. Hamul, in turn, was determined to press Michael back, hoping to keep the attackers bottled up in the doorway until help could arrive. By so doing, too, he forced Michael to fight with the body of the dead mercenary underfoot, thus placing him at an additional disadvantage.

For moments that seemed hours, the clash of metal upon metal and the grunts of the two men fighting for their lives filled the room. But Michael had gained considerable experience in battle during the fighting at Karkar and again at Ramoth-Gilead, while Hamul had lounged in the palace taking his ease as Jezebel's favorite. As the moments passed, the pace quickly began to tell upon the larger man. His movements became less agile, his thrusts less quick. And, seeing that his opponent was tiring, Michael pressed the battle even harder, fighting with both sword and dagger as he sought to deliver a fatal blow.

The opportunity came when Michael slipped in the pool of blood from the body of the dead mercenary, and Hamul leaped in triumphantly, slashing down in what he confidently expected to be the final blow. Michael tried desperately to evade the sword and in so doing slipped again. This time, however, he moved so rapidly that his body slid away from the path of the sword in Hamul's hand and the weapon struck the floor, momentarily numbing the renegade's wrist. From a half-kneeling position on the floor, Michael thrust upward with his sword and felt it sink into the other's body.

Hamul gave an indrawn "Ahhh" of agony, then as the sword dropped from nerveless fingers, he crashed to the floor, jerking Michael's weapon from his hand. Michael's own men were pouring into the chamber now in order to secure the other doorway against further possible attack. Still panting from the brief but desperate struggle, he drew his sword from the body of Hamul and, wiping it upon the fallen man's tunic, crossed the room to the other door. When he kicked it open, a dramatic—and chilling—scene met his eyes.

The chamber in which Michael found himself occupied the entire upper floor of the great tower that rose from the side of the hill to form the most prominent feature of Ahab's palace. Across from him an open doorway gave access to a balcony; through it he could hear the howling of the dogs Jezebel kept chained on the ledge far below to prevent anyone from climbing the sheer wall of the cliff and gaining access to her quarters. It was not the location of the room that sent the cold chill through Michael's body, however, but its occupants.

Jezebel stood in the doorway opening out upon the balcony. Beside her was one of the palace eunuchs with a drawn sword, the point resting against the breast of Prince Ahaziah. On the other side was Joash, the Governor of Samaria, with a swordpoint held against Miriam's throat. The queen was dressed in the royal robes she wore at state functions, and the golden tiara with the blazing jewel was upon her head. Joram was nowhere to be seen.

As he faced Jezebel across the room, drawn sword in hand, Michael was forced to admit that she had never been more beautiful—or more evil.

"What is the meaning of this, Prince Michael?" she demanded icily.

From the courtyard outside, Michael could hear the shouts of Jehu ordering his men into the palace itself. The gate, he realized with a surge of triumph, had been successfully taken and the stronghold was all but in their hands.

"We have captured the palace," he told Jezebel. "Order your eunuch to release the king of Israel."

"Stay where you are or Ahaziah dies," Jezebel warned. "Only my son Joram shall rule in Israel."

From the breast of his tunic Michael took the small parchment roll containing Ahab's decree naming Ahaziah king. "This is my authority," he said. "Kill Ahaziah and both you and your son will die."

Jezebel did not budge in the face of the threat, but when she spoke again, her voice had a softer note. "I know you well, Michael," she said. "You do not make war upon children and women. You might kill me, but Ahaziah and the girl will die first. And Joram is Ahab's son, so the people would still name him king of Israel."

Michael's eyes met Miriam's across the room. He saw her make an involuntary movement toward Ahaziah, as if to protect him, then draw back when Joash pressed the blade more tightly against her throat. Perhaps nothing except the sight of the sword against his beloved's white flesh could so completely have exorcised the demon that had entered Michael that night in the grove of Ashtoreth. Anything that still remained of his desire for Jezebel was destroyed in that instant; he knew he could kill her now without compunction. At the same time, he could not destroy Joram when the boy's only sin was in having her for a mother, for Ahab was the boy's father and, as Jezebel had said, if Ahaziah died, Michael's own loyalty to Ahab would force him to support Joram as king.

"Speak on," he told the queen, playing for time.

"What is it worth to you to save Ahaziah and your betrothed?" Jezebel asked.

"I will make no bargains that leave you alive," Michael told her.

Jezebel chose to ignore the threat to her own life, assuming as she always had that no man who had known bliss in her arms could ever go against her very long. "Tear up the decree and declare it was written in error," she said in the warm tone he knew so well. "Support Joram as king and I will let Ahaziah and your betrothed go free. In time, we can talk of other things."

Michael understood her meaning but the promise had no allure for him now. Before he could say anything, however, Miriam spoke.

"Let her have her way, Michael," she begged. "Not for my sake, but for Ahaziah's."

As Michael stood, desperately seeking a way to destroy Jezebel yet save the other two, Jehu's exultant voice floated up through the open doorway to the balcony from the courtyard below.

"Throw down the queen!" he shouted. "He who throws down Jezebel shall live. All others shall die."

Jezebel's laugh rang out. "The stupid fool! Does he not know that I am protected by the prophecy of Elijah? I shall die by the Wall of Jezreel, not here in Samaria."

It was like Jezebel to assume that Elijah's curse would protect her now. Distraught as he was, the words had no particular significance for Michael. But to one person among those making up the tense scene, the words did have a special meaning. It was Joash, the Governor of Samaria, whose sword was at Miriam's throat.

"The Wall of Jezreel." Joash seemed to be speaking to himself, yet his voice had a chilling quality that brought even Jezebel up short. "Everyone knows this very room rests upon what a long time ago was called the Wall of Jezreel."

Michael caught the meaning of the phrase at last and what it signified to Joash. And with the realization, he saw a way out of the impasse.

"The dogs drank the blood of Ahab by the Pool of Samaria when the king's chariot was washed there today," he said. "Be sure the whole prophecy of Elijah will be fulfilled this day and Jezebel will die here in Samaria. Save yourself while you can, Joash."

Joash nodded slowly, a strange look in his eyes. Obviously the reference to the Wall of Jezreel by Jezebel had reminded him of the strange way in which Elijah's curse had worked out in the case of Ahab.

"Abandon the queen, while there is time to save yourself, Joash," Michael urged. "Let the dogs eat her flesh by the Wall of Jezreel and the prophecy will be fulfilled."

Joash hesitated no longer. Dropping his sword, he seized Jezebel in his hands, lifting her as if she were a doll. She had time to scream only once before he stepped through the doorway to the balcony and tossed her over the rail. The eunuch who was guarding Ahaziah also dropped his sword and Michael rushed to take Miriam in his arms.

From below came a horrible snapping and growling, broken by one more scream of pure terror that turned into a keening wail of agony, before it trailed off and became silent. Then there was nothing save the dreadful sound of the dogs as they battled over their meat by the Wall of Jezreel and the exultant shouting of Michael's men in the courtyard below.

Turning to Ahaziah, Michael lifted the boy's right arm as Jehu and his troops burst into the room.

"Hail Ahaziah!" he shouted. "King of Israel!"

With a mighty shout, Jehu and the soldiers took up the cry and, straightening his shoulders, Ahaziah stepped forward to receive their pledge of allegiance. Miriam had buried her face in Michael's breast when he took her into his arms. Now she raised her head and looked toward the balcony.

"The curse of Elijah," she said in a tone of wonder. "Who could have thought it would be fulfilled here in such a horrible way."

"It was not Elijah's curse that destroyed the queen but the curse of Jezebel herself," Michael corrected Miriam gently. "Her overpowering ambition would not let her rest, even when her cause was lost. Israel lost a great king in Ahab because Jezebel was evil." He looked across to Ahaziah, standing straight and regal as he received the homage of Jehu and the soldiers. "But perhaps we have gained another who will be just as great."

Keep Up With The BESTSELLERS!